# DEDICATION

*For Leonard . . . Always*

A Mattie O'Malley Mystery

# PAST SECRETS, PRESENT LIES

# Deborah L Stempien

**Editor Wendy VanHatten**
VanHatten Writing Services

http://www.vhwritingservices.com

**Cover Design & Layout by Ginger Marks**
DocUmeant Designs

http://www.DocUmeantDesigns.com

ISBN: 978-0-9897635-1-6

# PROLOGUE

Then . . .

Dry cornstalks rustled in the light breeze, randomly disturbing the peacefulness of the night. A night so still the disharmony of the frogs down by Echo Creek could be heard from a quarter mile away. Recognizing the tranquility could be shattered at any moment, and he had no time to give it more than a cursory thought, he focused all his attention on the mission at hand.

Fingers tingling from the lack of movement, he waited, forcing himself to breathe. Taking a deep breath, he slowly let it out.

In and out.

In and out . . . in . . .

He sensed, more than saw, movement in the cornfield, that habitual feeling creeping back into his senses taking over his psyche. The hair on his nape stood straight up as steely gray eyes scanned the field beyond where the corn whispered and sighed.

"Head's up," his headset crackled. "We have movement."

After re-checking his M40, he shifted into position, and it wasn't long before he acquired his target. Peering down the length of scope, he centered the crosshairs at the halfway point on the target's damp brow, the perspiration on his forehead glimmering in the midnight moon.

He shook his head, willing himself not to think about the target . . . *he never let himself think about his target* . . . he drew a deep breath and held it as he gently squeezed the trigger.

Allowing the breath he had been holding to escape silently, he simultaneously tried to quiet the thunder rumbling through his head. It took sheer will and several steadying breaths to bring him back.

His partner's peculiarly calm voice crackled through the headset, "Scarecrow connected."

Heaving a sigh of relief he responded, "Scarecrow out, now let's get the hell outta here and let Raven get to work."

# CHAPTER 1

N ow . . .

I rolled over and grimaced as I squinted my eyes at the clock . . . again. Having been awake for the better part of the night I was convinced sleep was no longer an option. Not sure if it was excitement, fear, dread, or a mixture of all I couldn't stay in bed a moment longer. My mind constantly going over the same issues . . . with the same results.

Quietly, I slipped from under the covers, gathered some clothes, and slowly made my way toward the bathroom in the dark.

Showering quickly, I corralled my shoulder length red hair into a clip at the back of my head, and put on my usual small amount of makeup. Studying my fatigued face in the mirror my mind wandered back to the evening before . . .

*. . . the reflection of my own determined heart-shaped face stared back at me in the computer screen as I typed out those last two words . . . THE END.*

*With a satisfied grin I leaned back in my chair and looked out the window from the workstation I'd set up for myself when I first moved in. I set my office in the front of the house because I liked to see what was going on in the neighborhood when I surfaced from the world I was creating into the one around me.*

*I saw Roger's car pull in the driveway. Finally! I couldn't wait to tell him. Things had been somewhat strained of late. Now that my book is finished maybe, we can get back to normal. Normal being relative . . . I'm sure.*

*Excited, I met Roger at the door with my manuscript.*

"What's this?" he asked suspiciously, as I held out my book to him.

"It's my book. I want you to be the first to read it," I crowed proudly.

"Oh . . . So, you finally finished it, huh?" he said as he walked past me and crossed the room to the door that separated the living room from the kitchen.

I nodded, letting my eyes follow him, recognizing the slight twinge of anger in his voice but deciding to ignore it.

"When I sell it I can finally open the bookstore we've talked about."

"All you've talked about, Mattie! You . . . not we. That bookstore is your dream. Not mine, it never was," he snapped, turning back to face me. "What about my business, my real-estate office? Huh? It's one of the largest in the area. I built it from nothing and I want you to be part of it. I thought that was what you wanted, too."

"That's your work, but it's never been mine." I walked over to him and laid my hands on his arm. "Roger, don't you see? If I ever intend to know my potential I have to try to get this book published, and I have to do it now. Why can't you understand?" I stopped and looked at him with tears in my eyes, wishing he would come to his senses, wishing he would finally begin to see me as an individual with a mind of my own. Dropping my hands from his arm, I shook my head and said, "I'm sorry Roger, I can't keep doing this."

Making a u-turn in his attitude he said, "No, Mattie, you're right. I'm sorry. I am excited for you; I'm just wound a little tight tonight. That's all." Looking down at the three hundred-page manuscript he said, "Is it okay if I start reading this tomorrow? I'm dead on my feet tonight."

I nodded. "Sure, tomorrow's fine." Turning so he couldn't see the disappointment on my face, I said, "I'll just go order a pizza for dinner."

With a weighty sigh, I finished dressing and made my way downstairs looking for Harry and coffee. *Not necessarily in that order.*

"Come on Harry, it's time to go outside," I called after checking all the favorite hiding spots of my two-year-old Irish Setter.

I decided to flush him out with food, so I poured some doggie biscuits into his bowl and filled his water dish. After I got my coffee brewing I found a couple slices of questionable bread. *I have been known to eat food after the expiration date.* I sniffed the bread, checked it for green spots, and deciding it wouldn't kill me I dropped the bread in the toaster. Glancing out the kitchen window,

I saw the sun just starting to rise. This is my favorite time of day. Harry and I normally share it together.

Picking up my cell phone, I punched the #1 key.

"Hey, have you seen Harry this morning? I haven't been able to find him."

"No, haven't seen him yet and . . . good morning to you, too."

"Sorry . . . could you help me look for him or are you expecting a patient?"

"Not until eleven, so I can help search for Houdini." Karen said affectionately. She loves Harry as much as I do. "I'll check around here first. Make me a cup of coffee."

"You got it."

Just then, Roger came into the kitchen looking extremely handsome in his dark grey suit, white dress shirt, and red *power* tie.

"Hey, have you seen Harry this morning? I can't find him anywhere," I asked, not sure what to expect after our argument last night. He barely said two words to me while we ate our pizza then went right to bed after that.

Shaking his head, "Nope, haven't seen him since last night. He's probably hiding out somewhere. Don't worry about him; he'll be back."

"Yeah, you're probably right." I held out a cup to him, "Coffee?"

"No thanks, I don't have time. I have an early closing today. I'll grab something on the way." He kissed me on the cheek then pushed through the kitchen door, back through the living room, and out the front.

*"Huh . . . I guess that explains why he's looking so handsome this morning." I thought to myself.*

Calling back over his shoulder he said, "I heard that. And I look handsome every morning," he chuckled as he walked out the front door toward his black Jeep Grand Cherokee sitting in the driveway.

Turning back he said, "I called Paul, the plumber. I'm meeting him here tonight after work to check out the red water that's coming through the pipes."

"Ummm . . . thanks. That's great."

*Wow; turn on your blinker.*

I could hear the old hoot owl from the tree in the front yard waking up as I smeared peanut butter on a piece of toast, poured coffee into my favorite mug, and started toward the back door thinking out loud, "I'm glad to see his mood has improved but I still need to think about . . . things."

When I moved to Hopewell a year ago the last thing I wanted was a relationship. I tried and tried to tell Roger that. However, as an attorney he managed to sidestep every argument I had. Also as top selling real estate agent he never took no for an answer.

Shoving the toast in my mouth, I unlocked the back door and stepped out onto the porch.

"Son of a . . . !" I cried out as the toast flew out of my mouth and my cup of coffee shot toward the shrubs as I slammed into the porch with a groan. A sudden surge of pain in my arm told me I'd probably cracked or torn something. The wind knocked out of me as I laid there struggling to breathe.

"What the hell . . . " I moaned and glanced around to see what I tripped over. "Harry?" My right arm, taking the brunt of the fall, felt useless as I attempted to get to my knees. Leaning over my heap of an Irish Setter, I shook him, trying to wake him. My jaw, throbbing from the fall, ached as I yelled for Karen who I could hear out front calling Harry's name.

"Mattie, what happened?" Karen asked running around the side of the house and onto the back porch.

"It's Harry. He's been hurt or something. I can't wake him," I said not able to contain the quiver in my voice.

"Okay. Scoot over and let me take a look at him."

Karen bent down over Harry's motionless body and laid her head on his side. Looking over at me she said,

"Well, he's breathing. In fact, he appears to be snoring. Did you give him some Benadryl or something? You know . . . for a cold or to help him sleep."

"God no! Harry doesn't need any help sleeping. Why won't he wake up?"

"Mattie, he's fine. He just needs to sleep it off. He obviously got a hold of something. Maybe he went through the trash. We'll just keep an eye on him but as long as he's breathing, he's fine. If he doesn't wake up in the next hour or so we'll give Glen, at the veterinary clinic, a call."

Noticing the bruises beginning to form on my arm, Karen reached for my hand.

"What happened to your arm?" She examined my arm closely.

"I tripped over Harry. I think it's just bruised."

"Honey, I'm taking you to the hospital. I think it might be more than a bruise."

"Finally," I said as Karen and I left hospital. I was anxious to get back to see how Harry was doing. But, worrying was obviously a waste of my time since he didn't seem any worse for the wear. After we left Karen's Harry and I entered the house; he in front of me with a rawhide from Karen and me with the pain pills the doctor had given me. The diagnosis . . . bruised ribs and a sprained wrist.

With a heavy sigh and heavier eyelids, I eased down into my overstuffed chair and put my feet up on the ottoman. Laying my head back and closing my eyes, I thought I'd just rest here for a minute. Something was nagging at me; I just couldn't get a handle on what it was.

"Mattie, wake up," Roger whispered as he squeezed my leg. Startled, I jumped up from the chair and tripped over the ottoman falling into him. Thankfully, he caught me because I don't know how many more falls this 35-year-old body could take in one day. Sitting back down I struggled to wake up, not even realizing I'd fallen asleep, *except for the drooling,* which I don't ordinarily do when I'm awake.

"Hi. I didn't hear you come in."

"I'm not surprised, the way you were snoring. What happened to you?" Roger asked staring at my bandaged arm.

Looking into his eyes, I shook my head in a reflex action to clear the confusion.

"Rough day. Oh . . . and please, I do not snore."

He shrugged, "Have it your way."

"Remember, I couldn't find Harry anywhere in the house this morning? After you left, I went out back to look

for him and I tripped over him lying on the porch . . .
Karen thinks he was drugged. Anyway I fell flat on my face
and on my arm." I said holding up my bandaged hand as
proof. "Do you know anything about that?"

Shaking his head, "No . . . what are you asking me?"

"I guess I'm asking if you know anything about
Harry being drugged."

"Why would I know anything about that?"

"I don't know. But you were the only other person
here besides me."

"You think I drugged Harry?"

"Honestly, I don't know what to think."

"Why would I do anything so inane?"

"You have to admit you are a little jealous of him." I
shook my head. "Jeez, when I say it out loud it sounds a
little ridiculous."

"A little ridiculous?" Roger's voice was getting
louder.

"Okay, calm down. I understand you're angry."

"You're damn straight I'm angry." Shaking his head
he said, "I can't talk about this right now; I only came
home to tell you I have a meeting tonight and won't be
home for dinner."

"All right, we'll talk about this later. What time will
you be home?"

"I have no idea and don't bother waiting up," he threw back over his shoulder as he stalked into the kitchen.

I sat for a minute with my head in my good hand. After taking a few deep breaths, I rose and followed him into the kitchen.

"Want some wine?"

"No, I'm working tonight."

"Right. I'm sorry. I forgot."

"That's right, you forgot. It's not like I just told you two seconds ago, or anything."

"Roger, I'm sorry. It must be these pain pills the doctor gave me today."

"Just drop it." Roger's voice was abruptly calm. "I don't want to argue with you tonight."

"Neither do I."

Making an effort, I started fresh. "I was thinking maybe we could go out to dinner tomorrow night and celebrate me finishing the book. What do you think?"

"I don't know. Let's just play it by ear, okay. I've got to get back to the office. I'll be late tonight so I'll see you in the morning."

"Ummm, okay," I said to his retreating back. "Hey, what about Paul the plumber? I thought you were meeting him here tonight."

"I'll call and cancel," he called back over his shoulder.

The contented feeling that had been with me the night before was long gone. Something was wrong with Roger. His mood swings were abrupt and emotionally charged. It had been on the tip of my tongue to mention therapy, but I'd been too aware of what the response would have been. Roger would have given me one of those harsh, withdrawn looks, and the conversation would have ended. Besides I'm not sure I want to go there either.

Too restless to sleep, I went to my office and turned on my computer. I should get started on sending out query letters to publishers. However, I wasn't thinking of work.

By nature, I was impulsive and trusting. But since I'd been burned so badly prior to moving here, I vowed to temper that side of my personality. Now, I think Roger and I have some serious talking to do.

# CHAPTER 2

O ne week later . . .

I struggled to free myself from the dead weight that was trapping me on my bed . . . it felt as if I was suffocating.

"Dammit, Roger get off me," I ground out once I realized what was cutting off my breathing. With a grunt, I managed to shove his body until he flipped off the end of the bed and landed on the floor with a loud thump.

"God, Roger what the hell are you doing here? You moved out last night, remember?" I was standing over

Roger waiting for him to talk to me. "I can't believe you have the nerve to come back here."

Roger was sitting at the kitchen table staring into a glass of wine when I finally made my way home. He glanced up as I limped through the back door.

"Jeez, you look like hell Mattie. What happened to you?"

Ignoring the sarcasm in his voice, I said, "Someone broke into Karen's office, tied her up, and trashed the place, as if they were looking for something. The door was locked and I thought I could kick it in. You know, like Sami has been teaching me. Anyway, the only thing I accomplished was bruising my foot. The doctor at the ER said it wasn't broken," I explained, while hobbling further into the kitchen. I looked at my reflection in the glass door of the microwave, and startled myself. My red hair, although always a little unruly, was crazy, kind of like a cat that stuck his tail in a light socket. I winced as I pushed my fingers through it turning toward Roger who was sitting and staring into his wine glass again.

"Is something wrong?" I asked. "You didn't like my book . . . right? Is that what this is all about?"

Shaking his head no, he rose from his seat at the table, and retrieved another wine glass from the cabinet before answering me.

"You and I need to talk," he said while pulling a chair out for me. After pouring a glass of wine for me, he sat down before speaking again.

"Mattie, something's going on here I don't understand. First, you accuse me of drugging Harry. How could you even think I would set it up for you to hurt yourself?

Plus, all we do is fight anymore and you're very secretive. Is there someone else?" Holding up his hands and shaking his head, he continued. "No, don't answer that. It doesn't matter anyway. You were supposed to be home three hours ago and when you do come in; you look like you've been in a street brawl. Obviously, it never even occurred to you to call me. I don't know what's happening and you don't seem to want me to. Apparently, this whole living together thing was just one big mistake. I shouldn't have pushed you. I knew you weren't ready. Lord knows you told me enough times. Anyway, I'm moving back into my house tonight. I used the last two hours to pack up my stuff. I've just been sitting here waiting for you. To say goodbye."

Staring into my glass, I tried to wrap my head around what he had just said. I couldn't look him in the eye. If I did, he'd know I was thinking the same thing. Although I do care about Roger and I don't want to see him hurt, things just haven't seemed right since he moved in. I think we're just too different.

He drank the last of his wine, walked over to the sink, placed his glass in it, and with his back still to me, he sighed, "Goodbye, Mattie." He walked out the door.

I sat there too numb to move as I listened to the door close.

"What the hell just happened here?" I asked, to no one in particular. Not able to come up with any answers and too tired to care any longer, I limped up the stairs and into the bedroom; a slight breeze blew softly through the screened window, ruffling the sheer, pale curtains.

In the dim light, I was drawn to the empty spaces that used to house Roger's personal items. The dresser top that would have normally held the possessions from his pockets . . . cell phone, scribbled notes to himself, loose change, and the leather wallet I'd given him last Christmas . . . all gone. There was no longer a stack of real estate books on his bedside table. The closet door was wide open and what was left of my clean clothes still *hung there. Roger's clothes were gone. Shoe boxes from the top shelf . . . gone. Ties hanging on the rack. Gone. The cold feeling in my gut spread. I stepped over to the dresser and opened the top drawer, even though I knew what I'd see. Nothing. It was empty. Scanning the room, I saw Roger had taken everything, even the picture of him and me down by the pond last summer. All gone. Turning toward the bookshelves, stacks of CD's and DVD's . . . all gone. Roger had taken everything that was his . . . and left. It's as if he were never here.*

"Come on, Roger you're scaring me." I leaned in to get a closer look at his face . . . dead blue eyes stared back at me, vacant and transparent. I reached out to touch his face.

Dead!

Shuddering at the touch of his cold skin I tumbled backward landing hard on the floor. Rolling onto my stomach, scrambling on all fours I crawled toward the hallway. Just as I was about to stand, claw-like hands grabbed me from behind and yanked me to my feet. Daring to look back over my shoulder, I gasped as reptilian eyes stared at me through slits of a mask.

I realized the stare, ruthless in its intensity, was filled with unspeakable purpose. The sight of the knife firmly grasped in his claw-like fist launched a scream shooting straight through my mind.

In that split second, I knew.

*I'm going to die.*

A sliver of panic pierced the last of my control and worked its way through me like a shard of glass penetrating the flesh.

"Where'd he hide 'em?"

Spinning on the balls of my feet I dashed toward the stairs. Aware he was right behind me, I picked up the pace. I heard the sound of his boots echoing off the pine floor, his breathing rising above my own labored gasps.

Blindly I ran. Tripping over a carelessly placed rag rug, I flung myself toward the stairway, conscious of his proximity.

Hands grabbed me from behind, yanking me to my feet.

"Last chance."

I shook my head, more to clear it than in answer to his statement.

Jerking me tight against his bulky chest a low, gravelly voice whispered in my ear, "Keep the faith." A beefy fist struck the center of my back flinging me forward.

I cried out, more in surprise than fear, plummeting halfway down the stairs before I actually hit with a dull thump. A searing pain gushed through me. I whimpered softly. Waves of grayness rippled over me. There was ringing in my ears as I slid into a dark void.

# CHAPTER 3

Someone switched off the lights leaving me in total darkness.

"How are you feeling?" the soft voice asked. "You're looking a little better."

Better than what? It was that voice again. I laid still feigning sleep, hoping it would be enough to discourage the voice as l willed it to leave me alone. *Sleep*.

*Whispering*. I attempted to turn my head toward the voices but stopped quickly. The pain was so intense it felt as if someone had taken an ice pick to my brain. I sensed, more than saw, Karen. Somehow I knew her honey-colored hair would sweep gracefully across one eye as she stared down at me from the foot of the bed.

Sneaking a look, I noticed she was paler than normal and the skin around her brown eyes bore a shadowy, bruised appearance that made her look very fragile and very weary.

"The CT scan showed no significant brain injury. A concussion, definitely. She needs quiet for a few days. Keep the noise level down. Her head will be pounding when she wakes."

"Did she say anything at all?" Karen asked the doctor. The line of her mouth was tight with worry and her eyes looked tormented.

"She took quite a beating considering what she went through yesterday morning and again last night. It's not uncommon for a person to forget the event that caused the injury; she may never remember. And honestly Mrs. Kavanaugh, you really shouldn't push her."

"Doctor." Karen informed him.

"Yes, Mrs. Kavanaugh?" He replied.

"No, I mean its Dr. Kavanaugh, Dr. Harmon."

"Oh, I'm sorry Dr. Kavanaugh. What is your specialty?"

She smoothed back blond hair from a pale oval face and forced a smile to her lips. "Criminal behavioral psychology."

"Well then Dr. Kavanaugh, you should realize pushing her to remember could be dangerous to her mental stability."

I closed my eyes, and immediately, gratefully, found myself sinking once more.

Glen Echo Road curved atop a ridge that swept through Hopewell's finest wine country. Limestone fences marked boundaries of the expansive wineries. Excited and a little apprehensive, I drove through Hopewell toward my new home. At the bend in the road I turned, taking in the magnificent views. Through the stands of huge pines, I glimpsed rows and rows of well-kept grapevines. Finally, I arrived at the drive that led to an impressive old Tuscan farmhouse. The drive continued beyond the house to the back where a small garage stood.

I turned my old Volkswagen into the drive behind the house and parked by the back door.

Colorful planters filled with brilliant purple and yellow pansies stood on either side of the expansive back steps. They added a welcome touch of color that contrasted greatly to the darkness of the ivy wrapping the back of the house.

Turning the key the lawyer had sent me, I let myself into my new home. Noiselessly on its black iron hinges the large wooden door swung open. I stepped directly into an inviting kitchen that revealed hand-troweled stucco walls and an antique heart of pine floor. Dark wooden beams stretched across the ceiling lending to the coziness of the room.

The silence of the empty house felt like a haven to me when I entered it, but I sensed something, no someone, was missing.

Moving further into the room, I opened the shutters to let the afternoon sunlight flood in, illuminating the floating motes of dust in the still air. A large cast iron range and a bath size sink hunkered beneath the window overlooking the backyard and out into the vineyards.

The first time I ever set eyes on Karen she was walking down the small hill from her house, crossing the street toward mine. At first glance, she appeared almost plain with beige dress slacks, a white sleeveless silk shirt, white flat sandals, and her long blond hair pulled back exposing her oval shaped face. But . . . she was anything but plain.

Knowing she was a psychologist did nothing to prepare me for how drop-dead gorgeous she was, with a body that could only be acquired with the assistance of a personal trainer and a face that was agelessly beautiful. Her refined features were touched with warmth. Yet, she appeared remarkably casual and unaware of the effect she had on just about every man within eyesight of her. She crossed the street armed with paper cups and a jug of iced tea; a welcome sight for the movers . . . in many ways.

Extending my hand, Karen politely shook it with a strong, firm grip taking me totally off guard. This petite woman exuded strength and confidence, but it was obvious she didn't trust easily. Being a psychologist, she had probably already figured out that was a two way street.

"Mattie how do you feel, honey?" Not waiting for an answer, she turned toward the man in the white coat, "Do you remember Dr. Harmon? He treated you here in the ER after you tripped over Harry, as well as last evening when you tried to kick in my door. Do you remember any of that?" Lifting my head off the pillow, I leaned forward, winced as my body protested, then slowly sank back into the pillow.

"Hello, Mattie. How are you feeling?" he asked in a hushed tone.

*Ahh . . . the voice.*

My eyes glazed over and closed; my head ready to implode. Sleep . . .

"Mattie, Stryker is here. He wants to ask you a few questions." Watching me with an expectant look, Karen asked, "You remember Special Agent Stryker, don't you?"

Stryker?

I was in so much pain that even my eyelashes hurt as I eyed him suspiciously. He was handsome, with the mark of a man used to shouldering authority. His eyes were dark, as was his hair. He was probably about my age, but his eyes seemed . . . older, albeit wiser. And, the hint of dark stubble on his square jaw made him look just a little bit dangerous. Whatever his age, his strength was obvious, and there clung to him an indefinable air of power. He would be a hard man to forget.

*Glancing up from my seat at the table, I got my first good look at my potential knight in shining armor as Stryker walked into the restaurant. I gasped a sharp breath as I felt the air being sucked out of the room. My eyebrows shooting up to my hairline.*

*"Wowie zowie! Hello Agent Sexy Pants," I said to myself.*

*I smiled over at Karen, who was giving me her best 'get real' look.*

*Stryker made his way to our table as Karen rose and offered her hand. He pushed her hand away drawing her into a hug so fierce I thought he was going to hug the stuffing out of her. Pulling back, she looked him up and down, "You are looking handsome as ever Special Agent Stryker. How are you?"*

*"I'm well and pleasantly surprised by your phone call Dr. Kavanaugh." He replied, using the same formal greeting. He then turned and fixed me with a perceptive eye. Wow, he was handsome and now that he was closer I could see his eyes were coffee colored and his dark hair was sprinkled with silver at the temples.*

*Turning to me, Karen said, "Mattie O'Malley I would like you to meet Agent Beau Stryker of the FBI-CBU."*

*"Agent Stryker, it's nice to meet you." I extended my right hand, but quickly pulled it back remembering it was still in a sling from the fall I'd taken yesterday.*

*"Please, it's just Stryker." Pointing to my bandaged arm he asked, "Have an accident?"*

*"No thank you, already had one . . . Just-Stryker," raising my wrapped hand, and wiggling my fingers.*

"Ha . . . ha . . . very funny." He laughed, his eyes taking on an evil twinkle. Turning to Karen he said, "I'm glad you've finally got someone to add a little humor to your life, Kavanaugh."

As he was sitting down at the table I asked, "So Stryker, what does CBU stand for?"

Looking me in the eye he explained, "Criminal Behavioral Unit. We're a special unit, obliquely connected with the FBI. Actually, I'm not surprised you've never heard of us; most people haven't. Our area of expertise is the psychological behavior of violent repeat offenders. We are a little like the proverbial . . . don't ask, don't tell branch of the family. The Bureau can't really justify how we go about gathering our information, so the director feels it's in his best interest to pretend we don't exist."

"Exactly how do you go about gathering your information? If you don't mind my asking."

"Dr. Kavanaugh's never filled you in on what it is she does?"

Stealing a glance at Karen, I shook my head.

"Well . . . it's the study of wills, thoughts, intentions, and reactions of the offenders. You could say we read their minds. Sometimes it works . . . most of the time it doesn't."

Our server appeared just then cutting off any more talk about the CBU. As she filled our water glasses, her appreciative gaze never strayed from Stryker.

She informed him her name was Skky. "That's spelled with two k's," she said, leaning forward as she pointed to the nametag pinned to the front of her form fitting uniform. "My momma said they made a mistake at the hospital when they were printing up my birth certificate. I kinda like it spelled that way. It makes me different."

That's not the only thing that makes you different I thought to myself, while shaking my head and doing an eye roll. I must be getting more coordinated if I can do all three of those things at once. My time at Gil's is really beginning to pay-off.

At a second glance, a perceptive observer might note Skky had a demure quality about her. The saucer shaped doe-like eyes had a self-assured quality, her rosebud mouth, adorned with a blood red lipstick, curved in a blend of shrewdness and determination, and her spiky black hair, framed a smooth, round dumpling face.

I might not have given Skky that second, careful glance except that she was all over Stryker.

"Well Skky, with two k's, I believe the ladies and I are ready to order lunch," he said with a grin that just had you knowing he was used to this type of attention from women.

With our burgers ordered and eaten and Skky with two k's waiting on another table, Stryker leaned back in his chair and crossed his muscular arms over his chest. He looked somberly at Karen and asked, "What's up Kavanaugh? I haven't heard from you in . . . what . . . five, almost six, years and now out of the blue I get an SOS." Although his low words seemed to be devoid of emotion, I recognized the pain behind his statement.

Karen looked at Stryker while nodding her head in acquiesce, "I just heard you were back in the States and I've been meaning to call."

"Okay, shoot."

Without preamble, Karen enlightened Stryker on everything that had been happening over the last few days. Stryker sat listening as Karen recounted the events of the morning I headed out my back door, and went on to explain about the break-in at her house. Without warning, Stryker barked out a laugh. I jumped causing him to laugh even louder, "Kavanaugh you have been out of it for a while. The CBU does not investigate simple B & E's. You might want to contact the Local Leos."

"Beau, I was hoping you might be able to give us a new perspective on the situation. As you were good enough to point out, I have been out of the game for a while now. Since we're just trying to figure out if Mattie's accidents and my assault are connected, we thought a fresh pair of eyes might help." Karen said, sounding, for the first time since I met her, very unsure of herself.

"Come on, Kavanaugh, you and I both know there is no such thing as coincidence." Pointing his finger at Karen he continued, "You just have to get your head out of your butt and look at it like the professional you are. You are better than anyone I have ever worked with. And believe me there have been a lot since . . . "

"Since I quit. Go ahead and say it, Beau. You have never forgiven me for quitting."

"God, Karen," Stryker sighed as he shook his head, "It wasn't my place to forgive you. You need to forgive yourself and move on with your life." His voice soft, he took Karen's hand and said, "Babe, it's been six years. It's time to stop beating yourself up. I know you still blame yourself, but it was never your fault."

"Then whose fault was it?"

"Not yours. Contrary to popular belief, you can't control everything. You know better than most, no one can control a monstrous act of evil. Except, of course, the monster that performed the act and mark my words, he will pay for that act."

"Spoken like someone who's moved on." She said ironically.

"Karma's a bitch," he said smiling.

"You don't believe in karma."

Shaking his head, "Kavanaugh, get your head back in the game," he advised as he threw some money on the table, "And call me when you're ready to come back to work."

He started to walk away then turned back.

"Things change Karen, people change. Hell, even me," he said with a shrug.

Karen turned down our street and we saw the dark SUV sitting in her drive. "I guess Just-Stryker changed his mind."

*Karen shook her head and did her throaty little laugh, "Nope, he knew he was coming all along; he just wanted to get my goat."*

*"And did he?" I asked innocently.*

*"Always."*

*"Can he really read minds?"*

*She shook her head and laughed, "No, Stryker can't read minds. What he does is stalk killers who are, without a doubt, the most dangerous threat to society. He gets into their head. That can be a dangerous thing for one's own psyche. He is more focused than anyone I have ever observed. No matter how relaxed he may appear, there is an inner wariness and tension in him; an alertness to his surroundings. He has good instincts. Very good instincts. And quite probably more than mere instincts." She said all this while staring at her house.*

*"It sounds like you have a lot of faith in him. I'll leave the two of you to your tug of war and talk to you later," I said, and limped back across the street to my empty house. The last few days have taken a toll on my thirty something body.*

Remembering Karen's question, I nodded.

"Ms. O'Malley do you remember anything about your fall down the stairs?" Stryker asked.

In an anxious tone I replied, "I couldn't breathe . . . " I stopped, feeling as if I'd run into a wall. "Something heavy was on my chest," I continued. My gaze slid around the room, taking stock of my surroundings item by item. As I forced myself to relax and to shake the confusion and panic, I tried to remember . . .

I shook my head, winced. "Something . . . " Raising my hand to my head, my fingers touched . . . bandages. "What's this?"

A woman in my peripheral answered, "We've had an accident, dear," she said by way of explanation. I could only assume she was a nurse since she was on the other side of the bed pouring water from a carafe into a plastic cup.

"We? Then why aren't you in this bed?" I moaned.

With a placating smile she asked, "Do you want to sit up?"

At my slight nod, she pushed the control and the head portion of the bed rose slowly.

"Is that better?" Karen asked with concern. Her voice was both touching and grating at the same time.

I nodded and gently touched the bandages once again.

"What happened?" I grimaced, surprised by the drained sound of my own voice.

"You tell us," Stryker pushed.

Karen laid her hand on Stryker's arm trying to rein him in, turned to me, and said, "Harry was scratching at my door. I ran across the street and found you lying at the bottom of your steps unconscious. I couldn't wake you so I called an ambulance."

"I don't remember falling." I gave an almost imperceptible shake of my head, then jerked forward, "Wait . . . I was grasping for air . . . " I clawed at my chest. "I couldn't breathe. It was Roger . . . again." Laying my head back on my pillow I continued, "I just assumed he was drunk and we were having a Groundhog Day."

Stryker glanced at Karen, eyebrows raised, question in his eyes.

Karen shrugged as if to say, *just go with it.*

"Oh my God, Roger's dead, isn't he?" Tears springing to my eyes I laid my head back on the pillow.

"What makes you *think* Roger's dead?"

I felt a chill crawl through me as I stared at him. Blinking, I struggled to get my sluggish mind moving.

"I don't know. His eyes . . . his eyes looked . . . empty. He is dead, isn't he?"

Not answering my question Stryker continued, "How did you end up at the bottom of the steps?"

"I don't know."

"You don't know, or you don't remember?"

Struggling to raise my head off the pillow I glared at him. "What's the difference?"

"Okay. How often does Roger come home drunk and fall on top of you?"

"He's only done it one other time, a few days ago. And it isn't his home anymore!" I said, a little louder than my head would have liked. "Do you always answer a question with a question?"

"I'll stop as soon as you start giving me some answers."

"Agent Stryker, that's enough!"

I felt a rare surge of relief.

That compelling voice, soft yet always heard, seemed to rise above the conflict around me. Her concern for me, palpable. Standing in the doorway of my hospital room was my mom, elegant and agelessly beautiful.

Her once golden hair now had shining white strands shooting through it, and her beautifully made-up face was smooth, as if time had never touched her. Determined blue eyes sparked with a perception of all present.

That perceptive gaze came to rest on me.

Violet crossed the room, frowning. She was a small woman who kept herself trim by doing yoga. Her golden hair and demure stature had skipped over me. Except for our brilliantly blue eyes, anyone would be hard-pressed to tell that Violet and I were mother and daughter. As a matter of fact she was more apt to be mistaken for Karen's mother than mine.

As often in dealing with my mother, I remained silent, wondering, yet again, if I would ever achieve her compelling presence. The answer was instantaneous.

Not in this lifetime.

When she reached me she smiled, drawing me into a gentle embrace. I felt the whisper of Violet's lips on my cheek as I inhaled a faint hint of lilac, her preferred scent.

She managed to keep her voice even, but an edge of concern was evident. "How are you dear?"

"I'm fine, Mom. What are you doing here?"

"Where else would I be, Matilda? You've had an accident and I came to care for you."

I glanced over at Stryker who cocked an eyebrow.

"Mom," it sounded more like a whine than a plea. "There's no need for that. I'm fine."

"Darling, you are not fine. If you were fine you wouldn't be in a hospital bed right now needing peace and quiet." The last half of that statement directed toward Agent Stryker.

"Beau, Violet's right. Mattie needs to rest," Karen said taking Stryker's arm and leading him toward the door. They stood just inside the doorway talking to each other in hushed tones, giving me a chance to check him out. He was wearing a white v-neck t-shirt, butt-hugging jeans, and black boots. He had a bad boy, motorcycle rider look about him. I lifted my eyes in time to see him looking back over his shoulder at me, with a smile on his lips, his straight, even teeth were white against his five o'clock shadow.

"Okay, we'll talk when you get out of here. Goodnight Mrs. O'Malley. It was nice meeting you," he nodded to my mother. Looking back over his shoulder at me, he winked, "Matilda."

*The eye roll hurt my head.*

As he exited the room he gestured to the doctor. I watched as they stood in the doorway whispering.

One couldn't help but compare the two men.

Dr. Harmon had the physique of a runner: broad shoulders, small waist, and long legs. Handsome, almost too handsome, with all the natural grace of a gazelle.

Stryker, on the other hand, standing a head taller, wearing a darker temperament, was ruggedly handsome. Stryker was more warrior-like with ninja fighting skills. Both extremely sexy.

Absorbed in my own thoughts, I hadn't realized Dr. Harmon had moved over to my mother. Catching only the end of the conversation, I realized her intent was to stay the night here, with me, in the hospital.

"No! Mom you can't stay here. You'll be very uncomfortable. Karen can take you back to the house and you can sleep in a nice comfortable bed. Right, Karen?" I pleaded. "Dr. Harmon, tell her she doesn't need to stay here. I'll be fine," more pleading.

"Well, no, she doesn't need to . . . " turning toward my mother, he said, "Mrs. O'Malley, maybe you should go home and get some rest. Mattie will be monitored through the night. We should be sending her home in a day or two and she'll need someone there to help her, someone who is well rested."

"Well, doctor, if you're sure. Karen, can I stay with you though? I really don't want to stay in that house alone, at least not until we talk to Roger and clear up this mess."

"Sure, Violet, that sounds great. Your furry grandson is already at my house. I know Harry Allen O'Malley will be excited to see you." Karen said as she picked up my mom's suitcase.

Mom looked at me shaking her head, "I can't imagine why you gave that dog three names. Most people are satisfied with just one name for their animals."

"Be nice to Harry, Mom. He's one of the family and you'd do well to treat him as such. He gets his feelings hurt easily and has a long memory."

"Alright dear, don't get yourself all worked up," Mom said as I felt the light touch of her lips on my cheek. "We'll be back in the morning."

"Night Mattie, call me if you need anything," Karen said while guiding my mother out of the room.

"Karen?" She nodded to my mother to go ahead.

"Yes, sweetie." She turned around and came to stand next to my bed.

"Why can't I remember? I mean . . . I remember Roger's dead eyes staring up at me. But I don't remember falling down the steps."

"The doctor says it's a mild form of amnesia not uncommon with a concussion. You'll remember everything when you're ready." She patted my hand and turned to leave the room.

"Karen, how long have I been here?"

"You fell early this morning."

Sighing I said, "He left me. Last night."

After they left, my hospital room seemed too quiet. I closed my eyes for a moment, fighting the tears that threatened. I looked around the small private room.

Flowers and balloons adorned the cabinets and cards were taped to the wall by the foot of my bed, probably so I would see them when I first opened my eyes.

Remembering Dr. Harmon was still in the room, I looked over at him, "Thanks Dr. Harmon for helping me out there. I wouldn't have gotten much rest with her here all night."

"You're very welcome Mattie, and please, call me Jonathan."

"Are you leaving for the day, Jonathan?" I asked. He was dressed in a grey suit and a white shirt open at the collar. His blue eyes were bright behind neat rimless glasses. Tall and slim, he had a handsome face, with a straight nose and fine cheekbones, framed by a thatch of wavy blond hair that most likely took copious amounts of product to tame and was possibly the only unruly thing about the straight laced Dr. Harmon.

"Yes, I am. I just wanted to check on you one more time before heading out as you seem to have had your fair share of accidents lately."

"Yes, it seems I have. Don't let me keep you. Goodnight."

"Ms. O'Malley . . . Mattie, I wanted to ask if I could visit you . . . at home after you're released from here, as . . . say a friend."

"Ummm . . . sure that would be great. Just give me a call . . . and when I'm able to show my face in public again, in a year or so, we can do dinner or a movie . . . or both . . . or you could just come over and we can talk, or whatever. I'm sorry I'm babbling. I do that when I'm tired or in pain. I go straight to babble mode."

"No, that's fine; as a matter of fact it's kind of cute. You get some rest now. Doctor's orders. I'll call you . . . soon. Goodnight, Mattie."

# CHAPTER 4

Someone is in my room. I can sense them. A faint presence. An apparition? Too exhausted to open my eyes, my brain is shouting fight or flight. But, I'm not capable of either right now.

I'm not afraid as a hand gently strokes my hair. Lips press my cheek and something wet, like tears, bathe the side of my face. A soft voice, a voice I hadn't heard in a lifetime, other than in my dreams, whispered close to my ear, "I'm here angel, I'm always here."

Standing in the doorway, tie askew, hair mussed, he looked strong and tired, as if his shoulders carried the weight of the world. He was an old soul, with a soothing air and quiet certainty that seeped into those around him. Worldly cares seemed less important to him than making someone smile.

Despite all efforts to suppress them, the tears came.

"Allen?" I called. My twin advanced further into the room, using his white cane to guide him. "What are you doing here? It's the middle of the night."

Following the sound of my voice, he came to my bedside. "I couldn't wait until tomorrow to come. I had to see you, figuratively speaking of course," he chuckled softly to himself. "I knew something was up so I called Karen."

Tears running down my cheeks I tried to reassure him, "I'm fine, just some cuts and bruises."

"I can't believe Mom didn't call me. What the hell is she trying to protect me from? You're the one who's lying in a hospital bed, Mattie. What's going on here?" I could hear the concern for me, beneath the anger, in his voice.

"There's a chair right next to you; pull it over by the bed here. You need to sit down, before you fall down. You look exhausted. Maybe you should be in this bed instead of me."

With a fatigued smile he reached for the chair, pulling it closer to the bed. I took hold of his hand.

Remembering the dream I had earlier I asked Allen, "Did you just get here?"

"Yes. Why?"

"No reason. I'm glad you came. Thanks."

"Where else would I be?"

The calm I was looking for earlier finally seemed to settle over me. Everything would be fine. With our hands still clasped, Allen laid his head down on them. He was softly snoring in seconds.

The pleasant scents of dinner drifted from the kitchen as Allen and I sat on the sofa in my living room. Dr. Harmon had finally released me from the hospital this afternoon telling Mom I needed peace and quiet. So, just like she did when we were ten years old, Mom made us sit quietly on the couch and wait for her to finish making dinner.

"Allen, I'm so glad you're here. Now I have someone to run interference with Mom," I said to my twin. "Maybe she'll even go home early, to see Mr. Wonderful, if she knows you're staying here to keep me in line. Although . . . he's something we need to discuss." I said, recalling the night she phoned me about him.

After struggling through my nightly routine, I finally laid down in bed, hoping to get some sleep and not think about the scene with Roger tonight. However, as soon as my head hit the pillow my phone started playing Bad Moon Rising, my mother's personal ringtone.

*I picked up the phone and said, "Hi Mom, what's up?"*

*She hesitated before she spoke, "How do you do that?" she asked, clearly amazed by my psychic abilities.*

*"Do what?" I asked innocently.*

*"You're more like your grandmother than I would ever care to admit. I thought you were going to call me when you got off work tonight. I decided you either forgot or you just didn't want to talk to me, in which case it didn't matter to me because we need to talk."*

*"Seriously, Mom I've had enough talking today. Can't we do this in the morning? I'm tired and I just got into bed."*

*"No, I've put this off long enough. I have something to tell you. I was going to wait and surprise you when you came for a visit but that doesn't seem to be happening anytime in the near future, so I'll just tell you. I met someone. His name is Peter Dawson. He's a widower. I know this comes as a surprise to you and I don't want you to be upset. He's a wonderful . . . "*

*Cutting her off in mid-sentence, "Really, Mom? Wonderful?"*

*She went on as if I'd never spoken, " . . . he's a wonderful man. He lost his wife two years ago to cancer and has no children. His only family is an aging sister who never married. And he is wonderful with her."*

*"Wow, two wonderfuls, he must be something. How did you and Mr. Wonderful meet?"*

*"If you're going to be juvenile about it we can just talk about this when I come up there." She threatened.*

*"Okay, Mom, sorry," I said duly chastised." How did you and Mr. Dawson meet?"*

*I knew Violet O'Malley well enough to know that if I didn't change my attitude quick she'd board the next plane to Michigan, and l would be on the wrong end of a full-blown lecture on how to act like an adult and why can't I be more like my brother.*

*"Well, if you're really interested?" she nudged.*

*I remained silent . . . fearing my mother would start sharing the most intimate details of her love life with me. Eeeww!*

*"I met Peter at Speed-Dating for Seniors. Actually, it was the Single-Jingle-Mingle. Peter and I first met last Christmas.*

*That got my attention. "Last Christmas! And I'm just now hearing about this . . . why?"*

*Mom continued as if I'd never uttered a word.*

*"Clarisse had been going for about nine months or so and finally wore me down. I went, Peter approached me, and the rest as you children say, is history. Clarisse is there all the time. You know she's very popular with the men."*

*I think I detected a slight touch of awe in my mother's voice as I proceeded to do a full body shiver at the thought. Clarisse Duggan is my mother's best friend and she's been around for as long as I can remember and has been looking for a man about as long as that*

*"She can't believe I met Peter my first time attending. She told me I was lucky I saw him first otherwise she would have torn into him like a monkey on a muffin!" Violet giggled.*

*I was speechless and could only cringe at the thought. The only thing I knew for sure was that I would never be able to look at muffins . . . or monkeys in the same way again.*

*"Mother, what were you thinking?"*

*"Don't 'Mother Me' young lady . . . I was thinking I was tired of being alone. I hardly ever get to see you and Allen. You're both so busy with your lives. I was hoping you and Roger were going to get married and give me grandchildren. You know how much I want grandchildren."*

*"Mom, I'm sorry. And yes, I do know how much you want grandchildren. I promise you will get them someday, just not today. Okay?"*

*"Maybe Allen will meet someone. I guess I'm getting tired of waiting for you two to make my life meaningful again. And since I was forced to retire last year it's worse than ever." I think she was talking more to herself than to me.*

Drawing my attention back to him, Allen said, "Listen Mattie, I would like nothing better than to stay here and keep Mom off your back. I am the big brother after all."

*By two whole minutes.*

"However, I really have to get back to work. I've been gone long enough and anyway you're doing great. You don't need Mom or me here any longer. You haven't tripped or fallen and sprained or broken anything in four days. I'd say you're making progress. From what Karen's been telling me it was starting to be an everyday occurrence." His smart-ass on autopilot.

Allen's hand was reaching toward mine so I placed my hand in his, "Mattie, I have something I want to tell you but I don't want Mom to know just yet." His head cocked to the side as if listening for her. After I assured him the coast was clear he continued, "I met someone. Her name is Allison Bailey; she's a librarian at the research library across from the Perkins School for the Blind. She was helping me with a research project. We spent a lot of time together and one day I offered to buy her a cup of coffee. She really loves her coffee, just like you. I told her all about you and she's excited to meet you. I think you two will really get along. Mattie . . . I think she's the one."

*What's up with these people knowing all about me and me knowing nothing about them? I guess I'm not the only one in this family with secrets.*

Hugging him I said, "Allen, I'm so happy for you and look, she and I already have something in common. So, when are you going to tell Mom? You know with news like this, it'll take some of the heat off me. Not that I'm just thinking about myself. I really am happy for you. Now that Mom has "Mr. Wonderful", she wants everyone to jump on the bandwagon. What did you think of him anyway? Speed dating, really? How could straight-laced Violet do something so common? I understand they came out for a visit."

"Honestly, I don't know what to think about him. He doesn't seem right for Mom. I don't know. He seems a little rough around the edges for her. He sure asked a lot of questions about you," Allen said shaking his head. "Something doesn't feel right about him."

"Are you sure you're just not being a little possessive here? You know, with Mom being single all these years and us having her all to ourselves. I don't know about you, but I'm more than ready to let someone else divert some of that attention away from me."

"No, now that I've found Allison, I do want that for Mom. However, he just doesn't feel like the one. I don't want Mom to settle."

"So how did you hide Allison from Mom while she was there visiting you?"

"I didn't have to hide her. Allison was at a conference in Florida while Mom was visiting me. How ironic is that? She was only about ten miles from Mom's house. Good thing Mom was in Boston with me otherwise her radar would have kicked in and she would have honed in on Allison down there. I figured it was best if I said nothing just yet. Allison and I are still in the getting to know each other stage. Anyway, I'm not ready to expose her to Mom or you, for that matter, just yet. Maybe for the holidays . . .

we'll see." Allen doesn't like keeping secrets, so I know this is weighing on him.

"So, you don't really have to be back for work, you have to get back to Allison," I said with a wink wink, nudge nudge. This was totally wasted on him. "Okay, so don't make me ask the obvious."

"No, she's not blind. If that was the obvious question you weren't going to ask."

"Cool. She went for you even knowing what you look like." I said teasing my twin. Sitting there wearing his worn out jeans and baby blue polo shirt open at the throat Allen is the stereotypical tall, dark, and handsome. So totally opposite of my tall, fair, and some might conclude, cute . . . on a day I really work at it. I use the term 'cute' loosely as I sit here with a swollen nose and two black eyes that are turning all shades of purple, green, and yellow. Since I haven't done anything with my red hair for a while, I think Carrot Top would be seriously jealous of me right now. I think I'll ask Karen to take me to Judy's Curl-Up and Dye-It for a haircut.

I was just taking a drink of water when Allen said, "Allie is more astute than that. She . . . " Before Allen could finish that thought, I snorted my water and it went shooting through my nose (*man that hurt like hell*) and all over him. "What the . . . " he said jumping off the sofa and wiping water off his face.

I stood up still choking and laughing at my brother with water dripping down his face, "Really? Allen and Allie O'Malley? If you care anything about her you'll let her keep her name when you marry her. I have got to talk to this girl and set her straight."

"No one said anything about marriage. And, I wouldn't care if she did keep her name."

"If who kept their name?" Mom asked, pushing through the swinging kitchen door. She walked into the living room, wiping her hands on a dishtowel. Looking at us she let a little frown settle between her strawberry blond eyebrows. Without skipping a beat she continued, "Are you two ready for dinner? I made a pot roast with carrots and potatoes. I also made a peach cobbler for dessert. I invited Karen to join us, but she's busy catching up with some patients. She said she would come by for dessert though and she's bringing vanilla ice cream to serve with the cobbler. Allen, how did you get all wet?" She asked, disappearing back into the kitchen. Our mother liked to ask questions but rarely waited for answers.

My kitchen is small; some would say cozy. Wide plank pine floors are the shining glory, literally. I refinished them myself when I first moved in and all the hard work was well worth it. Above a large porcelain sink the only window overlooks the entire backyard, including a small apple orchard, a pond, and miles of vineyards. I always feel close to my grandmother here. Well-worn pine cabinets may have seen better days but still serve their purpose. Glass fronts on all the upper cabinets display dozens of wine glasses my grandmother collected over the years. These are the very same ones I use on a regular basis.

"I talked to that nice Ethel Tams when I was in town this morning shopping for dinner. We agreed you shouldn't rush back to work. She said for you to call her when the swelling on your nose goes down and your eyes don't look so bruised. What a nice woman." Mom said while dishing out our food.

"We agreed? I'm sorry, but how is it the two of you agreed? Don't I have any say in the matter? And how does she know my nose is swollen and my eyes are bruised?"

"She saw them when she came by the hospital to see you."

"When . . . why would she come by the hospital to see me?"

"Why wouldn't she? She's your superior at the library, isn't she?"

"I just never thought we had that kind of relationship, that's all."

"What kind of a relationship does one have to have with someone else to show a little human kindness?"

"I don't know, Mom. Forget I said anything. This pot roast is great. It's been a long time since that old oven was used." I like to think of myself as a master of redirection.

"I gathered that, since I had to take down the picture of the turkey you had taped to the oven door, so I could use it." Mom said. So much for those super powers.

When am I going to stop opening my mouth and sticking my foot in it? I looked up in time to see Karen walk in the kitchen door. "Good, you're just in time."

"In time for what?" Karen asked while putting the ice cream in the freezer.

"Nothing. Karen, would you like something to eat? We have plenty," Mom asked Karen while pulling a plate out of the cabinet.

"Well, if you're sure you have enough?"

"Sit down and I'll fill your plate for you." Mom set the pot roast filled plate in front of Karen. "Did you finish with your patients, Karen? I'm sorry you had to cancel appointments for Mattie, but we certainly appreciate you doing it."

"It really was no problem, Violet. My patients aren't usually that eager to see me anyway. They'll probably get together and send her a thank you gift," she said glancing over at me and winking.

"Helloooo . . . sitting right here. I can hear you." I looked over at Allen who just sat there stuffing his face. I don't know if he was oblivious to what was being said or just trying to stay out of it. His head came up just then and he had a shit-eating grin on it. Figures. He was enjoying this.

"Karen, would you mind giving me a lift to the airport in the morning? I've got a nine o'clock flight." Allen asked.

"Allen, you're leaving already? I thought you would stay through the weekend?" Mom asked.

"No, Mom, I've really got to get back to . . . my students. Besides, Mattie is doing much better. The doctor said she could even go up and down the steps now. You know Mom, you could probably head home, too, as I'm sure Mr. Dawson is missing you by now. Mattie will be just fine."

*God Bless you, Allen.*

Mom shaking her head said, "No . . . I don't think so honey. I'm going to stay for her doctor's appointment on Monday and see what he has to say. Then, I'll decide after that. Besides Peter decided to visit his sister since I was here with Mattie."

"You know, Violet, I'm right across the street if she needs anything and I can take her to her appointment on Monday." Karen said, adding her two-cents to the conversation . . . about me!

"No, you've done too much already. You need to get back to your patients. We'll be fine," Mom said to Karen.

"Well, you know I'm here and I'll do what I can." She said, looking over at me with a gleam in her eye and raising her perfectly shaped eyebrows.

"Hello . . . still sitting right here. You can all go home for all I care. Contrary to popular belief, I can take care of myself." I jumped up, knocked my chair back, and stomped out of the kitchen through the living room toward my office/bedroom. I've been using my guest room since I was released from the hospital. Dr. Harmon advised me not to climb stairs for a while because of the concussion and maybe getting dizzy and maybe falling down the stairs . . . again. I think he was laughing when he offered up that piece of advice.

# CHAPTER 5

The doorbell stopped my rant in mid-stomp so I turned around and continued to stomp over to the front door. I pulled it open harder than I intended and it went flying back into the wall. Great! Now I have to patch that hole, I thought looking up at my visitor.

He was attractive as sin with dark hair and gleaming dark eyes. Men that tall and that sexy should not be allowed to show up on a girl's doorstep without giving some kind of notice, I thought wearily. I leaned against my front door and tried not to dwell on the fact that I had two black eyes and hair so big it looked as if I was wearing a red fur hat.

As I stepped back to let him enter the living room, I couldn't help but notice he looked just as good from the back, in his white t-shirt and butt-hugging jeans, as he did from the front.

Did I mention he was really tall?

"Hey, Matilda, am I catching you at a bad time?" Stryker teased with a glint in those discernible brown eyes, and a sensuous mouth made only slightly sinister by a two-day-old beard.

"No. Not at all. Your timing couldn't be better. If you're looking for Karen, she's in the kitchen with Mom and Allen; you can go on back there. I'm sure they'll give you my dessert." Why am I being so whiney?

"No, as a matter of fact it's you I came to see. Can we sit?" he said motioning to the sofa.

"Sure, come on in and sit down. Can I get you something to drink?" I said trying to be a little more hospitable as we sat on my overstuffed couch teeming with comfy pillows.

"No, nothing; thank you," Stryker said, his gaze taking in the gleaming pine floors that were accented by Navaho rugs, and the black and white desert prints adorning the walls. The southwest touches should have been at war with the Tuscan farmhouse style of my home, but they weren't.

"Interesting place."

"Thank you," I said as followed his gaze around the room. "I think."

"Have you had a chance to think about the other night when you woke up and found Roger lying across you?"

"Yes, I have."

"And, you still believe that Roger is dead."

"Well, he certainly looked dead. However, I haven't had much experience in that field. Since you and Karen couldn't find a body, I guess I was mistaken. You know I've been on pain killers for the last couple of days," I said by way of explanation.

"I've been to Roger's office and his house but haven't been able to locate him. As a matter of fact, no one seems to know where he is."

"Did you talk to Crimson? Crimson Ravensky, his secretary and sentinel. No one gets past 'The Crimson Tide'. Even me. She knows where he is and what he's doing at all times." I sat there for a second thinking. "What about Joel Simmons? He's the assistant Roger hired about six months ago."

"Yes, I've talked to both of them and no one has seen him since the night you fell down the stairs. He was supposed to meet a client the next morning and never showed. Joel took the meeting and I got the impression from Crimson that was a big no-no."

"Yeah, that's a fact. Joel wasn't allowed anywhere near the clients. Roger said he was still schooling him. In fact, you're further ahead of the game than I am; I've never even met Joel. I was beginning to believe he was Roger's imaginary employee. Anyway, I haven't given it any thought since Roger walked out that door three days ago." I leaned back on the sofa shaking my head, "Man, has it really only been three days? I feel like it's been months." I glanced over at Stryker; who was staring at me like my hair was on fire. "Is something wrong?" I asked, patting down my hair.

He shook his head no. "I was just wondering what you've gotten yourself into. You seem nice enough, maybe a little flaky and naïve but nice none the less."

"I am nice; and I'm not flaky or naïve! Anyway, what are you basing that assumption on?" Trying to muster up as much dignity as my ailing body would allow.

"This assumption, as you call it, is based on the fact that you're sitting here with a broken nose, two black eyes, a concussion, sprained wrist, bruised ribs, and bruised foot. Now you may call that an assumption . . . I call it fact."

"Those were all accidents. It doesn't make me a flake." I was getting another headache, which seems to happen every time he's around. "Not to change the subject, but how do we go about finding Roger?"

"We're still looking but there hasn't been any activity on his credit cards and we still haven't located his car. I've checked at his house but nothing there either. I can't go inside and look without a search warrant and honestly, I don't have enough to justify a warrant. Do you have any idea where he could be? We have to assume he ran because of the assault on you but there may be other factors we aren't aware of yet."

"I don't know where he would go. His whole life is that real estate office. He doesn't have any family that I know of. I don't know anything anymore and my head hurts." There I go whining again.

Stryker, feeling sorry for me, placed his arm around me, "I'm sorry. I don't mean to upset you but there seems to be more here than meets the eye," He said while pulling me into his hard chest to comfort me, his chin resting on the top of my head.

I liked it. The feel, the sound, and the scent of him. Damn, he smells good. I wiped my eyes with the back of my hand. "Thanks," I sniffled.

"Eh . . . hemmm." Someone cleared his throat.

Abruptly I jerked my head up and hit Stryker under his chin so hard I knocked his head back and into the wall behind the sofa we were sitting on. He yelped and jumped up, holding his hand over his mouth. "Why the hell did you do that?" he mumbled. "I damn near bit my tongue off. Not to mention putting a hole in the wall with my head." *Oh, great another hole to patch.*

"Sorry . . . I didn't mean to disturb you." Standing on my front porch, staring through the screen door was Jonathan.

"No, you're not disturbing anything. Please come in." I said while pushing open the screen door to let Jonathan enter the living room.

"Ummm . . . Dr. Harmon. I would like to introduce you to Agent Stryker."

"Do you want me to take a look at that, Agent Stryker?" Jonathan asked, walking further into the room.

Shaking his head, Stryker recovered and held out his hand to Jonathan, "No, thank you. I'm sure the damage isn't permanent," he said, his eyes leveling on me. "I'm considered pretty hard headed. Please call me Stryker. We met briefly at the hospital while I was visiting with Ms. O'Malley, Dr. Harmon."

Jonathan shook Stryker's hand, "Yes, I remember and it's Jonathan. Are you sure you don't want me to look at your head? You hit that wall pretty hard."

Shaking his head, while scowling at me, Stryker asked, "Are you making a house call? I didn't know doctors did that anymore."

"Well, it's more of a social call. I have something I need to discuss with Mattie and I figured while I was here I could check up on one of my more spirited patients."

Laughing aloud Stryker said, "Spirited? Is that the new word for accident prone?"

Not giving Jonathan a chance to answer, I steered Stryker toward the front door. "Agent Stryker was just leaving. Thank you so much for stopping by. I'll call you if I remember anything else."

"And thank you for your help Ms. O'Malley. I'll be in touch. Good bye Jonathan; nice seeing you again."

Turning back to the man standing in my living room, I said, "Jonathan how would you like some homemade peach cobbler and ice cream?" I took hold of his arm and dragged him into the kitchen.

Pushing through the kitchen door I said, "Hey everyone, look who I found on my front porch. Jonathan, you remember my mother Violet, my friend Karen, and my brother Allen."

"Oh doctor, it's nice to see you again. Please sit down and join us for dessert. How good of you to come and check up on our Mattie." Violet smoothed back a strand of silver hair and fixed Jonathan with a beguiling gaze.

"Well, I'm not really here to check up on her. I stopped by to ask her something." Jonathan explained, clearly beguiled.

"Oh really? And what would that be?"My mother asked innocently. She was so damn graceful I felt like a clod even though I hadn't moved a muscle.

"Mom! That's none of your business." Turning toward Jonathan I said, "Don't answer that. We'll talk after dessert."

"No, that's okay. I don't mind talking in front of your family. I was wondering if you would like to accompany me to the largest affair of the season, the Black and Blue Ball. It's a fundraiser the hospital puts on every year at this time."

"And you're asking Mattie because she's all black and blue?" My brother was laughing, obviously finding himself very amusing. I knew he was going to get back at me for that Allie O'Malley crack.

Jonathan chuckled a little and said, "No, that's not a prerequisite, just a bonus. It's called the Black and Blue Ball because it's black tie and our boys in blue help sponsor it. The proceeds go to Harbor House, a local shelter for abused women and children. I thought it would be fun and after all she's been through lately, she could use a little fun. Anyway, if she does happen to get hurt there, she'll be in good hands because the place will be lousy with physicians and cops." Looking back at me he said, "I'm just kidding, Mattie. It's not for another few weeks and you should be pretty much healed and back to normal by then."

*Normal? What the heck is normal?*

"Thank you, Jonathan. Can I think about it for a while? I'm not sure I would be comfortable going to something as fancy as a ball looking like this."

"Oh, honey it's a wonderful opportunity and so nice of Dr. Harmon to invite you." Mom said, injecting herself into the conversation.

"I know it is, Mom. It's just that I'm not sure how healed I'll be by then."

"Oh honey, you'll be fine by then and Jonathan can keep an eye on your health . . . "

With a resigned sigh, I sat back in my chair and watched. There was no stopping Violet once she got rolling. The best I could hope for was just to live through it.

I regarded my family with both love and frustration. Mom, always the ringleader, resolutely believed everyone in the world was meant to find someone. Violet saw interfering in her children's lives as not just her right, but also her obligation.

"Don't worry about it Mattie, it's always a lot of fun. I know you'll enjoy yourself and it is for a good cause. Just let me know when you decide. Now let's enjoy this delicious looking dessert you made, Violet." Jonathan said rubbing his hands together and smiling at my mom.

Jonathan went home, Mom and Allen went up to bed, and Karen and I were sitting at the kitchen table having a glass of *BellaRosa's* finest merlot. My grandmother left a very well stocked wine cellar.

"Should you be drinking wine so soon?" Karen asked, as she picked up her wine glass and downed half the contents . . . I think Mom is getting to her, too.

"Yes, I should and don't even think of taking it from me. After the week I've had, I not only deserve it, I've earned it. Forget the last week, after the day I've had, I earned it."

"What happened out there in the living room between the time you stomped out of here and then re-entered with Dr. Harmon? I thought I heard you and Beau going at it." Karen said while helping herself to more wine.

"Do you know he had the nerve to call me flaky? Naïve and flaky, that's what he called me. Oh, and let's not forget nice enough. That's what he said, I was nice enough."

"Oh sweetie, don't take anything Beau says personally. He's a little rough around the edges and being a former Marine, he has no delicacy what so ever." Karen assured me.

". . . and it wasn't just him. Jonathan joined in by calling me spirited."

"Spirited doesn't sound so bad to me."

"Well the two of them did see eye to eye on one thing. They agreed that I was accident-prone. Not one of the things that have happened to me in the last few days was my fault. I just happened to be in the wrong place at the wrong time . . . on several different occasions." Oh God, I'm whining again. Holding my glass out, I said, "Hit me again, Karen. Maybe I'll get drunk and pass out on someone, instead of the other way around."

"I don't think you want to do that, Mattie. I think you've had enough trouble lately. Speaking of passing out on somebody, can we talk about the other night when Roger was here?"

"Sure, what do you want to know?" I asked.

"Well, nothing looked as if it had been disturbed. In fact, your bed was made. Like you hadn't even gotten into it yet."

"Of course I'd gotten into it. It was three o'clock in the freakin' morning for goodness sake! How long did the doctor say I was out?"

"Mattie, they couldn't tell us how long. We assumed it wasn't long because you said Roger woke you at three. They really have no way of determining how long you really were unconscious."

"Karen, at the risk of repeating myself, I don't understand. Roger was there lying across my chest. I looked at my clock it was three o'clock. Harry was nowhere around. Roger must have let him out when he came in because Harry *was* in bed with me. There was no other way Harry could have gotten out. I've been locking this place up tighter than Fort Knox. I'm guessing Roger took his key with him when he moved out. I really didn't pay any attention. Besides, have you ever known me to make my bed? I never make my bed. Didn't that seem strange to you?"

"Yes. I have to admit that was the first thing I said to Stryker."

"You mean someone came in, and decided to make my bed? Did Mom go up there before you and Stryker?"

"No honey, it was just us. So either Roger wasn't really drunk or dead, and is just doing all this to scare you or . . . ?" She was looking at me as if I had the answers.

Hmmm . . . fat chance. I'm more confused now than I was before, if that's even possible.

"Jesus, Karen, weren't we just sitting here a couple of days ago having this same conversation. What the heck? I feel like I'm losing my mind."

Karen got up and walked around the table, "Come on Mattie, and let's get you to bed. You, Stryker, and I will all sit down together after Violet goes home and sort through this."

"Karen, will you take me to get a haircut tomorrow? I feel like I'm wearing a fur hat on my head, my hair is getting so big." I whined again.

"Sure, honey. I'll call Judy first thing in the morning and get you an appointment."

I lay in bed for a long time after Karen left, just listening. Listening for anything out of the norm.

There was nothing.

Maybe I am losing my mind.

Harry must have sensed something was bothering me because he jumped up on the bed and laid his head on my chest. I wrapped my arms around him and fell into a deep sleep.

# CHAPTER 6

I t was a golden Indian summer day with the temperature reaching a pleasant eighty degrees. Despite the heat, there was no denying autumn was here. Sidewalks displayed a colorful carpet of leaves that scrambled with every breeze.

Strutting out of the hair salon, I was on the verge of actually feeling human again. Judy not only cut my long auburn hair in wavy layers, she highlighted it. After giving me a manicure and a pedicure, she threw in a make-up lesson that included a demonstration on how to cover my bruises with concealer and contour my high cheekbones.

When she turned me around in the chair to look in the mirror, I was startled. Who knew I could clean up so well?

The unseasonably warm weather allowed me to wear my little turquoise sundress, which according to Judy made my blue eyes bluer. My white sandals showed off my beautiful pedicure. The turquoise nail polish, Blue Moon, matched my dress exactly. I was feeling very self-confident.

Admiring my reflection in the windows of the shops as I strolled down the street to meet Karen, I failed to notice the bicycle lying on the sidewalk. Before I knew what was happening I stepped on the rear wheel, my foot wedging between the spokes. Falling forward I hit my shoulder on the handlebars and ended up doing the horizontal mambo with it. Feeling very exposed, I pulled at my dress as I tried to roll off the bike but couldn't because my foot was caught in the spokes.

Out of the blue, a pair of hands hooked under my armpits, yanked me upward, and I found myself looking into Stryker's amused face. He rose to his feet, lifting me easily with him. Hearing a whimper, I looked around and realized it must have come from me. My legs felt like rubber, and I was forced to wrap my arm around his neck to keep myself upright.

"O'Malley, are you okay?" He asked with that irritating and ever-present smirk, all the while backing me up against the building.

I felt my jaw go slack despite my efforts to maintain control. I looked around to see if anyone else could help me.

"I gather I wasn't expected." Dark amusement toyed with his mouth, but his eyes were unreadable even as they probed mine.

"Uh . . . no, no, you weren't." My voice came out a tight whisper.

I was disconcerted by the sexual appeal of this man and shaken by the feelings he stirred within me.

"Well, you see, I got a knot the size of a golf ball on the back of my head . . . "

He lowered his head to show me, his hands braced on the wall behind me.

I combed my fingers through his hair until I found the bump. Couldn't miss it, really. High and hard, and wow, it must hurt. "Ouch."

"You know, O'Malley, I've been all over the world, encountered any number of killers, but I've never come away with a lump quite this large before."

"Would it help if I kissed it?"

"Not as much as looking up your dress did," he said, wiggling his eyebrows at me. "Seriously, are you okay?"

"I'm fine." I said, tugging at my dress. My legs weren't working right, but somehow I managed to step around him.

"So . . . where you headed?" he asked, giving my dress an appreciative glance.

"I . . . I'm running some errands and then meeting Karen at Coop's for coffee," I returned awkwardly, feeling uncomfortable under his steadfast gaze.

"Hmmm . . . it just so happens, O'Malley, that is why I'm here. Karen asked if I could meet you. She got hung up with a patient. I told her I'd be happy to have coffee with you and bring you home. I think she was hoping you'd still be in one piece when you got there, though. How do I explain you getting hurt on my watch?"

"That wasn't my fault. I was walking, minding my own business. What was a bike doing lying in the middle of the walkway anyway? Anyone could have tripped over it."

*Why was I working overtime trying to justify my clumsiness?*

"Weeeelll," he drawled, "It kinda was your fault, although I don't blame you for sneaking a quick look. I was having a hard time taking my eyes off you myself. You look amazing."

Oh jeez!

Shaking my head to clear it, I said, "I wasn't checking myself out. I was looking at the window display." We both turned to look at the window in question and saw the back of a stainless steel pizza oven with our own reflections staring back at us.

Stryker looked back at me and raised one eyebrow. "Okay . . . what do you say we go get that coffee? But, you might want to put your shoe back on first."

I looked down at my feet and sure enough, there was my sandal wedged in the spokes of the bicycle. Working my shoe out from between the spokes I said, "No, that's okay. You can just take me home. We don't have to go for coffee."

"No can do, O'Malley. Kavanaugh said you needed coffee and coffee you shall have. Come on, you can lean on me just in case you're tempted to attack another bicycle." Leaning in with a *stage left whisper* Stryker added, "Today's Friday."

Shaking my head with a big question mark over it, he clarified, "Your panties . . . think its Wednesday."

*Crap!* I rolled my eyes and turned three shades of red.

That got a smile from Stryker.

"Ha-ha . . . you're quite the comedian Stryker. Karen is right, I do need coffee and Coop has the best. It's been so long I'm afraid of going through withdrawals."

Stryker grinned wider and slung an arm around my shoulders, "I like a girl with a sense of humor," Stryker said as he led me toward Coop's Coffee.

Stryker and I walked to the end of the block where Main Street and First intersect. Coop's is on the northeast corner and across from Coop's sits Hopewell Travel. Directly across from there is Lucy's Diner, where the special of the day is always meatloaf and the help is always crabby.

In the middle of the block, I slowed down to look in the window of a three-story brick building. There was a FOR LEASE sign in the large front window. The building appeared to have been vacant for a long time. Above the door was an engraved plaque stating the name and year it was built. Humphrey House 1916.

"Old man Humphrey's father built it in 1916 and the family lived in it until about 1946, when he lost all his money in the stock market. They split it up, made the top floors into apartments, and rented the bottom floor to any business that could afford the rent.

My book store is going to be in this building someday." I said to no one in particular while I was peering into the front window of the building. I had my hands cupped around my eyes to block the glare of the afternoon sun.

"You want to open your own book store?" Stryker asked, seeming genuinely interested.

Nodding, I said, "Yep. I love books. I love the way they feel in my hands, the way they smell, and the sound of the paper when you turn the pages. Everything about them. You can trust books. They don't cheat on you. They don't lie to you. They don't leave you. I couldn't imagine my life without them." I said getting lost in my own thoughts. "For a while, I thought I wanted to be a photographer. In fact, I studied photography while I was getting my teaching degree at ASU. I owned my own photography studio in Arizona.

When I inherited Gramma Rosa's house last year I sold the studio to my assistant and moved back here. I still have some pieces hanging in an art gallery in Scottsdale."

"So, you're a photographer?"

"Ummm . . . more like a frustrated picture taker."

"Oh . . . is there a school for that?"

"It's self-taught."

"I noticed a couple of striking black and white desert prints hanging in your living room while I was there last night. Are they yours?"

"Guilty. And thank you. I only frame my favorites. The rest are up in the attic in a box." I explained.

"What type of photography did you do?"

"Well, I made my money doing headshots. But my first love is natural scenery."

He stared at me for a moment.

"What?" I raised my hand to pat down my hair in case it went wild while I was tango-ing with the bicycle.

"Nothing. It's just that you seem pretty clearheaded for someone who thinks she's such a wreck."

"I do have some moments of clarity," I countered. "But trust me, they're brief."

It was a nice compliment, though.

We were standing very close. Stryker reached out and ran a finger over the bridge of my nose, "I like your freckles."

My hands went immediately to my cheeks.

"Freckles, the bane of my existence," I laughed.

*Sometimes a certain scene brought back a distant memory from long ago, resurrected from a forgotten past. I would catch a fragmented glimpse of my father, Michael O'Malley, his voice filled with laughter. A memory from a happier time, before the disappointment settled in . . . before his departure shattered a little girl's heart.*

*Some considered having lost my dad at such a young age I was too young to remember him, but I did. A perfect moment would come over me. In a flash of clarity, I would remember everything . . . his warm smile and caring eyes . . . just like the eyes I was looking into right now.*

"My dad always teased me about my freckles. Angel kisses . . . that's what he called them. He would kiss me repeatedly until I was laughing so hard I couldn't stand up anymore. And I would yell for help, screaming that I was getting attacked by a band of angels."

Smiling, Stryker asked, "Where is your father, O'Malley? This is the first time I've heard you speak of him."

"Dead."

"Damn, I'm sorry. I didn't mean to pry."

"It was years ago. I hadn't seen him for years even before he died."

"What happened?"

"Car accident, out west somewhere. We didn't get to ask too many questions." I turned, breaking the gaze we had been sharing. Stryker had a lot in common with Michael O'Malley, I realized. Outgoing, strong willed, as well as dangerously handsome. "Until I heard of his death, and maybe even for a while after, I dreamed he would come back for us.

"My parents split when we were little; Mom packed us up and took us to Florida. Dad didn't follow. After we moved, I convinced myself he was a secret agent or worked for the CIA and couldn't come home. Because, if he visited us he would be placing us in jeopardy so he had to stay away. I didn't want to believe he chose just to forget us. I've always had quite an imagination.

"Anyway," I continued with a sigh, "In the face of reality, I have out grown the need for happily-ever-after fairytales. But, to my shame and surprise, the need to hear that I hadn't been fundamentally unlovable at ten years of age has nagged at me all these years later."

Stryker's gaze had settled on something over my shoulder, looking deep in thought. He glanced back at me as if he just remembered I was standing there and said, "You know O'Malley, I think the hardest thing for children to realize about their parents is that they're just human. They don't come with guarantees that they're always going to do things perfectly," Stryker was suddenly sounding very wise.

"Oh, I know that," I said ruefully. "I learned that a long time ago."

Stryker glanced at me apologetically. "And, your brother?"

"Allen, my twin, lives in Boston. He's a teacher at a school for the blind there."

"And, he's blind?"

"Yeah. It happened when we were about six years old. He was hit by a car. We always had hoped that his sight would return . . . but so far nothing. He's always handled it better than I. It's been said by some I have survivor's guilt."

"What happened? What do you have to feel guilty about?" his voice was low and easy.

Not certain my legs would hold me up much longer; I leaned back against the building. His eyes demanded an explanation. One that I had a strong aversion to giving. I hated dredging up old wounds and re-infecting them. Yet, for some crazy reason I knew I'd tell him; it was as if he had the right to know my deep, dark secrets.

"We were in our front yard playing tag and I was it. I taunted and yelled and chased Allen into the street and right into the path of an oncoming car." I took a deep breath. "Allen never blamed me. He's a wonderful big brother."

"Big brother? I thought you were twins."

"Oh, we are. But, Allen won't hesitate to tell you he's a whole two minutes older than me. And better looking." I said with a smile on my lips.

"Well, it sounds like he loves you very much. You're lucky."

"Yes," I said, deep in thought. "Yes I am."

"Did he attend school in Boston?"

"Yeah. In fact I followed him there, positive he needed me to protect him. Because that's what I did. Boy, was I surprised when I found out he could get along just fine without me.

"I watched him for one solid week, going from class to class, building to building. Usually, with some good-looking girl on his arm. He was actually doing fine without me. Better than fine.

"Can you imagine the blow to my ego when I found out he could really have a life without me? It was pretty devastating," I shrugged, then added philosophically, "That was when I decided the best thing for him, was for me to go to school somewhere else."

Our gazes met. There was a sense of intimacy we shared that could not be denied. Talking to him was easy, despite the heat of physical attraction that could totally set me on fire. I pushed that aside and decided to simply enjoy being with him for the moment, feeling the heated tingle of attraction.

Stryker obviously feeling the tingle, too, cleared his throat and asked, "So, O'Malley did you always want to write?"

"To tell you the truth, it was something that just happened. There was a time in my life when things weren't going so great and I started keeping a journal"

"So it's an *autobiography*?" he asked with a quizzical look on his face.

I snorted out a laugh, "No, not at all. The ideas for the book are loosely based on a few things that happened in my life. But, it's purely fiction." I stopped . . . remembering the events that triggered my starting to write in a journal. Remembering . . .

Startling me out of my revelry, two crows choose that moment to fly screeching across the treetops and land in a nearby maple tree. The birds sat quietly on separate branches, as if their previous outburst had been an embarrassing lapse in judgment on their part.

Time to make a hasty retreat and maintain at least a little of my dignity. I grabbed Stryker's arm and said, "I need coffee . . . now."

"Then coffee you shall have. Lead the way," he said with a bow.

I pushed open the heavy wooden door and was immediately plunged into the welcome dimness of Cooper's. The cool air smelled wonderfully aromatic; coffee with an underlying scent of freshly baked muffins engulfed me. Inhaling, I took in my surroundings as we stood in the large front room that housed the retail part of the coffee shop/bakery.

Wooden shelves anchored to the walls near the ceiling displayed items from when the building was inhabited by his mother's dress shop. I imagined many of the items were from much further back, when it was just a dry goods store. Old sugar sacks were nailed to the walls. Dozens of old coffee tins adorned the shelves. Old-fashion display cases, with dark wood trim framing glass fronted cabinets, now housed assorted muffins and Coop's famous pies.

Behind the counter, Coop had hung photos. Photos of his parents, old black and whites, and photos of himself in uniform. *Wow, he was hot!* Funny how I'd never taken the time to look at those old photos.

Coop's appeared empty, except for *the man* himself, seated at the long mahogany counter, studiously working on what I assumed to be inventory. His feet were propped up on the brass rail that ran the length of the counter just above the floor.

A mug steamed gently at his elbow, and soft classical music played on a boom box. Inhaling deeply, I allowed the smell of Coop's to settle over me. Nothing relaxed me like the smell of fresh ground coffee beans and today was no exception.

"What cha drinking?" I asked softly.

"Green oolong tea, full of antioxidants. You should try some," he said without looking up.

"Over my dead body."

"A real possibility, since you insist on eating red meat."

Coop stood and smiled; his eyes full of easygoing charm.

I felt the emotional burn of hot tears. By the time I was halfway across the sloping wooden floor, Coop's strong arms were open and his smile replaced by a searching look of concern. I stepped into his embrace; clinging to him, I buried my face against his chest.

"It's okay, Mattie I'm here." His arms tightened around me. Pressing his lips into my hair he asked, "Want to tell me?"

Shaking my head, I pulled back a little and brushed away the tears. "I'm fine now that I'm here."

Setting me away from him, he said, "You look great, Mattie."

"Liar. But thanks anyway. I just left Judy. She's a miracle worker.

I adored Nicholas Cooper from the moment I bumped into him, *literally*, two years ago.

*I had just arrived in town after driving cross-country from Arizona. Needing a cup of coffee I stopped at the first coffee shop I saw, which happened to be Coop's Coffee Café.*

*I went barreling through the door and slammed into the chest of the largest man I had ever seen. At least the largest man I'd ever seen that close. Unfortunately, the large man was carrying a tray full of hot coffee and pie to a table. The tray went flying as he reached out and caught me. But because we were both in motion, we toppled backward.*

*Somehow, the very large man managed to land on the bottom and buffered me when I fell squarely on top of him. For a moment we were both so stunned we couldn't utter a word. Through eyes heavy with coconut cream pie, Coop squinted at me.*

*His face and lips were twisted but not from anger as I'd first thought, but laughter. I felt my own laughter building inside when I thought how we must look.*

His rich laugh and a generous sense of humor . . . part sarcasm and part goof ball . . . makes him very approachable, along with the mop of curly brown hair and bright brown eyes. His easy smile shows off the dimples in his cheeks. From the moment we met, I felt a bond with him as I'd never felt with anyone else. It was as if I'd known him forever. I would trust this man with my life.

As always, he was dressed in an unbuttoned plaid flannel shirt, over a black t-shirt, jeans, and boots. His baseball cap sitting backwards on his head was something I generally teased him about but, right now I found it especially comforting knowing things were still normal in my otherwise chaotic world.

"Here, I thought you could use some sugar." Stryker said as he approached us with two large cups of coffee and large piece of Coop's famous coconut cream pie.

Taking Coop by the hand, I pulled him toward Stryker.

"Coop, I want to introduce you to someone. Nicholas Cooper I would like you to meet Beau Stryker."

After placing the tray on the table Coop had led me to, Stryker extended his hand. "Nice to meet you, and please call me Stryker."

The two men shook hands eyeing each other pleasantly, but with a slight undertone.

I smiled and watched as they sized each other up.

Coop was half head taller than Stryker, had a broader frame, but was a good ten years older.

"It's Coop, and it's nice to meet you too, Stryker. Karen has mentioned you to me."

Turning his attention back to me, Coop took my hand, "Karen's been keeping me apprised on what's been happening. You know if you need me, I'll help anyway I can." He assured me while glancing over at Stryker.

Tears came to my eyes and I said, "Thanks Nicky, I appreciate that."

Wiping away the tears I looked over at Stryker, "You know, you guys have something in common. Coop was an Army Ranger, Special Forces, or something. And Stryker here was a Marine."

They both nodded eyeing each other.

Stryker waited until we were seated and I had taken a drink from the large cup before he spoke again. "O'Malley, do you know if Roger owns any other properties?"

*Wow cut to the chase, Stryker.*
"I'm sorry, but there's really no way to ease into this."

*Great he's doing it again.*
"No . . . I mean, I don't know. I didn't even know he still owned his house until the night he moved out. I guess I didn't know him as well as I thought." I grabbed a napkin to wipe my nose. Great . . . I'm going to cry in front

of Mr. Marine. "Will it freak you out if I cry?" I asked, wiping a tear from my eye.

"Yeah . . . kinda," he mumbled from behind his coffee cup.

*Jeez.*

"I have no idea where Roger is or where he's going. We haven't been close for quite a while now, in any sense of the word. I guess everything just fell apart when I started spending so much time writing my book. He thought I should work for him . . . but . . ."

With a heavy sigh of his own, Stryker said, "Jeez O'Malley . . . will it freak you out if I cry?"

"Sorry. It's just that I really can't answer any of your questions."

"Don't be too hard on yourself. You can think you know someone their whole life and still not know anything about them." He said, watching in amazement while I went back to inhaling my pie. It was so good I sighed and let out a little moan.

Stryker, clearly amused, asked, "Hungry?"

The bell above the door jingled, drawing our attention as Karen walked in. I looked over in time to see Coop's eyes light up, confirming what I'd always believed. He's in love with Karen. Unfortunately, I don't think she's even noticed.

I let my mind wander thinking they would make the perfect couple. Her . . . short, blond, and gorgeous and him . . . tall, dark, and handsome. They would be my idea of the perfect parents. I wonder if they'd adopt me.

"Karen sit, I'll bring you a cup." Coop called from behind the counter.

After Coop had seen to everyone's needs, he kissed me on the cheek and said, "Mattie, you take care. It was nice meeting you Stryker." He nodded at Karen and went back to work.

# CHAPTER 7

O kay Mom, you heard the doc. You can go home. I'm fine. As a matter of fact I believe his exact words were 'you're perfect'. I'm perfect; you can go home now."

My mother has been here for a week taking care of me, and I really do appreciate it but now it's time for her to go.

"I don't know, Mattie I'm not sure you're ready to be left alone."

"Yes, I am Mom. You need to get back. I'm sure Mr. Dawson is anxious to see you. You've been gone for a whole week. Go home, relax, and don't give me another thought. Please!"

"You're right. I should go home and maybe you should come with me. You said you were coming down for a visit anyway. Why not now? You've been through a lot lately. You could come back home with me and relax. You could go to the beach and lay in the sun. We could go sightseeing. There's a lot to do in Florida."

"I have to get back to work. Ethel isn't going to hold my position forever. You don't have to worry about me."

"Oh honey, I'm teasing you. You're an adult and I need to realize it and let you get on with your life. That life wouldn't happen to include Dr. Jonathan Harmon, would it?" She asked with a twinkle in her eyes.

"Mom, we haven't even been on a date yet! Let alone plan a life together. He seems nice enough." *Time will tell.*

"Mom, on a more serious note before you go home, can we talk about Dad?"

"What exactly is it you want to talk about?" Mom asked while grinding some coffee beans. This is serious. She never makes me coffee. She's always trying to push tea on me. I hate tea.

"Why didn't he ever come visit us after we moved to Florida?"

"Well, your father was a busy man. He had an important job to do and he took that very seriously."

"More important than Allen and me?" I asked hearing the tears in my own voice.

"Oh, honey no. Don't ever think your father didn't love you and Allen. You two were his world. There were just things that needed to be done and your father was the one who had to do them."

"What things, Mom? What was so important he couldn't visit us?"

"Mattie, just because someone doesn't love you the way you wish to be loved doesn't mean they don't love you with all that they've got."

I sat and pondered that for a moment. Sighing, I realized I was eventually going to have to accept the basic truth; my father loved me as best he could.

"Okay Mom. I'm sorry I didn't mean to upset you."

*There is so much I don't know about my father. So many missing pieces to the puzzle of Michael O'Malley left blank by my mother's reluctance to talk about the past. Nevertheless, there was no quieting my hunger to know about him.*

"I forgot to tell you, your aunt Patty is coming for a visit. I was hoping I would still be here but since you're in such a hurry for me to go home, she'll have you all to herself. She is going to love that." Talk about the master of redirection. I can see where I got my super powers.

"Pepper? Coming here? Why? It's not that I don't love having her but Mom the timing is bad. You know, with all the stuff that's been going on . . . I . . . I . . . "

"Sorry honey, it's a done deal. And just so you know it's because of all the stuff that's been going on that I asked her to come."

The next morning I awoke with a renewed sense of purpose. After putting Mom on the first airplane out, I called Ethel Tams to inform her I would be back to work next week, no matter what she and my mother decided. I assured her that most of the swelling and bruising would be gone by then. Any remaining bruising I could hide with make-up and sunglasses. Ethel told me not to worry. Oliver had stepped up, was reading to my preschoolers, and filling in for me where needed. She said Oliver was doing a wonderful job and they hardly missed me at all. *That was very worrisome.*

Next on my list was finding Roger. Stryker couldn't go into his house without a warrant but no one said I couldn't. I decided not to tell Karen where I was going just in case there is some kind of code FBI agents live by. *You know the one where they cannot stand by and watch their best friend break into their ex-boyfriend's house.* I don't want her to try to stop me and I certainly don't want her contacting Stryker. I'm sure he would stop me or preferably kill me without leaving any traceable evidence. However, I will take my trusty sidekick with me in case I run into any trouble. Every crime fighter needs a sidekick.

I changed into black cargo pants, black tank top and my Sketchers. I checked myself out in the mirror after pulling my hair back in a ponytail.

"Not bad, if I do say so myself."

Heading downstairs I called to Harry, "Come on Harry, we're going for a ride." Harry hasn't left my side since I got home from the hospital so finding him hasn't been a problem . . . for now . . . anyway. "Oh, Harry what a good boy. Do you want to go for a ride in Ladybug?" After removing a rawhide from Harry's goodie jar, I grabbed my purse and keys and set off for Roger's mini-mansion with my trusty sidekick, riding shotgun.

Pulling out of the drive, I noticed Mrs. Blackwell was outside watering her garden. Maybe I should go ask her a few questions. She has the perfect view from the upper wraparound porch that Mr. Blackwell built for her after the great poison ivy fiasco of 1987.

If the story is true, Mrs. Blackwell was peeking through the shrubs at Mr. Esposito. Known for his nude sunbathing, it was probably something Mrs. Blackwell couldn't help herself from investigating. Rumor has it she was covered head to toe with poison ivy. Mr. Esposito, big on privacy, had planted it all around the perimeter of his yard.

Anyway, Mr. Blackwell decided to build her a widow's walk around the top floor of their house so she wouldn't have to go skulking through the poison ivy. She has been known to stay up there all night keeping our neighborhood safe from nudists.

I pulled into her drive as she was rolling up the hose and hanging it on the fence that protected her garden from the wildlife . . . like Harry.

Mrs. Blackwell was well into her eighties with long frizzy white hair that draped half way down her back, which she coiled into an untidy braid. Her smile revealed a gap between her two front teeth, which were yellowed and slightly askew. Lipstick, applied with a heavy hand was dark as it bled into fine hairline crevices along her thin upper lip, which lent credence to the deep lines that hardened her mouth. The elderly woman, as always, was attired in a long, black, and distinctly funereal voluminous dress. I've often pictured an endless supply of those dresses stored in trunks in a dusty corner of her attic.

Noticing me she wobbled over to my car. "Hello Matilda, I see everything is healing nicely," peering over her glasses into my car. "Mr. Blackwell and I were getting a little worried about you. What with all those accidents you've been having lately. Did you get the basket we sent you? I'm assuming you didn't, otherwise you would have said something and since you haven't said anything I guess I'll have to call Annabelle over at the flower shop and find out why it hasn't been sent yet."

"I'm sorry, Mrs. Blackwell, but that's one of the reason's I'm here . . . to thank you for the lovely basket. It was very thoughtful of you and . . . Mr. Blackwell."

*She is clearly losing it . . . Mr. Blackwell passed away ten years ago.*

"You're very welcome, my dear. Mr. Blackwell and I do not know what is happening to this neighborhood. Young women being pushed down stairs in their own homes, dogs running loose all over the neighborhood, and even poor Karen getting attacked in her own office." Shaking her head Mrs. Blackwell continued, "You know none of this stuff ever happened when your grandmother was alive. She knew how to keep order around here. You know we were best friends and I still miss Rosa, that dear soul. She was truly one of the good ones." She sighed, obviously taking a walk down memory lane.

"I noticed Violet came to take care of you for a while." She continued not waiting for an answer. "I never understood what happened between her and Michael. They were such a lovely couple. I can remember their wedding day as if it were yesterday."

"I know you still miss Gramma." I said as I patted Mrs. Blackwell's hand, trying to avoid stabbing myself with one of the many oversized rings she wore on her long gnarled fingers. "Did you see my father much after my mom took us to Florida?"

"Oh, I don't really recall. Now that you mention it, I guess he wasn't around much. You know your mother was the belle of the ball around here. Everyone just loved Violet Jensen. She could have had her pick of the boys, but she chose your father. It was like a fairy tale."

Walking away from my car Mrs. Blackwell was shrugging her shoulders and shaking her head. I guess we were done here.

"Oh . . . before I go Mrs. Blackwell, I just wanted to tell you I'm sorry about all the commotion that's been going on here lately and ask if you have seen anyone hanging around here that doesn't belong?"

Turning back toward me she said, "Now Matilda, you know I don't pay much attention to things like that. But since you asked, I did see a car creeping down our street the other night with the lights off."

"What night would that be Mrs. Blackwell? Do you remember?"

"Well, I think it was the night you fell down the steps. You know I'm getting old and things like that are getting harder to remember. But I'm sure it was the same night I went to my support group."

"Support group? What kind of support group would that be?"

"It's my psychic group. We meet twice a month at the old fire hall."

"Why would you need a support group like that?"

"Because my dear I'm a psychic, just like Rosa was. You didn't know? I'm not surprised Violet never told you. She never believed." My eyes as large as saucers, I shook my head no.

"Let me tell you there are all sorts of mistaken tales about our abilities. People look at us like we can fly or turn people into toads." She shook her head as if that was absurd. "We're not witches for goodness sake; we're psychics. We don't use brooms and cauldrons; our tools are tarot cards and crystal balls.

"I, personally, am a natural born psychic with intuitive abilities. I just peaked later in life than most. I'm being trained as a spirit guide. In fact, the first spirit I spoke with was Rosa when she asked me to watch over you. You have a purple aura floating around you. And that's not good."

"You spoke with my grandmother? How?" Nervously I giggled. "Did you use a Ouija board or have a séance to conjure up her spirit?" I asked jokingly.

"Why, yes actually we did. Had a séance that is. We would never do anything as pedestrian as using a Ouija board; those things never work."

Letting my head fall forward I hit the steering wheel with a thud and taking a deep breath, I dared to ask, "So you spoke to my grandmother from the grave. And just exactly *what* did Gramma ask you to do?"

"Rosa asked us to help you out if you ever got in to trouble. She knew there would be trouble eventually."

"Trouble? What kind of trouble?" I asked drawing my eyebrows together with a look of concern. My eyebrows were getting a real workout today.

"Why . . . your inheritance. I noticed a black cloud being drawn into your atmosphere." Clearly, this woman was wicked crazy.

"A black cloud? My inheritance? Explain please, because I don't understand."

*Okay, I didn't totally buy into the whole physic thing she had going on, but I was too chicken to totally discount it, either.*

Squeezing my hand, Mrs. Blackwell said, "Be patient my dear, you will." Looking down at the Bewitched watch she had on her right wrist she said, "I've got to get going. Sorry."

"I've got to get going myself, but I'll come back to visit soon. Thanks again," I jammed the gearshift in reverse, "for the flowers," I blurted. Then we flew out of the drive.

What the heck was that about? Séance's and Ouija boards. I'll have to talk to Pepper about this.

# CHAPTER 8

Feeling the need for fresh air, I pulled over to put the top down on Ladybug. "Harry, we're going topless." Harry and I were just a couple of redheads cruising through town with our hair blowing in the wind and singing along with the hometown boy, Bob Seger. I love hearing his voice booming through the aftermarket speakers I had installed in Ladybug while I was in college. My oversized sunglasses were pulling double duty today, hiding my bruises and shading my eyes from the bright sun. Harry had his head hanging out the window drooling all over the side of my car. It was worth it just to see the smile on his face.

Roger lives on the other side of town in a newer subdivision where the houses are set back off the street and look like mini mansions. Roger sold most of these houses. It's a gated community and there is always a guard on duty. He's been the same guard since Roger and I started dating. Hopefully, Willy's still here.

I pulled up to the guardhouse and saw Willy sitting at the desk. With my little finger wave, "Hi ya Willy, how's it going?"

"Good, Ms. Mattie. How you been? Mr. Moore ain't here just now. As a matter of fact I don't recall seeing him the last week or so."

"I know, Willy. Roger sent me to pick up a few things for him. He's been real busy lately."

"Well, I guess that'd be okay. What with you and Mr. Moore being boyfriend and girlfriend and all." Willy said while taking off his hat and running his hand through his closely cropped hair. "Maybe when you talk to Mr. Moore again you could have him give me a call here at the guard shack. I need to tell him about some work that's gonna be done on the water pipes in front of his house."

"I'll tell him as soon as I see him. Thanks Willy. Bye." I did my little finger wave again and pulled through the gates. I hope I don't do anything stupid and get Willy in trouble . . .

Making my way through Rogers's well-manicured neighborhood where the silence was like a sanctuary and the stately houses were tucked away between huge oaks, dogwoods, and armies of pine trees I made my way up Roger's long driveway. I took some time to scope things out, but didn't see any neighbors and the lawn people must be done for the day. They're usually crawling all over the place; apparently people who live in mini mansions never want their lawns to look like they've just been mowed. That's like getting a haircut every two weeks so you never look like you just had a haircut. If I'm spending fifty bucks for a haircut, I want everyone to know I just got a haircut.

I pulled Ladybug around to the back of the house while I checked things out. I turned the ignition off and started to open the car door, which Harry took as his cue. He jumped over the back of the passenger's seat into the backseat where he bounced once and then onto the hood. Jumping off and onto the driveway he turned his head to look at me, as if to say let's play. Then he took off as if his butt was on fire. I started to give chase but decided my time would be better served looking around the house. Harry will come back when he hears Ladybug start up. He loves going for rides in her.

Pulling my hair back into a ponytail I reached into the car and pulled out the hat Karen gave me for Christmas last year. It's a black baseball cap with FBI embroidered in white across the front and "Fairytale Believers Inc" across the back.

I walked across the brick patio Roger had installed shortly after he moved in here. His beautifully landscaped yard is where he liked bringing potential clients to show them the sort of neighborhood they would be buying into. I should have realized Roger would never give up this place. He always hated my old farmhouse, always complaining about it being too cold in the winter and too hot in the summer.

*It was never just right for old Goldilocks.*

Roger hadn't set the alarm. That was odd. But, not wanting to take the time to wonder why, I reached under the rock/speaker sitting on the patio and found the extra key. I took a moment to let my gaze wander over the yard again. It looked as if Roger hadn't closed the pool yet. Again, that was odd but I didn't have the time to worry about that just now. I quickly slipped inside and closed the door.

Making my way through the mudroom, I stepped into Roger's state-of-the-art kitchen. Any chef would be proud to call it his own. Only the best for Roger; stainless steel appliances, granite counter tops, heated wood floors, and cherry wood cabinets. Copper pots and pans hang over a gigantic island on a huge rack. In the center of the island sits a large white ceramic rooster. By large, I mean about two feet tall. The rooster is the only thing on the counters. Everything else is hidden in one of the two appliance garages. Roger always says clutter kills a sale. My house must have been killing him slowly.

A search of the kitchen drawers revealed nothing. Just off the kitchen down a short hall is Rogers's home office. The office showcases three bookcases filled with impressive looking volumes, which Roger insists 'shows well'. Situated in the center of the room, facing the doorway, is Rogers's beautifully carved cherry desk. His desktop displays an oversized, leather bound calendar, a computer monitor, a telephone with about a gazillion little extension buttons, and a penholder. The message light on his phone was blinking double time. Uh-oh, not a good sign. Roger never lets the phone go to voicemail. A quick peek through the desk yielded nothing. However, I caught sight of a stack of files sitting on the corner of his credenza.

I took a quick glance over both shoulders in a totally unnecessary move that somehow made me feel safer. *Nope, nobody's watching.*

I opened the first file labeled Ottawa Properties. It contained what looked to be standard legal real estate forms and as far as I was concerned, they could have been written in Russian.

Dropping that one I reached for the next one on the pile hoping it contained a ransom demand for Roger or at least a death threat.

No such luck. This one was labeled Paramount Properties and the documents looked to be as foreign as the first. I looked at file after file and the only thing I was getting was a headache.

One thing caught my eye as I looked back through a couple of the files. The property address was the same on all the files; 1222 Tower Trail in Hopewell, MI.

The wire wastebasket in the corner had a stack of papers in it. Looking closer, I saw that it was my book.

"Of all the nerve . . . I can't believe he just chucked my book into the trash." I walked over to the trashcan and picked up the title page of my book. Glaring at it with tears in my eyes, I said out loud, "Okay, now you've really pissed me off, mister."

Leaving the office I turned right and made my way further down the hall. When I got to Roger's bedroom I walked in through a short hall with walk-in closets flanking both sides.

As soon as I stepped into the room, I felt the hair on the back of my neck rise slowly. Turning to the left towards the bathroom, I saw feet. The feet were hovering just above the marble tile floor in the shower. Slowly, I let my eyes run up the length of the man hanging from the showerhead. With a clear view through the glass door, I saw the face of the person to which the feet belonged.

Oh my God! A sudden rush of movement behind me snapped my head around. A gray blur exploded through the door.

Screaming, my heart leaped into my throat. I tried to get away, but it was too late. Something slammed hard into the side of my head.

I dropped like a rock, the floor rushing up to meet my face.

When I opened my eyes, I found myself looking into Stryker's worried face. It was close and shadowed, framed by a patch of sky coming through the window.

"O'Malley can you hear me?"

I summoned all my resources. "Yes."

"Do you remember what happened?"

Frowning made my head hurt, so I abandoned the attempt and stared blankly up at him without replying.

"Come on, O'Malley, we've got to get out of here before this place goes up in flames."

Flames . . . ? Struggling to get up I scurried after Stryker toward the open window.

He leapt through the window and after landing on the ground with a thud, reached back with large hands, and tried to pull me out. I was hung up on something. Stryker gave me a tug, the snap on my pants gave way, and I was jerked out of the window with such force that Stryker flew backwards.

"Jesus, O'Malley . . . " he muttered, before collapsing with an "oomph" as I landed on top of him. I had to admit, landing on him sure beat the ground, though I'm not sure which was harder. His muscled chest didn't give an inch as he rolled us over and stood, bringing me up with him.

"Sorry," I mumbled, sure I sounded as embarrassed as I felt.

"Come on; we've got to get you out of here before someone calls the fire department."

"Wait! I'm not going anywhere without my pants," I protested, keeping eye contact so he wouldn't notice I was standing there in my Sunday undies . . . and it was Tuesday.

"Fine, but make it fast," he said while yanking at my pants, material ripping. When he turned around he was holding my favorite cargo pants, with the pocket hanging by a thread and a big rip in the seat. He had quite the wolfish grin on his face as he handed them back to me.

Good I don't think he noticed.

It should have pissed me off, but instead I found my fighting stance fading. Man, he had a great laugh. It was rich and full and it totally transformed his face. For a second, I got a glimpse of the happy all-American guy he'd probably been in another life.

"Hey! You did that on purpose! These are my favorite pants."

"O'Malley get your Sunday butt into your Tuesday pants because I have something I need to show you."

*He noticed.*

I sucked my breath in over my teeth, self-respect a minor priority at this point. I put my pants back on, and filled Stryker in on what I saw hanging in the shower.

"That's not our only problem. Come with me. I've got something to show you."

Following him over to the pool, I looked down into the leaf-filled water. In the pool was a tall, slim woman with clouds of flaming red hair surrounding her head. Floating face down.

Seeing is not always believing. Because, if I believed what I was seeing, I would be seeing me floating face first in Roger's pool. She looked just like me.

"Stryker . . . who is that?" I asked disbelievingly. I felt Stryker's body turn rigid, though he didn't move. We matched each other breath for breath. Close by, a bird chirped while a breeze rustled the leaves in a nearby tree.

"Well, from this angle it looks a lot like you. I think what we have here is a mistaken identity. I believe whoever did this thought he was drowning you. He must not have realized, when he hit you on the head in the bedroom, who you were. That FBI hat you're wearing is covering the majority of your hair.

"We've got to get you out of here. Whoever did this thinks he succeeded and I would rather let them think that for now. Come on. Let's get the top up on your car and try to get you out of here without being seen."

"Wait. I've got to find Harry. He was out running somewhere."

"Don't worry. I've got him in my car over on the next block. I'll drive you over there and you can drive my car to Karen's house. I'll drive yours out of here and with a little luck, no one will notice. Its dark enough now and with all the emergency vehicles that will be coming through we should be able to get out undetected. I found a service entrance at the back of the subdivision. Hopefully, we'll be able to work our way out through there."

# CHAPTER 9

"Mattie, why did you go over there?" Karen asked, returning to the kitchen with a sweater to tie around my waist to hide the gaping hole in my pants. Karen watched as I glanced at Stryker, who was looking at me over his beer. He nodded at me as if to say go ahead. "Okay, spill it."

"Alright. But, first in my defense I didn't say anything to either one of you because I didn't want to get you involved. I know you have procedures you have to follow and breaking and entering probably isn't one of them.

"I went to Roger's looking for anything that would tell me where he went or if I could find something that would tell me why he's trying to drive me crazy. Everything looked normal until I got to the master bedroom and saw someone hanging from the showerhead. The next thing I know I'm being pulled through the window with enough centrifugal force to knock me out of my pants."

Looking over at Stryker I asked, "What the hell did you do when you were a Marine?"

Leaning in towards me his eyes acquired an evil spark, "I'd tell you but then I'd have to kill you."

*Obviously the answer was way above my pay grade.*

"What were you doing there?" I asked.

"Karen and I started talking about the case and decided we should look a little deeper at Roger. Thinking that maybe he wasn't the perpetrator but the victim.

"Your car was there, so I knew you had to be somewhere. I was by the pool when I heard you scream. O'Malley, was it Roger hanging there?"

"No, it wasn't Roger . . . " I swallowed the wine I had just sipped from my glass and looked Stryker in the eye, as I answered.

Stryker reached into his shirt pocket and pulled out a picture. He looked at the picture then turned it to show us. "Is this the person you saw hanging in the shower at Roger's house today?"

I took the picture from his outstretched hand and stared at it. Stuttering I said, "Ye . . . yes, that's him. He's the one who was hanging there just staring. Who is he? How did you get this picture? That's Roger standing there with him though."

Karen got up and stood behind me with her hands resting gently on my shoulders trying to calm me. "Beau, who is he?"

"Joel Simmons."

"Joel Simmons? As in Roger's assistant . . . Joel Simmons?" Karen asked recovering from the shock much more quickly than I.

"Yes. However, I'm guessing his name isn't Joel Simmons. I'm running his fingerprints as we speak. Something didn't set right with me after I spoke to him about Roger the other day, so before I left his office I picked up a frame with this picture in it and slid it into my pocket. I should be getting the results soon."

"I don't understand. He's not Joel Simmons?" The cold prickle down my spine suggested it wasn't anything good.

"Was there anything thing in the house that seemed out of place?"

"I don't know . . . this all seems so surreal. However, as far as the house goes it was all . . . So Roger. You know . . . there was one thing." Shaking my head I said, "It's nothing really. Never mind," I said awkwardly, embarrassed that he threw away my book.

Leaning in towards me Stryker asked, "What?"

"Okay, I'll tell you. That jerk threw away my book. It was in the trash can."

"Sorry. Anything else?"

"Well, there were some files sitting on the credenza. I went through some of them looking for a ransom note or something but they were just some real estate forms."

"Did they mean anything to you?"

Shaking my head no I said, "Not really and everything else seemed normal except for hangman and the redhead floating in the pool."

"This brings us back on point. Roger's house . . . man hanging in shower. Roger's pool . . . woman-floating face down. Coincidence?" Shaking his head Stryker said, "I think not."

"Roger did not do this. He's not a killer. He's a real estate lawyer for God's sake. If he's pissed at someone, he takes legal action. He could never, ever do this. You don't know him."

Stryker cocked his head to one side. "Do you, O'Malley?"

I bit my lip. Good question. "Did you see who hit me and set the fire?"

Shaking his head no, "He must have gone out the front when I was out back trying to coax Harry into my car. By the way, I hope it's okay that I bribed him with a hamburger. It's the only way I could get him interested enough to get into my car." He said while patting Harry on the head. Little did Stryker know he now had a friend for life in Harry.

I shivered at the thought of someone trying to set me on fire.

Resting her chin on my head and squeezing my shoulders Karen said, "Honey, you're staying here with me tonight."

"Karen, I can't stay here forever. I have to go back to work in the morning and Pepper will be here tomorrow night."

Injecting himself into the conversation Stryker asked, "Who's Pepper?"

"She's my aunt. Really, she's my dad's aunt. My mom called her to stay with me and keep me out of trouble."

Chuckling to himself, Stryker said, "Good luck with that."

"Beau, maybe you should go back to Roger's and see what you can find out from the police there. They may talk to you as a courtesy. They need not know of your involvement."

"My involvement? What is my involvement? It's pretty clear I'm swinging by the seat of my pants here." Looking over at me he shrugged, "No pun intended O'Malley."

"Yeah, right. Laugh it up, spy guy."

# CHAPTER 10

After Karen said goodnight and headed upstairs, I went into the guest bedroom and fell backward on the bed. I closed my eyes and a mental picture of hangman leaped into my head.

Crap . . . 3:00 . . . again. Why can't I sleep? Something is bugging me.

I need to know what's going on over at Roger's house and I need to talk to Stryker about going over to Joel Simmon's place, too. But, I can't take my car out of Karen's garage.

Then it came to me. Roger left his bike in my garage when he left. It's perfect. No one would be expecting me to be riding a motorcycle and once I put on my helmet and jacket, no one would recognize me.

"No, Harry, you can't go with me." I whispered while kneeling in front of him at Karen's back door. "Stay here and look after Karen." I opened the door, stepped out, and closed the door behind me. The night air was cool and eerily quiet . . . not even a cricket chirping.

Skulking across the street, I made my way to the garage and slowly pushed open the door. My fingers twitched wanting to flip on the light switch, but I had to depend on the night's full moon for enough light to see what I was doing. I couldn't take the chance and turn on the lights in case someone was watching for me.

I pulled on my leather jacket and pants. Gathering up my hair, I settled the full-face helmet on my head then pulled the cover off Roger's 2003 V-Rod. What a gorgeous piece of machinery. All black, sleek, and ready to roll.

Darkness cloaked the area, making the stars vivid and bright in the clear sky. I drove slowly, glancing occasionally at the side mirrors to be certain no one followed. The road lay black and silent in front and behind me.

I drove past an old mental institution, Tower-House Hospital. Built by Dr. Archibald Towerhouse, this was the local insane asylum.

Even though it had not been used as such for fifty years or more, it still conjured up visions of zombie-like people wandering, hollow eyed, through the peeling, puke-green painted hallways, trying to find a way out of their living hell. Never having been inside I wouldn't know for sure, but the wind blowing through the tree branches could almost be mistaken for pleas of help from inside the crumbling walls.

I got a cold chill down my spine as I drove by. Almost like someone was walking over my grave. I don't know . . . it just seemed spooky.

Shaking off that feeling, I drove out of town and headed out on a two-lane black top road that doesn't get much traffic this time of the morning. I didn't dare drive faster though; deer, possum, and raccoons all crossed these winding roads. The dark tunnel beneath the live oaks and the winding, twisty roads finally ended. I opened up the throttle and let the cool night air work its magic on me. Roger's right . . . *She does have the smoldering sexuality of a crouched Bengal tiger.* I was feeling confident that if anyone were following me, I would have lost him by now.

Taking a curve at a good clip, I glanced behind me and saw a flash. A second later I heard what sounded like a car backfiring. By the time I straightened up from the curve, I had the throttle wide open.

The back service road that Stryker and I exited from just a few hours ago was coming up fast, so I let up on the gas and turned the ignition switch to the off position. Everything went black and deathly quiet. I coasted over to a cluster of birch trees and parked beneath them. As I got off the bike and crouched down behind one of the trees, I saw a car moving slowly down the street. They drove right by and didn't notice the back entrance.

I waited. I listened to the sounds of night, the deep hooting "hoo-h'HOO-hoo-hoo" of the great horned owl hunting for unwary prey, the distinctive song of the whippoorwill, and the rustle of the fallen leaves beneath my feet. When the taillights disappeared down the road, I came out of my hiding spot. I took off my helmet, and made my way through the subdivision toward Rogers's house staying in the shadows.

There were no emergency vehicles around. The only thing different about the place was the yellow crime scene tape that surrounded the house. I strolled up the drive as if I belonged there and went around back, like I did earlier. *Do not enter* tape was plastered all over the doorframe.

Something . . . a flash of movement . . . caught my eye as I stepped up onto the deck. Quickly, I turned my head to scan the backyard where I'd seen it.

*Is someone out there?* I caught my breath. I felt the prickle of cold sweat along my hairline.

It was nothing. There was no movement. Not even the quiver of a leaf.

I turned the brass doorknob. . . . It was unlocked.

Unable to draw back now that I was here, I refocused all my attention on what I was doing and cautiously pushed the door open. My breathing ragged and my heart jitterbugging, I ducked under the crime scene tape and forced myself to go inside. Closing the door behind me, I leaned against it, remembering the last time I was inside this house.

I looked wide-eyed into the gloom of the empty kitchen, half-expecting to find someone else in there until I realized the heavy breathing I heard was coming from me.

After getting my breathing under control, I looked around the kitchen. It didn't look as if there was any damage in here. I hope the same can be said for Roger's office. I want to get another look at that stack of files on the credenza.

Making my way around the island, I turned down the hall toward the office. When I got to the door, I started to go in. Then, instead, I traveled further down the hall toward the bedroom, noticing considerable damage to the hallway.

The carpet felt wet and squishy under my boots. The bedroom door had been kicked in. I knew this because I tripped over it when I started to enter the room, and fell flat on my face. Laying there a second accessing my body for damage and determining there was none, I looked around the room from my horizontal position. Oh my Lord, Roger is going to freak when he sees this mess.

The mattresses were pulled off the bed, his dresser sprawled front first on the floor, his desk tipped over, and what looked like the shower door laid where his mattresses should be.

I stood and walked further into the room. I couldn't help but look over at the shower . . . remembering the body that had been hanging there earlier.

My left eye started twitching . . . oh no . . . feet . . . this can't be happening . . . not again. I started to walk closer to the shower. My ears perked up when I thought I heard the back door close. It was hard to tell with all the heavy breathing going on. When I turned toward the bedroom door, someone grabbed me from behind. With a cold fear prickling up my neck, he put a hand over my mouth, and pulled me into a body so hard it was like hitting a brick wall. I fought him, but he simply wrapped an arm around my middle and walked backwards, hauling me with him.

I bit down on the hand that was placed over my mouth, as hard as I could, to try to get him to release me. That's when I heard a very recognizable voice whisper in my ear.

"You bite me again and I'm going to bend you over my knee. And trust me *only* one of us is going to enjoy it. Do you understand?"

Nodding my head yes as adrenalin-laced sweat dripped down my back, I collapsed against him in relief, giving myself a mental head-slap. *Stryker.* He pulled me into the closet with him. Dropping his hand from my mouth, he turned me around.

I could feel him staring at me.

"What?" I whispered.

"You hit yourself in the face."

Sigh.

"Mentally," I said, correcting him and wishing it were true.

"I *mentally* slapped myself in the face. And . . . stay out of my head!" I whispered, "I think I heard the back door close."

"I know; that's why we're in the closet. I want to see who it is."

"No. I think I heard it again . . . after I bit you. We must have scared off whoever it was."

"We? Seriously?" I could tell he was rethinking taking his hand from my mouth. "God, you're impossible. What the hell are you doing here? You were told to stay put. Where's Kavanaugh?"

"She's sleeping."

"Still doesn't explain why you're here, O'Malley."

"I'm here because I wanted to check out Roger's office again." I explained, like it made perfect sense.

"And, you didn't trust me to do it? You think this is my first rodeo?"

"Wow . . . way to be snarky and sarcastic. I just wanted to see what was going on since we hadn't heard from you and to suggest that maybe we should check out Joel Simmon's place."

" . . . And again . . . I ask . . . do you think it's my first time?" I could feel his already dark eyes growing darker by the second.

"You know, we could go around in circles all night with this. Did you see the new body in the shower?" I asked.

Stryker opened the closet door and nudged/pushed me out of the closet and into the bedroom. "There is no *new* body in the shower. It was me."

"Maybe you could have just told me it was you instead of scaring the bejeesus out of me."

"I could have but what fun would that have been. Besides you weren't supposed to go out of the house without one of us." He said while taking in my leather outfit.

"No. That's not entirely accurate," I said. "You told me not to take Ladybug out. I didn't. I rode over here on Roger's Harley. He didn't take it with him when he left, so I used it."

"I stand corrected," Stryker said. His eyes darkened a little more, but aside from that, his expression was unreadable. "Now, tell me you didn't really ride a motorcycle over here in the middle of the night after someone tried to fry you just this afternoon."

"I was careful. When I spotted the guy tailing me, I pulled into the service entrance and lost him."

"I'll bet you didn't lose him. I'll bet you led him right here. Who do you think it was that we heard? He's probably got your motorcycle staked out right now so he can follow you out of here." He said, with his typical air of quiet aplomb.

"That reminds me, I think he shot at me. In case you're interested." I said with just the right amount of indignation. "I saw a flash behind me and heard what sounded like a car backfiring."

Stryker, looking like he wanted to pull his piece and shoot me himself, slowly said, "That . . . reminds . . . you? That reminds you. You didn't think that was something you should lead with. And . . . who are you anyway, Dirty Harry? No one calls it a piece. It's a gun or a weapon or a firearm . . . not a piece."

*Uh . . . oh . . . not him, too.*

"Come on; let's go back where you left Roger's bike and see if anyone is staking it out. If we're lucky, they've called it a night. If not, maybe I could use you as bait."

"Bbbait . . . me? You're kidding . . . right?"

"I wish I wasn't," he said grabbing me by the arm and leading me toward the kitchen. As we got to the back door, I remembered the files in the office. Trying to pull free from Stryker's firm grasp, he held on tighter saying, "Forget it, they're gone. Someone got to them before I got here." *I've got to watch what I think around this guy.*

Stryker and I crept back through the neighborhood, moving stealthily through the woods. We came around to the road and checked to see if any cars were lying in wait for me. Confident the bad guys went home to bed, Stryker told me to get on the bike and hightail it home. He would cover my rear.

*I found that very unsettling.*

Feeling slightly panicky, I shivered, my teeth chattering, having nothing to do with the temperature. My eyes shot to my side mirror, half hoping to see hordes of Tower-House zombies walking stiff legged, arms out straight and a dead look in their eyes. This would have been preferable to Stryker and his mustang covering my rear.

# CHAPTER 11

I t's like corralling cats with you two. I can't even go to
bed at night without waking up and finding you
going in all different directions."

*I guess this is Karen's version of reaming us out.*

"Oohhh . . . I haven't even gotten to the reaming
out stage, yet," she said pointing her well-manicured
finger at me.

"Do I have to handcuff you to your bed to keep you
there?" I stole a look in Stryker's direction and found him
smiling and nodding in agreement. Then Karen turned the
same accusing finger on him saying, "And you . . . would it

have killed you to call? Then she wouldn't have had to chase you down and put herself in jeopardy."

"You're saying I'm at fault? You do realize this chick is about two clicks shy of crazy, don't you? Besides, I was a little busy with a murder investigation. Oh, by the way, it sure didn't seem like one. When I arrived at the scene, I introduced myself to the officer in charge and offered my assistance.

"Officer Dillon," *Stryker said in a way that clearly inferred he wasn't impressed with Hopewell's finest,* "said the fire department was handling it. When I asked if there were any injuries, I was told no one was home. Officer Dillon did have the presence of mind to ask what the FBI's concern was though. I explained I lived in the neighborhood and would help any way I could. I got the impression he had no interest in the FBI getting involved."

"Beau, are you saying there were no bodies?" Karen asked.

"Not that I could determine. That's why I was still there, hoping I could find something in the rubble. And, if she would have just stayed put like she was told, maybe I would have." He said, pointing an accusing finger at me.

"How could there be no body? It was there when you pulled me out of the window. And . . . and . . . FYI . . . Mr.

FBI . . . , and any other letter in the alphabet I can think of, I am not crazy. I'm inquisitive . . . big difference."

"I've never heard of anything so insane in my life," he muttered. "This kind of crazy should be illegal."

"I. Am. Not. Crazy."

"How do you know? Did your mother have you tested?"

"Mattie, you really should quit while you're ahead. Do you have any idea what could have happened to you last night? You could be dead right now."

*Wow, Karen's channeling Violet now.*

"This isn't funny. And I'm not channeling your mother. But if you don't start listening to us," swinging her finger between Beau and herself, "I will call her myself. Is that what you want?"

I shook my head no.

"Then you'd better think long and hard before you pull a stunt like this again. You were damn lucky it was Stryker in that bedroom and not someone who wants to kill you." Exchanging a knowing glance with Stryker she continued, "The two not being mutually exclusive right now . . . I'm guessing."

"Beau, why don't you walk Mattie home and wait for her while she showers and gets ready for work. I'll take a shower and get dressed while you're over there. Then you can go home and get some rest while I take Mattie to work."

"Karen, I can take care of myself."

"We are not going to have this conversation. Pepper will be here tonight and you can go home then. But just so you know, I intend to tell her everything that's been going on so she can be prepared for . . . whatever. She can also decide if Violet should be told."

Crossing my arms across my chest I said, "I can't believe you're threatening me with my mother. I'm not five, you know."

*I'm way more than five.*

"I know you're not five. Go on now or you'll be late for work. We'll stop and get something to eat at Coop's."

"Come on, O'Malley. Let's get you in the shower," Stryker said wiggling his eyebrows at me. Looking back over his shoulder at Karen, he added, "And yeah, Kavanaugh, she's way more than five."

Throwing back my head, I glared up at the now brightening sky. Spreading my arms wide, I sighed, "Seriously? Would it kill you to cut me a break?"

Walking across the street to my house so I could shower and get ready for work was exhausting. All my nerve endings were tingling, just thinking about Stryker sitting downstairs waiting for me.

I showered quickly, the red water reminding me Paul, the plumber, never came to check out the pipes. I blew my hair dry upside down just like Judy showed me. Then used the product I bought from her to carefully run through my layered locks to give me *sexy-just-got-out-of-bed* hair. I used my new concealer stick to hide the bruising under my eyes and applied mascara to my eyelashes; apparently it made my eyes pop.

After shimmying into a soft coral, sleeveless shift, *I really need to do some laundry,* and sliding my feet into a pair of nude colored, sexy strappy heels, I stepped back to evaluate my new self in my antique standing mirror that had the place of honor in the corner of my bedroom.

A long, soft whistle startled me out of my reverie. I jumped, then let my gaze settle on Stryker who was leaning casually against the doorjamb, totally filling out the doorway. Arms crossed over his chest, his biceps strained against the sleeves of his t-shirt. The slow grin that tugged his lips was nothing short of wicked. His gaze locked on mine like a heat-seeking missile.

"O'Malley . . . that dress . . . those shoes . . . incredible." He said in a voice so rich and smooth that if I closed my eyes, I could hear the smoky undertones and practically feel the warm richness cascading over me.

Decadent and . . . "oohhh" . . . a moan escaped my freshly glossed lips.

"Jeez, O'Malley, it was a compliment not a proposal of marriage."

Under his breath, it sounded like he said, "Like I would make that mistake twice."

*Amen to that.*

I glanced sideways at him and him at me. Both with a question in our eyes.

"Come on, we've gotta go," he said as he stepped aside to let me pass.

I was rethinking these shoes as every muscle in my body concentrated on not tripping as I walked down the steps in front of Stryker, all the while pretending not to be aware of the eyes that followed me.

"Got the right day of the week on today, O'Malley? Cause the way you're walking in those heels it's a sure bet somebody's going to get a peek at them."

I had that jittery feeling in my chest . . . again.

# CHAPTER 12

Leaning in, I whispered to Karen, "I don't know why he had to come. I thought you told him to go home and go to bed."

"I'm not his mother, you know. Besides, he's been up all night and hasn't eaten either. You two need to learn how to get along. I'm not a referee."

"Doesn't he have a job to get to?"

Karen shrugged her shoulders and said, "He's on leave for a while."

"Great. How long is a while? He seems to be around all the time."

"You need to be a little nicer. He is trying to help you, in case you haven't noticed."

Stryker was up at the counter giving our order to Skky with two k's.

*Jeez, when did she start working here?*

Today, she was dressed like a gypsy. Her round eyes were heavily made up with black eyeliner and purple eye shadow, giving her a very intense look. Her full lips were outlined and filled in with blood red lipstick. Her usually spiky black hair was lying flat on her head and feathered chaotically about her face. Her lavender peasant top, slipping haphazardly off her shoulder, and a colorful gauzy skirt completed the picture. Boy, she looked like she just hit the jackpot by the smile on her face. She giggled and batted her intense eyes at Stryker . . . like he just said the most hilarious thing. How obvious can she be?

"It's just a little harmless flirting. Let it go." Karen said while patting my hand.

"Well, if they don't stop flirting and get me my breakfast I'll be late. You know I haven't had any coffee yet."

"Yes, sweetie I know . . . believe me . . . I know."

"Where's Coop anyway?"

"I'm not his mother, either."

"Don't be sarcastic, Karen. You aren't good at it, and it makes your face go all scrunchie."

"That's comforting. Thank you. And I am sorry, but you seem to be bringing out the worst in me right now."

Stryker finally returned to the table carrying a tray weighted down with three coffees and four of Coop's humungous muffins. Handing out the coffee, Stryker leaned in with a secret little grin and said, "Did you notice who is working behind the counter?" Karen and I both turned our heads to look, pretending we hadn't seen him flirting shamelessly with her. "It's Skky, that waitress from the burger place the other day." Karen and I just nodded.

"She asked me if I heard about the fire at Oak Haven Subdivision last night. I told her I hadn't, so she filled me in on what she'd learned from a friend of her cousin. His brother is a firefighter for Hopewell. According to this fireman, it was a small electrical fire started by an extension cord in the master bedroom. The damage was contained to that area. I asked her if anyone had been injured. She was told no one had been home at the time of the fire."

"Beau, did you get the fireman's name? Maybe we should ask him a few questions. Something's not right here."

Taking a breather from my muffin, I looked at Stryker. "You never did answer me this morning . . . you did see Joel's body hanging in there didn't you?"

"No, O'Malley I didn't. But I do know his name isn't Joel Simmons. It's Joey Coulter."

Dropping my muffin, I said, "Coulter? As in Roy Coulter, the guy who's running BellaRosa Wines, my family's winery?"

"Beau, what's the relationship?" Karen asked, clearly in FBI mode.

"Joey is Roy Coulter's nephew." Stryker answered, going into alphabet mode also.

Karen stood up abruptly. "Come on Mattie, you're going to be late for work. I'll walk you over to the library."

"Wait a minute. I'm not going anywhere until you tell me what's going on. How does this connect to Roger disappearing? How could Roger not know Coulter's nephew was working for him? Are they the Mafia or something? Oh my God," I said grabbing my head, "my headache is coming back."

"Jeez, O'Malley, you're going to be my downfall yet," Stryker said indignantly.

"And yet you persist in hanging around," I said, lashing out at him.

"Mattie, enough! You are going to work. Beau and I cannot ride herd on you right now."

"Excuse me! Excuse me!" I said, disdainfully. "I do not need *herding*."

"Yes, you do," Karen retorted. "Pepper will be here by the time you get off work and you can go back to your house then."

"Okay. I'll go, but I'm not happy about it." Pinning Stryker with a stare that would do Violet proud I said, "I'm taking the extra muffin, too!" My Irish was up and that was always a dangerous thing, as Allen would say. He should know; he'd been witness to it often enough. Grabbing the muffin and my coffee, I stalked toward the door totally ignoring Skky who was waving and trying to get my attention.

Before I opened the door, I heard Karen saying to Stryker, "Why, *Agent Sexy Pants,* I don't believe I've ever seen you speechless."

*Again . . . seriously?*

Stryker's deep resonating laugh followed me as I tried to run down the street in my high-heeled strappy sandals. Making me realize exactly what the phrase 'running like a girl' meant.

*It's not pretty.*

Stumbling into the library, I noticed Oliver had already started my reading-time with the preschoolers . . . *an hour early!* Ethel was sitting at the checkout desk sorting files, so I wandered over to find out what was going on.

"Oh, hi Mattie. You're looking much better than the last time I saw you." Ethel said, finally noticing me standing at the corner of her desk.

"Eh . . . hmmm . . . yes. My mother told me you came by the hospital to see me. Thank you. That was very thoughtful."

"It was nothing. But I do have to tell you your mother is a delight. I enjoyed getting to know her. Will she be back soon?"

"Well . . . no . . . I just put her on a plane to go back home."

"I know that dear. She called me when she arrived in Florida. She wasn't sure when she would be getting back here, though. She seemed to think it would be soon. It all depended on whether or not you could stay out of trouble."

"What do you mean, she called you? I wasn't aware you and she were friends." I was getting more baffled by the moment. "And what did she mean about my staying out of trouble."

"Your mother is justified in being concerned about your welfare. I think it was very clever of her to have your Aunt Patty come to stay with you."

*WTF!*

"Anyway," I said shaking my head to clear it, "not to change the subject, but why is Oliver leading my preschooler reading group . . . an hour early? You knew I was coming in today."

"Oh . . . the parents seemed to like it a little earlier and the children really have gotten used to Oliver being in charge since you've been under the weather. I hope you don't mind, but I wasn't sure you were going to be up to the task when you returned." Ethel said, like it was the most natural thing to happen.

"I've only been gone a week! How could they get used to anything?"

"Mattie, you need to lower your voice; remember this is still a library. Let's just see how this goes for a few weeks. If you're still unhappy, we'll revisit it. Okay?"

"Fine! But I can tell you right now I won't be any happier about it. I implemented that program and I intend to see it through." I couldn't have seemed more whiney if I had stomped my foot. I needed to calm down and start over. "Okay. So, what do you want me to do then?"

"Well, you can start by putting that cart of books back on the shelves, then check-in and put away the new order that came in. The boxes are on the back wall by the magazine reading area. I'll be leaving for lunch in a little while. Oliver will cover the desk up here."

"You're leaving Oliver in charge?" I asked in disbelief.

"Why, yes dear. He has been such a tremendous help since you've been convalescing. He has my complete trust. We'll just ease you back in. So, let's get cracking on those books . . . okay," she said with that can-do attitude of hers.

"Sure . . . just let me put my things in the office and I'll be right back for the cart." Walking back toward the office I thought to myself, "That whole conversation was more than a little surreal."

*I wonder if I'm dreaming . . . again.*

A few hours later the books on the shelves were straightened and organized and the books that were stacked on the cart were put where they belonged. Fortunately, putting away the books was the one job I truly enjoyed here. But now it was time for a coffee break.

I walked up to the front to take the cart back. "Oliver, I'm going to Coop's for coffee. I'll be back in a minute," I said as I walked past the front desk.

"Umm . . . Mattie, I think you should wait until Ethel gets back. She really doesn't like anyone leaving the premises when she's not here."

Turning toward him, I said, "Since when? She's never said that before."

"Since that's what she said before she went out the door. I can call Coops and order you something. I'm sure someone will bring it down for you. They have a new girl there. Her name is Skky and she spells it with two k's . . . isn't that every kind a crazy? Anyway, I'm sure she'll run it down here for you." Picking up the phone and dialing, Oliver said to me, "That's a large coffee, black. Correct?" Nodding my head I walked away wondering yet again . . . *WTF!*

"Here Mattie, Skky just brought your coffee. I went ahead and paid for it. You owe me five dollars," Oliver said as he came around the corner carrying my coffee.

"FIVE DOLLARS? Coffee is only two fifty."

"What can I say? I'm a big tipper. Anyway, it was nice of her to bring it down. Don't you think? She wanted to give it to you herself but I told her you couldn't be disturbed because you were in the middle of a big project."

Looking around at the stacks of books that surrounded me I could see how he came to that conclusion. Besides, he did save me the agony of having to deal with Skky myself. I guess it was worth the extra two-fifty. "Thanks Oliver. I'll pay you back before I leave today."

"Okay. I just wanted to let you know Ethel is back and I'm going to lunch. I'll help put these away as soon as I get back."

"Thanks. I could use the help. These books are stacked so high I can't see over them. I'll just finish checking them in and we'll start putting them away as soon as you return," I said while turning a complete circle and not seeing anything but stacks of books.

Concentrating on checking in the books, I lost track of time. Bending over and counting the books was killing my back not to mention what the heels were doing to my feet. What the hell was I thinking? Convinced it was time for a break, I grabbed my coffee, skirted the wall of books I'd just created, and headed toward the magazine area.

This library has always filled me with amazement. As I walked slowly between the tall oak bookshelves, I ran a hand across the spines of the books. I'd always considered the library a refuge, a safe place to let my dreams take flight.

I glanced around the room and felt for a moment as though I'd stepped into the company of distinguished ghosts. Authors looked down from their perches high on the bookshelves: Ernest Hemingway, Jane Austen, Charles Dickens, TS Eliot . . . Leo Tolstoy. Real people, with real lives.

I continued to wander between the rows of shelves, envisioning the comfortable chair, that's just around the corner. That's where I can sit and ease the pain in my back.

I gasped as my gaze found him and stopped, riveted. My eyes went wide with shock. My hands tightened on my cup of coffee. My heart threatened to leap out of my chest. Roger was sitting in a corner of the library, partially hidden by some boxes of books I hadn't opened yet. He sat on the carpeted floor with his legs splayed out in front of him and his head slumped toward his shoulder.

And, unless my eyes were playing tricks on me, there was a bullet hole in the middle of his forehead. I was almost one-hundred percent certain he was dead. Murdered.

Oh, God. Oh, God, Oh, God.

Terror ran like ice water through my veins. At the same time, it occurred to me that if Roger had been murdered, someone had to have done it. They had to have been in the library, and they might very well still be somewhere nearby. Gasping with fear, my heart slamming against my chest, pulse racing, I looked wildly around, making sure there was no one else there. I trembled with foreboding of a bullet finding me at any second.

*Call 911. Call Stryker.*

I pulled my phone out of my pocket, hit the #1 button, and listened to the call connecting. At the same time I backed away from Roger.

"Stryker," he answered, his voice groggy with sleep.

Stryker's voice in my ear was the most welcome sound I had ever heard.

"Stryker. You need to come." Even as I gasped the words out, I was reminding myself that I've been through this before.

"O'Malley? What's wrong?"

"Roger he's in the library. He's dead."

"*What?* Jesus fucking Christ. Is anyone else there with you? Are you in any danger?"

"I . . . don't know. I don't think so. Ethel's here."

"Go get her. And stay with her. I'm on my way. O'Malley? O'Malley? Did you hear me?"

My stomach churned, bringing my trembling fingers to my lips I murmured, "Oh no . . . oh no . . . not again.

Please . . . please . . . please," I muttered, my eyes darting back to Roger.

"O'Malley!"

"Yes . . . I heard you."

As I whirled around, my ankle went one way while one of my sexy strappy shoes went the other. I tripped and fell and the wall of books, not being able to support me, collapsed. I scrambled to get up, tripped again and stumbled into a row of shelves containing all the books in the history section. The rack swayed and then proceeded to fall over hitting the shelves next to it going down like a giant game of dominos, until six sets of shelves, each full of books, were laying one on top of the other.

I was laying there dazed as Ethel came barreling around the corner. "What on earth . . . Mattie are you alright? Here let me help you up. Did you lose your balance on those insanely high shoes? I knew you came back too soon."

She pulled at my dress to cover my ass before she rolled me over to get a look at my face. Looking up at her I sputtered, "Roger . . . over in the corner . . . its Roger . . . hhhe's dead. Go look, please. I can't bear to see him again . . . please." I stammered through chattering teeth, pointing over to the magazine area where Roger was propped up in the corner on the floor.

"Alright dear, you just sit here. I'll go over and check on Roger. I'm sure he's fine." Ethel stood and walked around the books, mumbling to herself as she disappeared around the only wall of books I managed to leave standing.

I don't like to think of myself as a coward but how many times do I have to see Roger dead before it's not supposed to freak me out. Because . . . I am freaked out.

It seemed like an eternity before Ethel came back around that corner. When she did, she had an odd look on her face. "Is he dead?"

"Come on, honey. Let's get you off this floor and give Karen a call."

"What about Roger? I called Stryker and he's on his way. Maybe you're right. We'll call Karen and then she'll call the police." I said as all my sentences were running together.

"Mattie . . . slow down. Come with me. I want you to see something."

"No. I don't want to see him again. Let's just call Karen like you suggested."

"Come on. You need to see this." Ethel insisted, pulling at me to follow her.

Limping because I'd lost one of my shoes in my hasty getaway, Ethel pulled me to the magazine area and over to the empty corner. No Roger . . . again.

"Mattie, I don't know what you thought you saw but it wasn't Roger. Believe me if he was here, in the library, I would have seen him."

"That's not possible. I saw him. He was sitting right there on the floor. He . . . he had a bullet hole in the middle of his forehead. You've got to believe me. I saw him."

Taking me by the arm Ethel commanded, "Sit! I'm going to go call Karen. I think you need to go home . . . now."

# Chapter 13

I would trust this woman with my life.

Which I have and still do.

*My whole life.*

Holding me in her strong embrace, the shaking my body had been experiencing since finding Roger was finally subsiding.

I was fifteen years old again and Pepper came to Florida to tell us our father had been in a car accident and was dead.

Pepper held me then, too.

*Violet came into my room where I was reading aloud to Allen while he followed along in his brail book.*

*She said she had something important to tell us.*

*"Your Aunt Patty is here and she just informed me your father has been killed in an auto accident out west. She really didn't have too many details for me."*

*Allen jumped up and ran to his room slamming the door behind him. I heard him sobbing most the night. Pepper tried to get him to open the door, but he said he was fine and wanted to be alone.*

*She came to my room and picked me up off my bed, holding me in her lap with her arms wrapped tightly around me until my sobs finally subsided. I fell asleep there.*

*When I woke the next morning, she was still holding me. I asked her questions about my father. Some she could answer; some she couldn't.*

*My mother would never speak of him again.*

*Allen became very quiet and withdrawn after that. He wouldn't discuss him either.*

My Aunt Pepper is in darn good shape for a woman her age. She is tall, thin, and strong; her once brown hair is now white, glossy, and sleek, pulled back in a low bun at the nape of her neck, her cheekbones still high, her gray eyes twinkle with delight.

The jewelry she wore was gold and chunky. Everything about her screamed estate sales and vintage clothing shops. Which, coincidentally, she happens to own one of the most successful in Mesa, Arizona.

Bedazzled Boutique . . . *A Vintage Clothing & Book store.*

Pepper has come to have a reputation for being slightly eccentric. This is a reputation she is well aware of and a reputation that has served her well over the years. It affords her freedom to do the things she really wants to do and not give a damn about what anyone thinks.

"Oh, Pepper, don't get me wrong. I'm glad you're here. But is it a good idea? Shouldn't you be home watching over . . . everything there?" I glanced behind us at the kitchen door, making sure we were alone.

"Honey, everything is fine at home. You don't think I'd come otherwise, do you?"

"No, I know you wouldn't." I confirmed, sighing deeply.

"It's just that I think someone is trying to drive me crazy and they just might be succeeding." I drew strength from her nearness.

"Then, maybe you should consider coming home with me . . . just until all this is taken care of. Mattie, I'm worried about you."

Shaking my head I said, "No, I can't take the chance and drag this mess back there. Whatever this mess is."

She patted the seat next to her. "Come, sit down. You need to tell me everything," she said, leaning in closer to me and gazing into my eyes as if trying to read my mind. I'm not convinced she couldn't.

Starting at the beginning, I didn't stop until I finished with finding Roger at the library with a bullet hole in his head.

A minute ticked by.

Finally, something shifted in her seeking gaze; perhaps a flash of fear or perhaps the momentary shock of me confronting mortality. Bejeweled fingers clutched at her chunky amber necklace.

"Sweetie, do you think Steven could have anything to do with this?"

"What do you mean?" I asked. "No! He couldn't have anything to do with this."

She paused and looked at me doubtfully.

"Steven came to see me a few times after you left. He asked if you left anything with me. Naturally, I told him no but I don't think he believed me." She chose her words with enormous care. "A few weeks later, my house was burglarized. I'm sure it was Steven but I couldn't prove it."

"Pepper, I'm sorry. Why didn't you tell me? I didn't mean to drag you into this." I said taking her hands in mine.

My thumb touched her ruby ring. I've often wondered where she obtained the magnificent ring in its ornate gold setting with a circle of diamonds. In the sunlight, it blazed with a glow equal only to sunrise on the desert. I did ask, just once, a long time ago she had looked longingly at the ring on her hand, her mind obviously going to another time and place. She never answered the question.

"Did you get all of Rosa's papers when you inherited the house?"

"The attorney sent me a large envelope with paperwork in it but I just thought it was normal everyday stuff. You know, like insurance papers and such. I'm not even sure where it is."

"We need to find those papers honey. Oh, someone's at the door. You just stay there and I'll go see who it is," Pepper said walking through the swinging kitchen door into the living room.

I sat there gazing into the glass of wine Pepper poured for me the same way Roger had the night he told me he was leaving. What exactly did he say to me that night? Trying to think back and remember our conversation, I really couldn't come up with anything that was pertinent to what's been happening to me on a daily basis. I just know *that's* when everything started. I miss my sanity, I thought, wiping away the tears that started to trickle from my eyes.

"Hey you." Stryker was standing there dressed in black motorcycle boots, faded jeans, and a leather jacket. His dark, dangerous look had me feuding between wanting to run my fingers through his hair and running for my life.

Holding up the one sexy, strappy shoe I'd managed to salvage, I sighed, "I lost one of my shoes today."

Stryker brought a hand out from behind his back and dangled my other shoe from his finger. Handing it to me he said, "Listen, O'Malley. I've been over at the library all evening and there is nothing that indicates that a body was sitting in the corner or anywhere for that fact." Rounding the table, he took my hand and pulled me up, placing his hands on either side of my face, he bent his head down to mine. Forehead to forehead. Eyes closed. Bodies close, almost touching.

A long moment passed. I could feel him reaching out to me, but I couldn't let my guard down. Still the sense of him was overwhelming.

Breaking our trance, he whispered in my ear. "We'll figure out what's going on. Understood?"

I looked up admiring Stryker's square jaw that was now peppered with a five o'clock shadow. I nodded my head yes, while holding my breath as he lowered his mouth to mine.

The walls, floors, and ceiling all prickled and popped with energy. Power whooshed along my skin, raising the hair on my arms. As far as first kisses went, this one was like a lightning strike . . . intense, scorching, and dangerous.

When we finally came up for air all I could say was, "Wow!"

A corner of his mouth lifted into a lopsided grin with enough sex appeal to have my insides doing a series of somersaults. The energy was crackling so loud in the kitchen I didn't hear Pepper enter.

"Excuse me, Sweetie, but you have another . . . ummm . . . visitor." Tearing my eyes away from Stryker's, I looked over at the door and saw Jonathan standing there.

Jerking away from Stryker I clutched my hand to my chest just to make sure my heart was still beating, because I'm pretty sure it stopped for a while.

"Jonathan. How are you? Come in. You remember Stryker, don't you?"

*Oh God.*

"Hello, Stryker, it's nice to see you . . . again." Turning toward me he said, "I hope I'm not interrupting anything important. I should have called, but I was so worried about you. I heard what happened over at the library today and decided to take a chance and come over."

"Oh, Jonathan, that's fine. I'm glad you came. Stryker and I were just . . . ummm . . . "

"I was just leaving. It was nice meeting you Pepper. Jonathan," he muttered, as if he found the other man's name distasteful. "O'Malley, we'll talk soon. Thanks." Stryker pushed through the backdoor and into the still night air.

Turning to Jonathan I said, "Why don't you go into the living room with Pepper. I'll get us a glass of wine and be in there in a sec."

As soon as Jonathan turned around I was out the back door like a shot slamming into a rock hard body and a wicked grin. Stryker reached out and steadied me.

"Where's the fire, O'Malley?"

Tension sizzled like a live wire between us.

"I . . . I . . . I thought we should talk before you left."

"About?" He said feigning innocence.

Trying to ignore the way my body still hummed from the intense pleasure of Stryker's unexpected kiss I said, "About what just happened in there."

"It was just a kiss, O'Malley. Don't make a federal case out of it. Haven't you ever been kissed before?"

I had seen caring and tenderness in his eyes. Now only anger remained.

"Just a kiss? Really? You call that . . . just a kiss?"

Shaking his head and turning away from me he said, "Obviously, I should be calling it a mistake." He stepped off the back porch.

"A mistake? Is that what you want to call it?" My voice was definitely going up in decibels. In a few more minutes, only dogs would be able to hear me.

Turning back to me he said, "Well, O'Malley, *I tried to call it Bob*, but it would only answer to *mistake*," his voice dripping with sarcasm. "Listen, as much as I'm enjoying this . . . whatever this is . . . I've got to get back to work and you've got to get back to your . . . company."

His words stung.

I folded my arms across my chest and narrowed my eyes. "Well you can bet I . . . I won't ever make that Bob again," I vowed, trying to sound dignified and aloof.

I stood on the porch in the moonlight, peering into the darkness feeling a jumble of emotions. That guy's moods changed like the swing of a pendulum. I listened while Stryker fired up his motorcycle and took off down the road.

I knew there was definitely something happening here, something I couldn't explain, and something we were obviously going to call . . . Bob.

Jonathan was called away as soon as I got back into the house. Feeling guilty about him walking in on Stryker and me, I walked with him out to his car. Saying goodnight was awkward for me.

Jonathan's blue eyes gleamed. With unmistakable interest, he took my hands in his, "You and Stryker . . . ?" he left the question hanging.

"Nothing, nothing . . . he's just helping Karen and me with something . . . he and Karen used to work together . . . just friends."

*Lame.*

"Nope, nothing going on between us."

*Except maybe Bob.*

"Bob?"

*I swear I'm saying this stuff in my head.*

"Bob." I nodded.

"Meet me in the morning then. In the park . . . eight o'clock. Please."

I was hypnotized. Jonathan could be mesmerizing. From the first moment I met him I felt a strong attraction to him. Almost as if, I knew him in another life.

Jonathan's blue eyes gleamed with unmistakable interest. He reached for me. It felt a little awkward and forced.

Pulling me in closer he kissed me. Not the mind-melting kiss I got from Stryker, but a soft lingering kiss. Setting me away from him, he softly said, "I'll call you in the morning."

Being a doctor, Jonathan generated a certain amount of trust and respect from the people he cared for. He was also very good looking. The only problem was he was too kind, too agreeable. If anything this made me think of him more as a brother than a prospective lover.

A cloud slid across the moon and it was suddenly darker.

I sighed deeply after all the body blows I had taken that day. With a critical eye, I scanned the area around me while sitting on one of my front porch swings. A perfect glass of wine accompanied me. My farmhouse had the charm of a nineteenth century villa perched on the side of a mountain in Tuscany; except we were in Hopewell and there were no mountains. Hills, but no mountains.

Arched and constructed of wide wood planks with black iron hardware, the front door was the same door my grandfather carried my grandmother through when they were first wed.

The porch spanned the whole front of the house, while matching swings at both ends swayed in tandem with every breeze. Two one hundred year old oak trees soared above the second floor flanking the house on either side like sentinels protecting it from the enemy. Often, I've dreamed of climbing one of those trees and hiding where no one would ever find me.

The wind picked up; the trees seemed restless, stirring uneasily. Their branches swayed, bending and creaking in the wind. The old owl I had inherited with the house sent out a deep-throated hoot. Squirrels scampered up and down trees, busily hoarding their nuts, while dried leaves broke loose and swept along the sidewalks like brooms.

I stared into the shadowy night feeling very uneasy.

# CHAPTER 14

J onathan, true to his word, called first thing this morning. Pepper used the smell of freshly brewed coffee to rouse me. Coming down to the kitchen, I groped my way toward my first cup.

"How are you this morning dear?"

"Great," I said, from the depths of my early morning coma. "I'm meeting Jonathan for a walk in the park this morning." I explained to Pepper as I made my way back upstairs to get dressed.

When I got to the park, I saw it wasn't going to be the leisurely walk I was hoping for. Jonathan's a runner, and he runs in this park every day. After a little negotiating, we decided he would run his ten miles and I would run for as long as I could breathe. I don't want to run a marathon. I'm happy just walking to the mailbox and back every day.

Grateful I finally finished my run/walk with Jonathan, I decided I owed myself a cup of coffee and a muffin so I headed over to Coop's and let the aromas assault me as I waited in line.

Turning to me Mrs. Morgan said, "I'm sorry I'm taking so long Mattie but those darn women in my mahjong group can be so darn picky."

I nodded, not in any hurry since Ethel Tams told me not to come back to work until I was totally healed.

After promising he would call me later, Jonathan extracted a response from me that I would indeed go with him to the Black and Blue Ball. He then chastely kissed me on the cheek, and left to shower and go back to the hospital.

Mrs. Morgan finally made her choices, opting for all chocolate chip muffins, which if you ask me was a no brainer. What group of fifty-something women wouldn't prefer chocolate to bran?

Skky, with two k's, was working the counter. "Hi, Mattie, how are you today?" she asked in a sympathetic tone. "I heard you had an accident at the library yesterday. Oliver told me you're seeing *dead people*." She leaned forward, looked both ways and lowering her gaze she whispered, "I'll tell you something if you promise not to mention it to anyone. You swear? Cross your heart."

I leaned in toward her, looked both ways, crossed my heart, and held up my hand.

"I do, too . . . see dead people that is. I told Oliver and he understands. Most people don't like to hear about stuff like that, so I don't tell too many people about it. Oliver invited me to join his psychic support group. He says they're people just like you and me. I knew the first time we met we were a lot alike. Did you feel it, too?"

Skky is about ten years younger and three inches shorter than I am. Today she was dressed in Goth regalia, all black. Black t-shirt with skull and crossbones bedazzled across the front in rhinestones, black cargo pants tucked into black army boots, and a spiked leather collar wrapped around her slender neck. Her face looked as if it were dusted with flour. Her eyes outlined in kohl liner and her lips were painted black.

Skky is very diverse.

She'd mastered the art of talking without pausing to breathe and moving from one subject to the next without taking time to turn on her blinker. Now I'm being inundated with details of her marriage to, and I'm quoting here, 'revolting Bobby King' and a divorce in progress that sounded as though it might conclude in at least one felony.

*Skky King?* Rolling my eyes and nodding, I cut in when she took an unexpected breath.

"I'll have two large coffees, a dozen assorted muffins, and throw in a coconut cream pie for later."

Skky continued talking. I stopped listening.

My Stryker senses went on alert as a hand brushed the back of my neck and sent tingles down my spine. I tried to control the sensation but couldn't.

Stryker leaned in and kissed me on the side of my neck just below my ear.

"O'Malley?"

"Hey."

I saw his gaze shift to Skky filling my order.

"They're not all for me."

He laughed, his brown eyes twinkling. Good lord, the guy had twinkling eyes. He shouldn't hide them behind those mirrored sunglasses he always wore.

"How did you know I'd be here?"

"Just one of my many superpowers. Besides, I saw you in the park with Jonathan." It was hard to miss the brief flicker of annoyance that crossed his handsome face.

"He's a runner." My voice barely a whisper. A lock of dark hair had fallen over Stryker's brow. I had the strongest urge to brush it away with my fingertips, but I somehow managed to control the desire.

Stryker nodded. "Impressive."

As he stepped back just a bit to adjust his coat, I caught a glimpse of his handgun. Wearing a navy blue suit with a crisp white dress shirt and a charcoal silk tie, Stryker sparked with power.

He looked extraordinarily handsome this morning and I noticed more than one woman wobble a little as she passed by him.

"I'm going out of town for a few days," he said.

"Where you going?"

"Away."

"FBI business?"

"Not exactly. Kavanaugh can reach me." He wrapped his arm around my waist, pulled me to him, and kissed me.

Wow did he ever kiss me.

Releasing me he turned abruptly and walked away, leaving a very male scent behind in his wake.

Skky and I stared after him.

"*Da . . . aa . . . ammmn.*" Skky drawled, dragging the word out to three syllables.

"Yep."

# CHAPTER 15

P epper, is there anything odd in our family tree?" I flashed my aunt a fond smile. Pepper was the kind of woman I'd always admired: smart, insightful, independent, shrewd, and adventurous. She is a pilot, a teacher, a volunteer, and successful business owner.

She is also a sweet, quirky woman. She gives blueberries to her mail carrier every morning, because they are supercharged with anti-aging phytochemicals, and she believes they'll keep him safe from disease. She also keeps her next-door neighbor, Mr. Priestley the Elvis impersonator, informed on the stock price of Xerox.

So asking *her* if our family is weird is probably relative.

"Odd?"

"Maybe unusual is a better word."

"Well . . . your Uncle Phil could predict the weather after he was struck by lightning."

"Really? Where?"

"In the park, during a summer storm."

"No. I mean where on his body was he struck?"

"Oh yeah . . . uhm . . . he was running to hide under a tree when he tripped and fell face first into the mud. That's when the lightning bolt struck him in the butt. You see, he always carried his lucky silver dollar back there. After that, whenever Phil got a twitch in his right buttocks it would rain twenty-four hours later."

"Wow, how accurate was he?"

"Accurate enough to land a job at the local radio station predicting the weather."

"Really?"

*Come on Mattie, focus.*

"What I meant was, does anyone in our family have any special powers. Like turning a rock into a loaf of bread or leaping over tall buildings in a single bound."

"Why do you ask, Sweetie? Are you experiencing something? Other than seeing dead people, that is."

"I don't know why I'm asking. It's just that Mrs. Blackwell made some comments about Gramma Rosa."

"Humph . . . Bizzy Blackwell is someone you don't want to be paying too much attention to."

"I didn't think so. I think I'll take a walk down by the pond before it starts raining."

"Is your butt twitching?" Pepper asked innocently.

"Nope, not my butt. But my nether regions have been doing a lot of twitching lately." I replied, wiggling my eyebrows at her.

"The doctor or the secret agent?"

"Neither . . . both. I don't know. I'll be outside down by the pond."

I slipped out, swallowed by the gray haze that hung over the house as I crossed the porch and walked into the yard.

The air was chilly and the earlier pale sunlight had faded as the sky clouded over threatening the first hint of rain. The accumulating cloud cover had generated an artificial twilight, and the smell of gathering rain had infused the air.

Taking a deep breath I walked unsteadily down the sloping meadow to the apple orchard I observe from my kitchen window every morning. Thinking to myself . . . I couldn't ask for a better place to raise a child. *Someday.*

The small orchard has been here for decades, long before the house was built. The limbs were gnarled but strong enough to support the abundance of small green apples that grow every year despite no efforts on my part to encourage them.

Breathing in the intoxicating aroma, I wandered through the trees to a clearing that revealed a weathered wooden gazebo, which had seen better days, but still afforded a superb view of a serene lagoon rimmed by cattails. I stared out at the still, green pond with weary eyes. From the gazebo there is a spectacular view of the grapevines that produce the finest wines in the area. BellaRosa Wines, my family's very own mark on this land. How my grandmother must have struggled with her own inner demons when deciding whether or not to sell this family legacy.

Beyond the hundreds of acres of those picturesque grapevines a modern monstrosity hovers over all this natural beauty.

Roy Coulter built what seems to be, at first glance, something that should have been constructed on *I don't know*, Alcatraz. Huge grey cement blocks perch on at least three different levels. Each level comes with its own generous expanse of darkly tinted windows. One could only deduce these vast windows were bulletproof, used to deflect enemy fire . . . should the enemy try to invade northern Michigan that is.

It's purely speculation on my part, but I suspect there are bunkers in the mix and this design was most assuredly something Roy had to run by the Department of Defense in order to get the okay to have it built. Thankfully, my view of the Coulter Compound is obstructed by acres of grapevines.

When I first moved here, I would find myself drawn to this place to seek comfort, dangle my feet in the water, and dream. But, today everything seems restless; me, the air, the water, everything. Maybe it's nerves about seeing Roger dead all over town or maybe it's Stryker. He has me so tied up in knots I don't know which way is up. The man runs so hot sometimes I'm afraid of being scalded and then so cold I'm afraid hypothermia is going to set in.

Zipping my raincoat up to my chin, I sat down at the base of a tree and crossed my arms in a vain attempt to get warm. A sound escaped from me that was half sigh and half something else; tension, impatience, maybe simple weariness.

Lifting the collar of my jacket as another rumble of thunder echoed through the air, I thought back to a day not unlike this one. The thought sent a familiar pang of sadness slicing through me as I still found myself disbelieving that fate could be so cruel.

The devastating memories from six years ago deluged me, like a roiling, black sea, it's undertow threatening to pull me to the bottom. . . .

*His expression registered a look of confusion signaling recognition without context. He knew me. How? Not quite able to make the connection as he came down from his climax.*

*Leveling a gaze at me, in a tone filled with hostility and contempt, he said, "Put the camera down. I'm warning you. Stop taking pictures."*

*Another head peeked out from under the protection of the blankets at the other end of the bed. I jerked back abruptly with an involuntary sob.*

*He swayed between pleading and threatening.*

*Tired of pleading with me he picked up the alarm clock on the nightstand and let it fly.*

*Jumping out of the way, I tripped over a pair of men's shoes sitting in the doorway. Turning as I jumped, I fell, and landed on an iron doorstop we used to prop the bedroom door open; a duck shaped doorstop we had purchased together at an antique fair. As intense pain shot through me, I struggled to stand. Stumbling through the house, I took the same path I had just traveled minutes before. This time, making my escape.*

*In the shrubs at the back door, I heaved until my stomach was as empty as my heart. I finally made my way to the car and drove myself to the hospital.*

Shaking off the reverie, I was jerked back to the present by Harry's barking. One of those brainless activities dogs seem to thrive on, the fervor of his barking caused his whole body to quiver. "Harry! Harry!" My Irish Setter looked over his shoulder at me with regret, torn between his present obsession and his need to obey. Obsession won. Pulling myself out of my sedentary state, I noticed the light was draining from the sky and the air temperature was dropping. The rain wasn't falling hard, but it was annoying.

Walking toward the pond, I saw Harry chewing on something. At least the barking had stopped. "Harry come here, boy." I said while patting my thighs for him to come. "Whatcha got? Come on. Let me see." Instead of running to me, Harry decided to stop and drop. I closed the last few feet between us and knelt down to see what he was chewing on. It was a shoe. I reached over to pick it up but Harry took this as an invitation to play tug-of-war. I finally got the shoe from him and examined it closely. It was one of Roger's. He must have left this pair on the back porch and Harry decided to play with it.

Standing up with the shoe still in my hand, Harry ran around the edge of the pond to the cornfield that separates my property from the vineyard. Wading through the cattails around the muddy edge of the pond, he started barking again. Great! Now what? Walking over to where Harry's newest obsession was, I parted the tall weeds and cattails. Looking through them, I saw what had Harry so fired up. Roger's eyes, wide open staring at me, lifeless.

Disbelieving, I walked closer. I could smell the cold dirt and wet hay. Feeling faint, I crouched down, my knees sinking into the cold, moist ground, knowing this time he really was dead. Tears of frustration welled in my eyes. This time I wasn't engulfed in fear, as if I was finally resigned to the fact; Roger is dead. Shaking my head I pulled myself up and lost my balance, falling back and landing on my butt in the water.

My shoes had sucked in so deep; the mud wouldn't allow me to move. Wiggling out of them, I scrambled up to solid ground. On my hands and knees, I took a few deep breaths and concentrated on not losing my lunch. After getting my breathing under control, I turned around and looked at Roger, just to convince myself I wasn't crazy or seeing things, again. His face was ghostly pale and his mouth wide open in surprise or terror; hard to tell. Only now, he looked like one of the scarecrows I had hung up on the posts a few weeks ago. Moving closer I reached up, pushed back the straw hat, which was perched on his head, and laid the fingertips of my left hand on Rogers's forehead. The bullet hole that was there the day before was gone. Despite the grayish tone of his skin, it was still clear he had been a good-looking man. Sandy blond hair and delicate wings of eyebrows set off even, romantic features. He was still wearing the same suit he'd been wearing every time I'd seen him, which was no longer pristine. Now it was saturated with mud and in tatters.

Nervously I searched my pockets for my phone. I found it in my back pocket. Wet, cracked and no power.

# CHAPTER 16

Pulling myself from the water's edge, I ran to the orchard up on the hill and started yelling for Pepper. She was on the back porch when she noticed me.

Working her way down to me she said, "What's wrong, Mattie?"

"It's Roger! He's dead. I'll wait here you go call the police."

"Are you sure?"

Pepper was one of those elderly women who shaves her eyebrows and then pencils them in, giving her a permanently surprised look. Completely appropriate for this occasion.

"He really is this time, Pepper. Please call the police and Karen."

I could see Pepper was warring with herself. Should she leave me here alone with a dead person or should she go call for help. I nudged her a little and said, "It's okay, Pepper. I'll be fine. Go call the police."

Nodding at me, she turned and ran back up the hill toward the house. After calling the police, she called Karen to tell her we'd found Roger and that she was going to stay at the house to direct the police down to the pond as soon as they got there.

Karen came running down the hill still looking every bit the professional she was, wearing a suit suggesting she was seeing patients today. She waded through the mud to look at the body, making sure it was Roger and that he was definitely dead this time.

"Oh, honey, I'm sorry," she said as she walked back to me.

I sighed, unsure why I hadn't felt totally shattered as one might think I should be at finding Roger's body propped up on a bale of hay looking like a scarecrow.

Her phone rang. I turned my back on her looking out at the vineyards while she spoke in low tones into her cell phone.

Assuming it was Stryker, I asked, "Where did he go? He told me this morning he was leaving town."

"He went to Arizona." She paused for just a second, no doubt she noticed my intake of breath, and then continued, "He went to check out Steven Angelo."

My back stiffened. "I don't believe this." I said with my back still to her trying not to let her see how much that fact affected me. *What had he found out?*

The wail of sirens shattered the atmosphere and any further discussion of Arizona, Steven, or Stryker.

Red and blue lights flashed. Ray Adams, of the Sheriff's homicide detail, was the detective in charge. His face was grim as he walk toward us after he had checked the scene. "You touch anything?"

"I checked for a pulse." Karen glanced down at one hand, smudged with dried mud.

They both looked at me standing there full of mud and barefoot. "I lifted the hat to see if it was Roger."

"ID certain?" Adams asked, looking up over his glasses at me.

"Yes." I nodded, starting to tear up again. "It's Roger Moore, my ex-boyfriend."

"Ex, you say?" The balding, middle-aged detective asked, while writing in a small notebook. "Come with me."

We turned as another cruiser and the crime van slid to a stop leaving their headlights on to light up the scene. Detective Adams turned his attention toward them. "Don't touch anything until the M.E. certifies death. One of you head the other way around the pond. Go slow, look for anything, everything, trash, footprints . . . " He looked back at me to continue.

"Roger lived here with me until a few weeks ago. We broke up and Roger moved back to his house in Oak Haven subdivision, on the other side of town." I explained.

"Detective! Detective!" The call came in a rasping voice that carried like a crow's caw. Bizzy Blackwell, dressed in her usual abundant folds of black cloth that would have been perfectly appropriate for a funeral, was making her way slowly down the hill toward us. Her cottony white hair, damp from the rain, hung haphazardly around her parchment face. Mrs. Blackwell lifted her ebony cane to point toward the pond. "I understand you found the body."

"Ma'am, go back up the hill. You'll have to read about it in the paper," he said ignoring the doggedness in her voice as he turned back toward me.

"Was it Roger?" Mrs. Blackwell persisted. "Did he have a ring clutched in his left hand?" She peered up at me, her wrinkled face expectant.

I shrugged.

Adams stopped and turned, "Ring?"

"Yes, a silver claddagh ring," Mrs. Blackwell expounded.

He turned and trudged down toward the pond where the medical examiner had Roger's body lying on the grass.

Treading wearily back to where he left us Detective Adams thrust a small plastic bag toward Mrs. Blackwell to look at. "Is this the ring you are referring to, ma'am?" Mrs. Blackwell nodded eagerly.

Turning toward me he asked, "Ever seen this?"

I shook my head. "Never."

Turning back to Mrs. Blackwell he asked, "What do you know about this ring?"

"Just that the claddagh can mean love of the heart or true friendship."

"Ooo . . . kaaay," he drawled, "but how did *you* know he was holding a ring in his left hand?" More than a little exasperated, obviously trying to get Mrs. Blackwell to speed things up.

"Because I put it there." The "duh" was implied.

"When . . . and why would you place this ring in his hand?"

"When? Last night during the full moon. Why? So Roger would find love on his journey." Looking over at me she said, "I'm sorry dear but I knew the two of you were wrong for each other. This way Roger had a chance at true love."

"How did you know he was dead?"

"It didn't take a psychic to figure out something was very wrong here."

"Why didn't you call the police when you found him dead?"

"I didn't actually find him dead . . . here. It was in a dream and I wanted to make sure his passage to the other side went smoothly." There was reverence in Mrs. Blackwell's raspy voice.

"Uh-huh . . . strange lady." Adams muttered, turning from her.

"Yes," she agreed thoughtfully, "Even among psychics I'm considered a bit of a freak." Mrs. Blackwell's thin lips spread in an approximation of a smile.

"I see," he said. "And just so I have it straight, you dreamed that Mr. Moore was dead, and in order to make sure his passage to the other side went smoothly, you beamed yourself over here and placed a ring in his hand, correct?"

"Correct."

"Okay, Mrs. Blackwell we're done here for the moment. Could I get your phone number in case I have any more questions?"

"No."

Turning back to look at her, he repeated, "No?"

"No. I prefer to communicate over the astroplane."

Adams eyes blazed, and his mouth was a thin straight line. It looked as if he'd swallowed his mustache.

"Detective, a word," Karen asked, taking Adams by the arm, trying to pull his attention away from Mrs. Blackwell. This was difficult since he was staring at her as if she'd grown a second head.

Dragging him away from the car, Karen and Adams talked. I saw her hand him her phone. I could only assume it was so Adams could talk to Stryker. Several times, they looked over at me. I shivered, from a combination of the cold, and the prospect of being questioned. "He thinks I killed Roger." I mumbled to myself. I felt like that should trouble me. However, I'm not sure it did.

"Oh, honey, that's not true. We all know you wouldn't do that to Roger." Mrs. Blackwell said, stroking my hand.

"Thanks."

"That's alright." Glancing down at the oversized watch on her wrist she exclaimed, "Oh no, I'm late. An emergency meeting has been called. Gotta go."

"Wait! Detective Adams may have more questions for you. You can't just leave."

"He knows where to find me if he does. Bye Matilda, we'll talk later." She flicked her gnarly-ringed fingers at me and was gone.

After about an hour Adams trudged uphill to where I sat in the back of his police car. He opened the door.

"Out," he said.

*A man of few words.*

I slipped across the seat and eased my bare feet into the damp grass feeling the chill all through my body.

"A question, Miss O'Malley. Do you know anything about Mr. Moore's finances?"

I pushed my hands through my damp, tangled hair, winced, and shook my head no.

"Do you have anything to gain from his death?"

"No . . . not that I'm aware of."

"Start at the beginning and tell me everything, Miss O'Malley."

With a deep sigh, I told Detective Adams about everything that had happened the past few weeks since

Roger moved out. He didn't seem convinced that I had nothing to do with Roger's death.

I studied the detective. His face unreadable, as he gazed down at his cheap brown shoes that were now soaked and ruined.

"So what brought you down here by the pond today?" he asked.

"I don't know. I just needed to get away."

Pushing he said, "So you just happened to need to get away and you just happened to come down here?"

"I was upset Detective. I wasn't plotting a course."

"That's it, huh?"

I nodded as he glanced around, "Where'd the old lady go?"

"Said she had a meeting."

"Okay, I'll talk to her later."

"What happened to him? I mean how did he die?" I asked Detective Adams.

"Don't know," he said matter-of-factly.

After taking several deep breaths, I pulled myself together and stepped away from him. "When will you know?" My voice sounding more composed to my own ears.

"It'll take as long as it takes I imagine," he said.

Looking up I followed his gaze, the medical examiner was leaving and taking Roger with him. Clearing his throat, he called out, "Okay. Here we go boys and girls, it's gonna be a long night." Turning back to me he said, "Don't leave town. I have a lot more questions for you."

Detective Adams trudged back toward the pond mumbling to himself as portable work lights illuminated the crime scene so the police and crime scene technicians could do their job. Which they did, well into the night.

# CHAPTER 17

It was well after midnight and I could feel my butt dragging as the worn wooden treads squeaked in protest. I climbed the steep stairs of my old house and fell face first on my bed not bothering to change out of my wet muddy clothes and too bone weary to care. I wrapped my grandmother's quilt around me like a cocoon and fell asleep instantly.

*There was something in Roger's gaze. Fear? His lips were moving but nothing was coming out.*

*"Roger? Is something wrong?" I asked; dread mounting as I stepped toward him. "Roger?"*

*Suddenly his face changed. Panic distorted his features. He started moving backwards, away from me, toward the water.*

*"Roger, be careful!"*

*But he couldn't hear me.*

*Heart pounding, nerves extended to the breaking point, I walked toward him, arms outstretched, reaching for him.*

*"It's not your fault," he whispered.*

*"What? What's not my fault?" I cried desperately.*

*A deafening crack slashed through the night.*

*"It's not your fault," Roger whispered again and again, as he fell into darkness, and into the vast bowels of hell. "It's not your fault . . . "*

*I caught my reflection in the water, ethereal, otherworldly. It was as if I was standing outside myself. Watching . . .*

My eyes flew open.

I screamed and flailed.

The luminous dial of the bedside clock read four-thirty.

I was sweating, my heart pounding, the dream so real I couldn't breathe.

"Oh, God," I whispered, pushing the damp hair away from my face. When my eyes adjusted to the darkness I saw my bedroom door standing wide open.

There was the silhouette of a man in my doorway. "Oh, God!" I shrank back, terrified, the dream still lingering.

"O'Malley?" he said softly, and in an instant I relaxed my muscles, realizing who it was.

Swinging my legs over the side of the bed, I hung my head and said wearily, "Thought you were in Arizona."

Sighing, he pushed away from the doorframe, moved into the room, and around the bed. He was dressed in the suit pants he was wearing yesterday and nothing else. As he set the weapon he was carrying on the nightstand, he glanced around the room making sure I was alone.

I didn't protest when he sat on the bed next to me leaning forward resting his elbows on his knees resting his head in his hands. After a few moments of silence Stryker said, "I flew out as soon as I talked to Kavanaugh. Pepper suggested I sleep down stairs. I came up when I heard you scream. You okay?"

"Yeah, I'm good."

We sat side by side not touching.

We were silent. The rain on the roof was melodious. The atmosphere, oddly intimate.

Stryker pinched the bridge of his nose; I suspected he was battling a headache, which he seems to have a lot of when he's around me.

He glanced over at me with the strangest expression in his usually mocking eyes. Coming from anyone else, I would have called it concern. Sympathy. Maybe even compassion.

"Sorry about Roger," he said so softly I wasn't sure he actually said it.

I nodded.

"That's rough," Stryker said. "Seeing him like that."

I managed another brief nod. "Yeah," I said with a sniffle. "Why are you being nice to me?"

"I'm always nice," he assured me.

I didn't argue as his strong arm slipped around me. I didn't even put up a fight when he drew me so close I could smell the masculine scent of him and feel his heart beating in sync with mine. He pulled me to him saying nothing.

We sat like that for a while, not speaking, giving me time to let my mind wander to recent events and wonder who would want to kill Roger and push me to Mad Hatter status.

Laying me back on my pillows, Stryker wrapped me in my grandmother's quilt again. Lying down behind me, he encircled me with one arm around my waist. Pulling me close to him, he whispered in my ear, "You can't let this guy get in your head, O'Malley." His deep voice, combined with his warm breath, had flutters seeping down my spine and into my empty stomach.

"Too late. My head is his summer home." I whispered back.

Stryker's chest rumbled as he laughed quietly.

It felt good. I smiled.

I hadn't realized until now, laying here with him like this, how much I missed being with someone. Not just the sex, but the intimacy, the holding, the lying in bed for hours afterward and talking. I always imagined I would be with my knight in shining armor by now, someone who adored me as much as I adored him. Someone who would lie in bed with me softly talking about anything and everything. Someone who went to sleep holding me in his arms. A feeling of comfort surrounded me. I felt a sense of safety in Stryker's arms as I drifted off to sleep.

# CHAPTER 18

T he warmth of my cozy bed was seductive. Rare, early morning sunshine streamed in through my bedroom's multi-paneled window, making my brass headboard gleam.

Mingled aromas of coffee and the rich smokiness of meat woke me from my sleep. I stirred in my bed and drew my knees up to my chest, then stretched my legs out straight and my arms overhead. The warmth surrounding me beckoned me to stay put, but the smell of the most important thing to me in the morning, that first cup of coffee, forced me out.

Then I remembered, Stryker!

Recalling last night, I propelled myself into a sitting position. I looked over at the empty bed. Lying back on my pillow, I sobbed. Was Roger really dead? *Possibly*. Did I imagine Stryker held me last night? *Probably*. Sighing, I pushed myself from the bed, shed my muddy, still damp clothes, and walked across my bedroom toward a hot shower.

Twenty minutes later I was showered and dressed for the day. I chose a pair of khakis, white polo shirt, and a navy blazer. The effect was just what you'd expect . . . Julie; the activities director on the Love Boat. *I've really got to do some laundry.*

Shrugging at my reflection in the mirror, I turned on my heel and headed downstairs.

As I sailed into the kitchen full of courage and determination, Stryker was the first to notice me. He leaned casually against the kitchen counter wearing a black t-shirt with black cargo pants. He looked wide-awake.

I wasn't so sure about Karen though, casting a glance her way. She was noticeably pale and hollow-eyed this morning and definitely withdrawn. Stryker was watching her closely, if unobtrusively.

His long legs, stretched out in front of him, were crossed at the ankles. He looked fit, and tough; every inch an off-duty Dark Knight. Maybe he was a superhero. Super Stryker reads minds. I sighed, remembering him holding me last night.

Stryker's face didn't change, but his weight shifted slightly as he crossed his arms over his chest. As if he needed to move.

"Morning, O'Malley."

Eyeing my outfit, he said with a smirk, "Captain Stubbing called. He's waiting for you on the bridge."

"Thanks," I said in a withering voice. Then moved to the counter where I poured myself a cup of strong black coffee, relieved that I could justifiably turn my back to him.

Turning to face Karen and Pepper, I asked, "All right, who wants to explain why Stryker was out in Arizona checking up on Steven Angelo. That is a part of my life that is no one else's business. He has nothing to do with this. He wouldn't dare."

"What makes you say he wouldn't dare?" Stryker asked, now standing directly in front of me, arms across his chest, looking down on me, even with my three-inch heels on.

"I don't know. He just has no reason. That was a lifetime ago." I said looking up at him. I noticed his hair was wet, probably from a shower but he had a full day's worth of stubble on his jaw line. *Extremely sexy.*

He unnerved me by stepping even closer. I hoped he couldn't sense what had just been running through my mind.

"O'Malley?" He was standing incredibly close to me.

*You make me nervous. You're using up all my oxygen.*

"O'Malley." He smiled. "Stop talking."

"I did not say that out loud."

"You did."

"I swear, I'm saying this stuff in my head." *Jeez!*

Stryker left . . . to do whatever Super Stryker does. It was just Karen and I sitting at the table now.

"Mattie, did you know Angelo was being courted by a national news affiliation?"

"No, I didn't know. But then I haven't kept tabs on him."

"Why didn't you ever tell me you were married?" Karen asked.

"Because marriage to Steven Angelo was like riding on a burning rollercoaster. I got burned and it is not something I want to remember. Besides, it was a long time ago and only lasted about a minute. How did you find out anyway?"

"Pepper filled us in. Don't be angry with her. She's afraid for you. Do you believe Steven is capable of doing some of the things that have been going on here? It just seems like another one of those coincidences that keep popping up. And, Stryker did trace him back here. He's been in town for two weeks now."

"Steven? Here? How do you know?" I asked.

"It's not like he's been hiding it. In fact, he has been coming here every couple months for the last year. The only surprise here is why you've never bumped into him."

"I have no idea. I guess I'll see him when he wants me to."

"I imagine you're right."

"Karen, why were you so upset seeing Roger like that yesterday? It's not like you haven't seen stuff like this before."

"You're right. I have seen stuff like this before. Just like this."

"Anything you want to talk about?"

"Not at the moment, but thanks anyway."

Nodding, I said, "I need to go get a new phone. Mine died when I fell in the pond."

"Want me to come with?" I could feel her eyes examining me, looking for signs, watching for underlying tones. I hated it when she tried to psycho-analyze me, but it was simple instinct with Karen.

"No thanks. I think I just need some alone time." I knew Karen could sense my vulnerabilities, despite my efforts to hide them. It was one of the curses of our friendship, a comfort as much an annoyance.

"Well, solitude can be a wonderful thing. It allows one to ponder the perplexities of the universe, to examine one's strength and imperfections."

*Now she's just showing off.*

"Jeez Karen, I just want a cup of coffee and a new phone. I need to get my car out of your garage though." Ladybug was still hiding out in Karen's garage.

"How about you take Pepper's?" Karen suggested.

"Seriously? That thing is huge. I'll never find anywhere to park it in this town. There are no spaces large enough."

"Oh, quit being so dramatic. It's not that big."

"Okay, I'll drive anything just to get away from here and be by myself."

Sighing, I put Pepper's fire-engine red, vintage Lincoln in gear and started toward town. I can see why Pepper loves this car; it drives like a dream. The white leather interior and the daredevil doors give it a very classy look. *Very much like the woman herself.* Although, it's so big I could put Ladybug inside and still have room.

Ten minutes later, I was stepping into Lucy's Diner. Painted bright with polished metal chairs and tables, set off against red and yellow walls with posters of movie stars, the diner has a vintage look to it.

Lucy, the diner owner, was behind the counter in a white waitress uniform. Her curly, bright red hair (a color unknown to nature) was pulled back and held with bright yellow combs. Her thin lips were painted dark red, Lucille Ball style, to go with the fifties style of the diner, I imagine.

"Hey, Mattie, sit anywhere. What can I get for you?" Amber, the college student Lucy had working for her on weekends, asked as she looked up from a table in the corner where she was filling ketchup bottles. "You know meatloaf is the special today."

"Just coffee today, Amber. Thanks."

I tucked myself into a booth in an out of the way corner hidden from the world, holding the large cup of coffee Amber had just poured, trying to stop myself from shivering.

I glanced around.

It was becoming habit for me to make sure no one could hear my thoughts. What the hell is wrong with me? I'm creeping myself out.

There was a window on my left, overlooking the parking lot. After a lengthy battle with the town council, Lucy had placed glass and wrought iron tables, shaded by large red and white striped canvas umbrellas, for those who chose to sit outside and enjoy the view of the park. There was a large ficus plant between the next booth and me. So, unless you were looking for me, you would not find me. It was perfect. Maybe I'll see Steven walking around town.

Glancing out the window, I took stock of my surroundings. Across the street, in the park, the maple trees played host to bright splashes of gold among the thick evergreens crowding the hillside. Bushes that normally went unnoticed during spring and summer boldly proclaimed their presence, adorned now in pumpkin orange and scarlet red. Deep burgundy vines hugged the hillside and ran between rocks and into crevices. Color was everywhere.

A few days from now the park would undergo a transformation. The ladies auxiliary, with the help of many an unsuspecting volunteer, would begin decorating for the 32nd Annual Hopewell GrapeFest.

The park would be bursting with games and rides, craft displays along with an assortment of food and drink vendors, much like the Cherry Festival held in Traverse City every summer. There would also be a cooking contest centered on creative uses of grapes and wine . . . lots of wine. The annual Grape Stomp is a favorite for the twenty-something's. They love to jump in and get their feet purple.

Festival goers can sample some of the local wines and choose their favorites at the People's Choice wine tasting; a consumer judged wine competition at the Wine Pavilion. Always a healthy competition, but one my family's winery wouldn't be competing in this year.

There would be bales of hay, bright colorful mums, and scarecrows present in large quantities.

*Scarecrows* . . . I laid my head back and closed my eyes reflecting. I've always liked scarecrows but now . . . Roger looking like the scarecrow from the *Wizard of Oz* . . . I don't know.

Wiping the tears away, I found myself wishing there really was a Glenda the Good Witch and I could click my heels together and recite, "There's no place like home, there's no place like home, there's no place . . . " Wishing I were home right now with my . . .

Just then the ficus plant in front of me started shaking. Startled I lifted my head. Cloudy eyes glinting with amusement, intelligence, and a touch of defiance, peeked through the branches at me.

"Good morning, Matilda. Did I overhear you say something about a Good Witch?"

"I'm sorry, Mrs. Blackwell, I don't mean to be rude, but . . . " my new phone started playing Eye of the Tiger. Stryker . . . damn. I was hoping to get a few minutes alone. I let it ring.

Mrs. Blackwell looked back over her shoulder and said, "She's right here, my dear."

I dropped my head onto the table. "Shit," I said under my breath.

"Ouch," Stryker said as he sat down across from me. "Eye of the Tiger? Nice. O'Malley, you and I are getting so we can read each other's minds. You can't hide anything anymore."

"That's scary. I might want to get away with something sometime." Leaning in toward Stryker I whispered, "Mrs. Blackwell thinks she's psychic."

"From what I've heard, she is." At my dubious expression he continued, "Seems a bit unpredictable, though," Stryker said with a conspiratorial whisper.

"Uh-huh. If by that, you mean she's like totally whacked." I nodded in agreement.

We were silent for a few minutes before I asked, "Were you looking for me?"

"Were you hiding from me?"

"Dammit." I plowed my hands through my unruly hair. "You know, this answering-a-question-with-a-question shit is getting old. How did you get in here anyway? I never saw you walk in."

"That's because I move so fast I don't show up on anyone's radar. Are you setting yourself up as bait, O'Malley?"

"Hey, I was having a personal conversation with myself."

He sighed.

"Besides, this is exciting. Some of us can only dream about being used as bait. But I get to live the dream," I said unconvincingly.

Stryker closed his eyes for a second, battling that headache again I'm sure.

"I envy the way your brain works, O'Malley." He said shaking his head slowly.

"Excuse me."

Momentarily startled, I looked up at the strikingly attractive woman standing at the edge of our booth. She looked to be in her early thirties and was slender and athletic, with soft blond hair and liquid blue eyes. There was something geometrically appealing about her small face, delicate nose, and angular cheeks. She had a strong profile. The woman's navy blue suit was subdued and practical and yet still managed to show off her soft, supple curves despite her enormous stomach.

The camera would love her.

*Where did that come from? I haven't thought about photography for such a long time.*

The gold earrings dangling from her earlobes showed-off a long swan-like neck.

I let my gaze wander back to her eyes. She was nervously staring down at Stryker, waiting for him to acknowledge her.

I looked at Stryker, then at her, and back to Stryker again.

"Hi, Beau. How are you?" she asked. I detected a slight timbre in her voice.

His dark eyes looked the pregnant woman over once before an indifferent . . . no, almost hostile, "Stephanie. What can I do for you?" echoed back.

Rubbing a tale tell tear from her cheek with the back of her hand she answered, "I'd hoped we could talk."

"About?"

A shadow passed over the fragile woman's appealing face. She looked at me, her eyes growing uneasy.

"I need to talk to you. Privately. Please," she said softly.

"I don't think that's a good idea."

I raised my eyes in quick surprise. I took in her elegant maternity outfit, while trying to forget my pathetic appearance, and forced my mouth into what I hoped was a friendly smile. Not being able to stand the awkward silence any longer, I slid out of the booth and held out my hand, "Hi, I'm Mattie, a . . . *friend* of Beau's. Would you care to sit down?" I asked her as I glared at Stryker hoping to make eye contact.

*No such luck.*

He was staring down at the table as if it were about to sprout wings and fly him out of there.

She gave a determined nod and the gold earrings tinkled.

"Thank you, Mattie. That would be great. My feet are swollen and these shoes are killing me. I don't know what I was thinking." She giggled self-consciously as she slid into the booth across from Stryker, her gaze expectant. Looking back at me, clearly uncomfortable, she said, "Uhm . . . I'm Stephanie."

"It's nice to meet you."

Taking a quick look at Stryker, I said, "I'll just get going and give you two some privacy." Turning back to the woman I said, "I hope to see you again, Stephanie. Good-bye."

I turned. And, walked into over six feet of hard body and wicked attitude. Jeez *I never even saw him get up.* Stryker gazed at me for a long moment; I suspected he knew my thoughts. His eyes darkened ever so slightly. Aside from that, his expression was unreadable.

"I've got to do something," I said through clenched teeth, my hands balled into tight fists at my sides. "I can't let Steven get away with this," I said resuming our earlier argument.

"Let it go, O'Malley." Stryker's deep voice was grim. And commanding. He looked every inch a military man; his dark eyes stern and determined, his posture upright.

"Not this time, Stryker." I was breathing fast, my mouth a thin straight line.

"Listen to me." Stryker reached out, gripped my shoulders. "It could be dangerous to cross him."

"I don't care. Sometimes you can't look the other way. Sometimes you have to face down . . . " I broke off.

Stryker's face turned to a stony mask. His hands slipped from my shoulders.

"You are not going anywhere," he said in a tone that persuaded most people to drop the subject.

Unfortunately for him, I'm not most people.

"You think you can stop me?" I asked optimistically.

"I know I can." He folded his arms across his chest.

I shot a visual dart in his direction.

He arched an arrogant eyebrow. "You're going to get yourself killed."

"I'll take my chances."

"Forget it."

"What do you mean forget it? You can't tell me to forget it."

"I can and I am."

I got the impression he was struggling to hang on to his temper.

"You know Stryker, I'm not stupid . . . maybe a bit overly optimistic," a personality trait that my experiences in this particular field were stripping away at every fiber of my being.

He glared at me.

"I'm not on your payroll, Marine. I can do whatever I like."

Blocking my path, he frowned and said, "This isn't over."

"Understood." I said, with more bravado than I felt as I walked around him. Leaving him with the striking, pregnant blonde-haired woman, who sat gaping at us.

The squealing tires caught my attention, and of course I foolishly stopped in the middle of the street to see where the noise was coming from. This, in turn, made me a perfect target for the fire engine red Lincoln racing straight toward me.

At that moment, a mourning dove burst from a tree limb. The dove's ooh-ooh-ooh combined with the frenzied attack of a pileated woodpecker on a nearby trunk drowned out the scream that, I'm pretty sure, came from me.

Just as I was rehashing that whole bait thing and wondering what day of the week underwear I had on, something hit me like lightning.

Very fast and unexpected.

Energy so strong it was forcing me out of the way of the speeding car. I fell forward just before reaching the sidewalk, striking the curb with my knee and mashing my face in the grass. The rapid moving car swerved by as the other pedestrians screamed and scattered frantically.

"Are you all right?" Stryker shouted at me. His body covering mine felt like a lead weight pushing me into the ground.

"Stryker, you're crushing me." I said after lifting my head and spitting out the grass that managed to infiltrate my mouth.

He pushed himself up keeping his eyes on me the entire time. "Are you hurt?" he asked while running his hands over my body.

"I'm fine," I reassured him as I pushed myself into a sitting position to get a look at my knee, which didn't feel so fine. I sat there staring at the blood seeping through the hole in my khakis.

"You realize that was Pepper's car flying down the street don't you? She's going to kill me. She loves that car," I said, still panting with fear.

"She loves you more." Stryker reassured me. For all the anger and frustration, I could see in his eyes, his voice was gentle.

"What happened?" The soft cry came straight from my heart as my impatient fingers dashed away the tears that rolled down my cheeks.

"I don't know. But I'm damn well going to find out."

We heard the sound of approaching sirens.

Standing, Stryker looked around, and for an instant his sharp features were wolf like and predatory.

"Stay right here, O'Malley. Do you understand? Do . . . not . . . move," he ordered. He obviously wasn't going anywhere until I agreed so I nodded slightly and watched as he stalked across the street leaving me alone to stop the blood oozing from my injured knee.

Just then Detective Adams ambled wearily over to where we were; not seeming the least bit surprised to find me sitting on the curb injured.

"Can either of you tell me what happened here? Did anyone get a look at the driver?"

Stryker shook his head no. "Maybe you should ask them what happened," Stryker suggested, pointing to the crowd on the sidewalk across the street, in answer to the Detective's question. "I need to get her to the hospital. She's going to need stitches in that knee." Holding out his hand, I looked at it for a second before I took it and Stryker pulled me up and into him to lean on.

Adams turned in the direction Stryker pointed. Turning back to me he said, "Ms. O'Malley, you do seem to attract trouble, don't you?"

I noticed the ambulance and several police cars surrounding the area.

"I don't need an ambulance," I said, looking from Stryker to Detective Adams.

"It's not for you. It's for her." Adams jerked his thumb in the direction of the crowd. They parted giving me a full view of a gurney with a woman on it.

"Who . . . who's that?" I stammered.

Stryker eased me away from Adams. "What?" I asked, stopping, unable to wrap my mind around his sudden handle-with-care attitude.

Jaw set, he looked over at the medics, and moved his hand from my arm to the flat of my back to turn me and block my peripheral vision. The warmth of his hand, his nearness rushed pinpricks to my limbs.

"Who is it?" I asked a second time.

"Name's . . . Amber Watkins." Adams said, consulting his little notebook. "She's a waitress over at . . . "

"Over at Lucy's Diner. I know. I was just talking to her." I said finishing Detective Adams sentence. "What happened to her?"

"She was hit by a car. Pepper's car, precisely." Stryker told me, looking into my eyes.

If someone had doused me in ice water, the effect couldn't have been more paralyzing. I gasped, "What?"

"I need to ask you a few questions, Ms. O'Malley. Some of the witnesses said it looked as if the car was aiming for you. Did you get that impression?"

"Well, I'm not really sure. I heard the car, looked up, and stupidly I stopped in the middle of the street. I don't know if he was aiming for me or not."

"So it was a man driving?" Adams asked.

"I don't know. I all happened so fast. Is Amber going to be okay?" I asked, turning to Stryker.

"One more question, Ms. O'Malley . . . "

"She needs medical attention. She'll be at the hospital if you want to ask her anymore questions." He put an arm around my waist to turn me away from the crowd once more; I took full advantage of his support. I wasn't sure I could have made it on my own. "Come on O'Malley, let's go visit Dr. Delicious." Stryker lifted me into his arms and carried me away from Detective Adams.

"You don't have to carry me. I'm perfectly fine."

"I'd feel better if someone with some medical training told me that."

I started to reply but broke off . . . I sniffled. Great, I was going to cry again.

"Sorry, did you say something?" His voice was dry.

Being in his arms felt good and strange, all at the same time. For that matter, so did a whole range of other things that were far too confusing for me to sort through right now. I decided just to enjoy the moment we seemed to be having.

"Jeez, O'Malley you really should lay off the muffins." Stryker grunted.

# CHAPTER 19

Exhausted and drained, I slept restlessly. I was tired, so tired. Too many people, too many places, too much emotion. Phantoms drifted through my dreams.

The covers felt warm and my body relaxed. Then I moved. "Shit," I groaned and lifted the covers to look at my leg. My knee was red and swollen.

"The pain killers Dr. Delicious gave you must have worn off." Sami smiled at me from the doorway.

"Oh, Sami," I cried as she walked across the room and engulfed me in a strong hug. God, I love this woman.

Sami Gil is the owner of Gil's Taekwondo and my best friend, next to Karen.

An exotic beauty, her thick black hair hanging straight down her back, the blunt ends brushing her backside. Her almond shaped eyes, a testament to her Korean ancestry, were filled with laughter and a sassy, determined glint, while her perfectly shaped lips slid into a wide grin while staring at me. Wearing her Taekwondo uniform, her long black hair was now braided, and pulled forward, over her left shoulder.

I've been taking self-defense classes from her for the last two years thinking it would be good for my self-esteem and coordination. It doesn't seem to be working very well on either one of those avenues, I thought as I looked down at my throbbing knee. Maybe this will convince her to teach me how to shoot a gun.

"They were good while they lasted, huh?" She said nodding at me, bringing me back to the pain in my knee. "You took one last night and Special Agent Tall, Dark, and Brooding had to pick you up and carry your ass in here."

"Stryker carried me in here?"

"Yep. Did you know your FBI guy knows martial arts and is a seventh degree black belt?"

I shook my head impatiently and sighed. As much as I adored Sami, I understood that when it came to men she was a viper. After a heartbreaking relationship a few years ago that left her distraught and him, well, let's just say it was a while before he could *Walk Like a Man*, Sami adopted the viewpoint that when dealing with the opposite sex, you hunt them down, toy with them awhile, then walk away from them first. If Sami wanted him, she'd get him. She's a *real* man's dream.

"Oh, please," Sami, said reading my mind. "Your FBI guy has nothing on my militia man. He's all yours."

"Really?"

"I can hear you," Stryker said from the living room.

*Crap!*

"Sami, can you help me to the bathroom?" I whispered.

"Sure, then I gotta go. I'm between classes right now. Karen and Pepper should be back shortly."

Sami waited outside the door while I took care of business then washed my face, brushed my teeth and pulled my hair up in a high ponytail. Looking in the mirror, I saw I was wearing a white wife beater tank top and my pink boxers that had Sherriff Joe from Maricopa County printed across the butt. *I wonder who helped me into these.* Pepper's ratty old robe was hanging on the back of the door. It was that or the pink boxers.

Pulling on the robe, I opened the door and limped out. Sami wrapped one arm around my waist as I lifted one of mine over her shoulder and behind her neck. Guiding me into the living room, she sat me down on an overstuffed chair and lifted my leg onto the ottoman. Wincing at the pain, I shifted my leg and propped it on a plump throw pillow. My whole body ached.

"Okay, kiddo, I gotta go. I'm leaving you in Stryker's capable hands until Pepper gets back." Giving me a kiss on the head and giving Stryker 'the wink and the gun' she headed out the door.

Stryker was leaning forward on the sofa cleaning his gun on top of the coffee table. "Wowie zowie; that's a lot of fire power." I said amazed at the size of it.

He looked over at me with a smirk, saying nothing.

I laid my head back on the cushion and closed my eyes. "How is Amber?" I asked keeping my eyes closed. When he didn't answer, I opened them to see if he heard me.

He shook his head. "She didn't make it."

Without saying another word, Stryker got up and went into the kitchen leaving me alone to wonder about the events that led to her death.

The wafting aroma of coffee preceded his footsteps and a moment later he was back. Gratefully, I accepted the mug he offered.

"Here, I thought you might need this. Are you feeling any better today?"

"It hurts like hell, but I'll live. Do you have any idea why Amber was hit?"

Stryker shook his head.

"Where did Karen and Pepper go?"

"They went to see Mr. Benzer, your grandmother's attorney. Pepper went into the attic last night trying to find the paperwork for Rosa's estate but couldn't find anything. She's convinced all that's been happening around here has something to do with your grandmother. She called Benzer this morning and he agreed to meet with her right away. Her car is still in police impound so Karen took her."

"What's she hoping to find?"

"I don't know. She just thinks there is more to your inheritance than you know. Benzer would know better than anyone. If you don't mind my asking, what were the circumstances surrounding your leaving Arizona?" Stryker asked, leaning forward on the sofa with his sinewy arms resting on his powerful thighs.

"What do you mean? Gramma died, left me the farmhouse, and I was getting a divorce anyway. So, I moved here. That's it."

"Was your divorce final when you left Arizona?" Stryker prodded.

My tired brain struggled for an answer. "I assumed so. Daniel, my assistant, bought my photography studio so there was no reason to stay. But as far as the final divorce papers," I shrugged, "I really don't remember. It happened so fast; it's all kind of a blur."

"What happened? If you don't mind my asking?"

"When I first met him, I fell in love with him. I found him fascinating and funny. Now, it's obvious I didn't know him, didn't know a big part of him at all. Who was the man I married? Believe me; I would really like to know." I lowered my face into my hands.

I hated the regrets. The 'could have beens'. The marriage had never been picture-perfect. Maybe if I'd worked harder to make it better. Maybe then I wouldn't feel so damn guilty all the time. Maybe . . .

My brain cleared. It was as if I'd been looking through a fog for the past six years, since the day of . . .

"I'm sorry, O'Malley. I didn't mean to . . . " Stryker said. He looked uncomfortable, as if he might have to deal with a hysterically crying woman.

*Not this time.*

I jerked up and Stryker was privy to all the anger and pain I'd been carrying with me all these years. It radiated off me, like waves of heat, laced with poison. "Don't be sorry for me, save it for Steven. If I find out he's had anything to do with any of this, he'll need it."

"O'Malley, what's the deal with you and Angelo? Why so much hostility?"

"Do you know of many amicable divorces?" An oxymoron of the first order.

"No, not personally." He mused.

"Sooo Stryker . . . was that a Mrs. Stryker? Ex or otherwise at the diner yesterday?"

"Why do you ask, O'Malley?"

"There you go again, bob and weave Stryker. Can't you just answer a question?"

"Fair enough. Yes we were married . . . once," he said as he looked down into his coffee cup.

I thought about all the possibilities and decided to ask the obvious. "Do you still love her?"

I watched closely, but Stryker's expression didn't change.

"It wouldn't do any good if I did." He stopped speaking abruptly, pressing his lips together in a thin line as if to stop himself from revealing too much about himself.

I was intrigued. "Why?"

"Why what?" He asked with a smirk.

I shifted and still facing him, leaned against the back of the chair. "What happened? I mean only if you want to tell me. Whatever . . . "

My voice trailed off as a nagging thought occurred to me. Was he being evasive because she still mattered to him? *God, what do you care Mattie?*

"That's not the reason," he said.

I blinked at him. "What are you talking about?"

His gaze was unwavering. "I'm being evasive because I don't know what to say about her, not because she still matters."

Something inside me reached out to him. I wanted to smooth the creases from his forehead and around his eyes. "How is it you always know what I'm thinking?"

"It was a logical assumption."

"Uh-huh." I didn't buy it for a second. Super Stryker was reading my mind again.

"When I started working for the FBI," he said, "I quickly learned that emotional detachment was an asset. Nearly every situation is difficult on some level and leading with your heart is a good way to get yourself or others killed. Staying emotionally distant was something I learned while in the marines and has served me well at the bureau.

"In theory, Stephanie liked the idea of being married to an FBI agent. Unfortunately, it never traveled any farther than the idea. She started resenting the time I was away which left her alone. Kept telling me I wasn't there for her. I don't blame her for that, we were young, and . . . " he shrugged, "Stuff happens."

"So you two just drifted apart?"

"I guess you could say that."

"So, is this emotional detachment you're so fond of the reason you haven't gotten involved with anyone else?"

"No. I've avoided relationships because I loved Stephanie so much I can't ever love again."

I looked at him for several heartbeats, and then burst out laughing.

"Oh, come on. That's ridiculous. You can't ever love again. Wow that's quite a bit of melodrama."

I waited anxiously as he stared at me. I couldn't read his expression . . . not until one corner of his mouth twitched.

"Not buying my best line, huh?" he asked at last.

"Not for a second. Who has?"

"Everyone but you."

"I see. Then you need to start dating women with slightly higher IQ's."

He blinked, then his mouth twisted in a small, embarrassed smile.

"So the child she's carrying . . . ?"

"Not mine," he said, staring back at me, his eyes like tempered steel. His voice, however, lacked that hard edge, "This time."

"You mean you have . . . " I left the rest of the question hanging.

Stryker's gaze lowered to the gun he had been cleaning.

"No. She was pregnant but she miscarried while I was in Iraq," he said regretfully.

"Oh, Stryker, I'm so sorry. I didn't mean to . . . "

Raising his hand he cut me off saying, "Don't worry about it. I didn't even know she was pregnant until she lost the baby. After I came home."

"So why did she come looking for you yesterday?"

"To be absolved . . . I guess."

"Absolved? For what?"

"Probably because the father of her child is my younger brother Kyle."

"Ouch . . . And I thought my life was bizarre."

"It is, O'Malley . . . it is."

Clearly, it was time to change the subject. "Do you think Steven was the person driving Pepper's car?"

He lifted one hand and rubbed the back of his neck, a gesture I've come to recognize as meaning he was puzzled or thinking deeply. "I just don't know," he said slowly.

We fell silent, but this time it was a relaxed silence.

"Benzie couldn't find anything. But, then he couldn't find his hand if it was scratching his ass. His girl is gone for the week, so as soon as she gets back he'll have her locate it and send it over. He did say we weren't the only one's looking though. He said a man called some months back and asked about Rosa's estate. He wanted to know if your husband would have access to it. Benzie assumed it was Roger and the two of you were planning on getting married." Pepper said as her and Karen came in the door.

Shaking my head, I said, "No way. Roger would rather go into the witness protection program than get married. Also, he has . . . " I sighed, "Or, had no interest in this place other than maybe selling it.

"But, if that's the case, where does Steven get off saying he's my husband?"

"O'Malley, have you considered that he just may still be your husband?" Stryker asked. "That maybe your divorce was never finalized. You were in such a hurry to get away from there you might have forgotten that one little detail."

Pepper, sitting on the arm of my chair took my hand in hers. "Sweetie, I think it's time you told them. I know I promised never to tell a soul and I've honored that promise . . . until now. There have been too many "accidents" lately. And poor Roger's dead. If Steven had anything to do with that, you owe it to Roger to set it right. Especially, before something terrible happens to you or to . . . Please Sweetie, tell them. You can trust Karen and Beau."

I reached up to pat my aunt's soft wrinkled cheek. She leaned down toward me and I whispered, "I'm sorry Pepper, but I can't risk it." I kissed her soft cheek and said, "I'm tired I need to go back to bed. Karen will you help me?"

"Sure Mattie, let's get you back to bed. I'll get you another pain pill so you can get some rest."

Pepper stood so Karen could help me back to bed, her bag dropping to the floor, where it landed with a loud thud.

"What have you got in there, Pepper?" Karen asked, reaching toward Pepper's purse.

Pepper grabbed something and clutched it to her chest.

"Why Pepper," I blurted out with a choked laugh, "What a big gun you have."

Smiling, I stared at the cannon in my aunt's slightly shaky hands.

Pepper shrugged. "So, I'm packing heat. It just means you don't need to worry about any more trouble around here."

Karen finally found her voice, and asked. "Please tell me that's not a real gun."

"Of course it is, honey." Pepper's voice softened. "Mattie, this Colt Python was your Grandpa Paddy's favorite pistol. I'm licensed to carry."

Stryker chimed in just then, "Maybe in Arizona, but not in Michigan." He reached over and gently took the Colt from Pepper's hands. "I'll just hang on to this until you go back home."

Karen got me settled into bed and medicated before she spoke again. "Mattie, you know there's nothing you can't tell me. Beau and I will do whatever it takes to keep you safe, but you have to trust us."

"Thank you for your concern, Karen."

When it was clear I had nothing else to say, she nodded and left the room pulling the door closed softly behind her.

The next time I woke, it was dark outside. Pepper was shaking my shoulder trying to wake me. "Sweetie, Dr. Harmon is here to see you. Is it all right if I bring him in?"

"Um . . . sure. Oh, Pepper, is Stryker still here?"

"No, he left right after Karen helped you to bed. He was going home to shower and get some rest. Did you know he was up most of the night watching you? He told me to sleep up in your room and he would stay down here and listen for you. When I got up this morning, he was in that chair just watching you. I had to make him go lie on the sofa and get a little sleep. Anyway, I'll tell Dr. Harmon he can come in and then I'll make you something to eat." She turned and left the room.

I'm not sure how I felt about that . . . Stryker watching me all night.

"Knock knock . . . May I come in?"

"Hi, Jonathan. You didn't need to come check up on me again."

"Are you kidding? This is just where I wanted to get you." He did an evil doctor laugh while rubbing his hands together. "Only under different circumstances. Besides, I come bearing gifts." He said holding out a crutch toward me.

"Do I really need that?"

"I think it beats you trying to hobble around on one foot. That's a good way to get hurt again."

"I guess you're right. That must be why you make the big bucks . . . huh."

"Yeah, that and the long hours. So how are you feeling anyway?"

"The knee still hurts like hell. Will I be able to walk on it soon?"

"Sure, probably tomorrow. Just elevate it when it starts complaining and use the crutch. Don't be a hero. Use the pain pills if you need them. You'll be good as new for the Black and Blue Ball."

I nodded and said, "Good to know."

Jonathan turned to look through my bookshelves giving me a chance to study him. At roughly six feet, he was only a couple inches taller than me and a few years older. He was wearing a black sweater, cashmere, and black jeans. Penetrating blue eyes and dark blond hair, slightly tousled in that arty, I'm-too-cool-to-comb-my-hair way that you just *know* takes twenty minutes in front of a mirror to arrange. A square jaw with a wide white smile and thin lips. Jonathan, though not as imposing as Stryker, strikes quite a figure. He's slender where Stryker is magnitude. Besides his surreal good looks, there is a boyish charm and easygoing temperament, which is pleasant compared to Stryker's hair-trigger temper. Jonathan is a classic . . . but Stryker is . . . incomparable.

"I see you like the classics, Mattie." Jonathan said, startling me. *Could he read my mind too?* "I've read them all. Unfortunately, I haven't had much time to read since I went to med school." *Good he's talking about the books.*

"I'm sure your career is very demanding."

"Yes, it is. That's why I'm looking forward to the Ball. I don't get to go out much and I haven't had a date in ages."

"I find that hard to believe. I get the impression that you're very accustomed to having your way with women."

"Can't argue with that," he said, pushing his hair back off his forehead.

"I'm sure it makes for a very exciting romantic life."

"I'm not complaining," he said in an uncharacteristically arrogant way.

"Anyway . . . umm . . . I'm sure we'll have a lovely time. Thank you for inviting me to go with you. I just hope I don't embarrass you in front of your colleagues."

Turning back to me he exclaimed, "Mattie, you could never do that. You'll be the most beautiful woman there. I'm a lucky man."

"Hey," he said softly from the doorway.

I looked over toward the door and the sight caught my breath. There he was; tall, dark, and handsome, with thick brown hair and tired, penetrating brown eyes that missed nothing. His firm jaw was peppered with at least one-day's growth of beard. He looked as though he hadn't slept in at least twenty-four hours.

My heart skipped a beat.

Stryker was leaning against the doorframe watching me with those eyes. Sighing, I gave myself a mental slap.

"Hey, yourself. Pepper said you went home to get some rest," I said.

"I did get a little. You're looking better."

"Thanks." After a few silent moments I asked, "Are those for me?" Noticing the flowers he held in his hands.

He looked down at them as if he'd forgotten they were there. "Yeah, they are."

He made his way into the room. He looked wonderful dressed in jeans, an Aero-Smith t-shirt, and boots. As usual, his hair was tousled as if he'd just shoved his hands through the wavy strands.

Taking the flowers from his out-stretched hand, I breathed their scent deeply. "Thank you Stryker, they're lovely."

"No problem."

"Jonathan tells me I'll be able to walk tomorrow with a crutch and dance in time for the Ball."

"Well, I'm very happy for you. I was just checking in and since you're in such competent hands I'll be going." Turning his gaze to the other man in the room he said, "Jonathan, nice to see you again. O'Malley." He nodded toward me and walked out the door.

Maybe I imagined it, but he looked a little reluctant to leave me alone with Jonathan.

Pepper's timing couldn't have been better. She came in carrying a tray with grilled cheese sandwiches and tomato soup. I just realized how hungry I was. "Dr. Harmon, would you care to join us?"

Jonathan shook his head and said, "No thank you, Pepper. I was just on my way home as I have some work to do and have the early shift in the morning." Turning to me, "Mattie, I'll call you tomorrow." He leaned in and kissed me on the lips. A quick light kiss. Startled, it was all I could do not to jerk my head back into my pillow. "Goodnight. I'll talk to you tomorrow."

Laying my head back on my pillow I said, "What the heck, Pepper."

Munching on her sandwich, she giggled. "Child, I wish I had your problems."

# CHAPTER 20

Humming to myself, I ran the bathwater and sank into the steaming comfort of the tub. Settling into the bubbles, I exhaled a frustrated breath, letting the hot water command my attention as I relaxed, settling deeper into my old claw foot tub, closing my eyes.

Still, it was only a few minutes before little thoughts started creeping from the back of my mind. Trying to push them back, I thought about driving into Hopewell the first time as a full-time resident.

The Village of Hopewell was just that; a community glowing with fresh, exhilarating new hope. It was a village packed with antique shops, an art gallery, a full-service gas station, its very own accountant, health clinic, liquor store, and dentist. A dance studio that was still owned and operated by Miss Annie. And only one law firm in town . . . Benzer, Benzer, and Benzer.

Many years ago, the town boasted a clothing store owned by one family over four generations called "Coopers." The original store started as a "dry-goods" business in 1876 by Shamus Cooper, an immigrant from Scotland. The store is now a coffee shop owned by Nick "Coop" Cooper, a career soldier and bachelor, who came home when his mother fell ill. Coop ran "Coopers Clothing Store" until she died in 1992. After she passed, everyone thought he would go back into the service, but he surprised them all when he decided to stay and changed the clothing store to a coffee shop and bakery, leaving the original gold leaf lettering on the door and the original mahogany counter right where they were.

Returning to the Village of Hopewell was like entering a place where time had stood still. The lovely downtown area had a beautiful body of water on one side, dramatic hills on the other, and a spectacular park situated right in the center of town. Everywhere you looked, there were rolling hills with stunning views of the bay.

I drove out of the village toward Gramma Rosa's house, finding memories around every bend. The ditches on either side of the road were still as deep and overgrown as they had been when Gramma sent Allen and me into town to the bakery every morning for bread.

When I got to the house, I drove on, through rows of well-kept vines. This entire region was a wine lover's dream.

Locally, there are a number of family owned wineries in the Village of Hopewell. Hundreds of acres of vineyards surround the area. Wine is the main source of

235

*income in this area and everything else seems to revolve around it.*

I sunk deeper into the cooling water, closed my eyes, and my mind started to wander again. Worry niggled at me.

*I'd met Roger a few weeks after I moved here and since the day we met, he'd been pestering me to go out with him. He was an ardent flirt and yet very kind. Sandy blond hair, blue eyes, tall, and well-built with an engaging smile, he turned the head of almost every available woman in town. But I just wasn't ready.*
*"Come on Mattie, let me rock your world."*
*"Not gonna happen, Roger."*
*"I'm not giving up."*
*"I know." I sighed.*

Shaking myself from my self-imposed pity party, I decided to get out of the tub and make myself a cup of coffee, knowing I wouldn't be able to go back to sleep anyway. Maybe I can start working on the query letter for my book. It seems to have been put on the back burner for some time now.

My psyche, already primed for my first cup of coffee, I got the coffee beans out of the pantry. Opening the bag, I inhaled the aroma, losing myself in the heady scent as I closed the pantry door.

"Hey."

I nearly jumped out of my skin and barely suppressed a scream when I saw Steven standing directly in front of me. I felt myself sway, as I reached for my crutch. The blood had all rushed out of my head and settled in my feet making it hard for me to move. I dropped the bag of coffee beans and watched as they scattered across the shiny pine floor like cockroaches when the lights are suddenly turned on.

Regaining some of my composure, I fixed Steven with a malevolent gaze.

Not having seen him for six years, and no longer in love with him, I could look at him as a grown-up not some starry-eyed schoolgirl.

I never noticed how narrow his eyes were or how weak his chin was. Good Lord, he was puny. To think I had always thought of him as wiry.

*Jeez.*

I had an instant image of Stryker, all solid, muscular, and sexy, and that made Steven look even weaker. What in the hell did I ever see in this guy?

"What are *you* doing here?" I whispered angrily not wanting to wake Pepper who was still sleeping upstairs in my room.

"Hello to you, too, Mrs. Angelo." Steven said, his skinny chin jutted forward, a wry smile creating an evil look on his face. Steven always had a sardonic sense of humor.

"Get out," I said, the tension in my chest making me sound small even to myself.

We locked eyes, and his were filled with meanness.

He shrugged, "I don't think so. You and I need to talk," he said stepping closer.

I didn't like where this was going and I'll be damned if I was going to let him lead.

"Get the fuck out of my house," I wrenched out between clenched teeth.

"Nope. I kinda like it here. Anyway . . . that's what we have to talk about. *Pause.* Technically it's not just your house. It's our house. You see, *Matilda,* you were in such a hurry to get away from me you didn't stick around long enough to make sure I signed the divorce papers. Which I didn't. Besides there's this little thing called desertion. You disappeared for six years before you filed for divorce.

"It's a good thing I stayed in the house. I couldn't believe my luck when I saw those papers from the attorney informing us your grandmother had died and left us everything. Since we're still married I'm entitled to half of everything you inherited. Don't worry I'll leave something for you."

*Oh . . . I sighed . . . he just wants to talk about my inheritance.*

Everything he had done to me rose up like bile in my throat and all I could think about was how fucking infuriating it was that this puny little troll thought I was going to take this laying down.

"You are definitely certifiable." I snorted at him.

"I think I make a pretty compelling argument."

"In what universe?"

"It's only fair."

"Only in your warped mind."

"Hey! You ran out on me. I looked for you for six months before I realized you weren't coming back to let me explain. So, I think I'm entitled to half of everything."

"You looked for me for a whole six months, did you? Wow. That must have been very trying for you. And you have the nerve to accuse me of running out on you after what you did to our child. Steven . . . you are certifiable."

"I didn't mean to hurt you or the baby . . . I swear. You've only got yourself to blame you know. You should have stopped taking pictures," he said as if it all made sense.

*Sami settled in the back of my brain. Two years of self-defense classes assembled in one place, here and now. I had to take control of the situation . . . instinct told me it was now or never.*

"You want half of everything I have, you puny pile of shit? You have no fucking idea who you're dealing with now. I'm not that same star struck wimp you fucked around on when we were married. I'm not going down without a fight this time. And I'm sure as shit not running."

I jabbed my finger at him while I yelled at the top of my lungs.

Some of the bravado left the set of his shoulders. Steven took a step back. He looked around, his eyes growing uneasy as he forced himself toward me. Stepping forward, he reached out to grab me.

As he got closer, I leaned on my crutch for balance. I rammed my good knee so hard between his legs he gasped, forgetting all about grabbing me. Instead he doubled over and clutched his exploding testicles, giving me ample opportunity to rear my leg back a second time and slam my knee into his downward facing nose.

*Good fucking work,* shouted the Sami in my head.

When he collapsed on the kitchen floor, I watched as he writhed in agony, "My fuckin' nose," he moaned. Then whined, "God, my balls."

After watching a few minutes more, I asked innocently, "Do you need a ride to the hospital or something?"

His expression swiftly changed from pain to one of unmasked fury. "No! Smart-ass. However, you'll pay for this. I was going to let you keep this little shit hole house of yours and only take the vineyards and winery but now I'm going to take it all." It was hard to take him seriously since he was trying to stop the blood flowing from his nose by pinching it, making his voice sound like one of the Lollipop Kids from Munchkinland.

Still shaking, I gripped the crutch tighter just in case he was determined to try to attack me again.

"You're not taking anything. You're going to be in jail for killing Roger. I hope you rot there." I lifted the crutch again and hovered over his sensitive reproductive organs.

Scooting away from me and holding his hands up to shield himself he yelled, "Kill? I didn't kill anyone. The only thing I'm guilty of is not signing divorce papers."

His whiny voice grated.

Lifting the crutch I yelled back, "Liar. You were always a liar. You murdered Roger."

"I swear to you I didn't kill anyone. Do you think I'd be stupid enough to stick around, with this place crawling with cops and feds if I'd killed someone?"

"Well, you were stupid enough to break-in here in the middle of the night. That puts you pretty high on my stupid list. God . . . you're such a coward. I can't believe I never saw that before I married you."

"Trust me, I never touched Roger."

"And I'd be right up there, on the top of that stupid list with you, if I believed anything you said."

Steven tried to get himself up from the floor. Not sure if he should expose his testicles or his nose. Deciding he would risk the bleeding nose he reached out for me to help him . . . I watched as he screamed, his eyes rolling back in his head and he collapsed on the floor again. Looking up I saw Pepper standing there holding something that looked like a remote control.

"Pepper, what did you do?"

"I tasered him." She said with a gleam in her eyes and a malicious little laugh. "It won't kill him . . . unfortunately."

Bending over, careful not to get too close, I could see he was still breathing but his eyes were rolled back in his head and his whole body was twitching. I wondered if that was what Uncle Phil looked like when he was struck by lightning. *Focus O'Malley.*

"Come on, Pepper. We've got to get him to the hospital."

Her astute green eyes were shrewdly calculating. She hates Steven as much as I do. Pepper is the only one who knows what he did to me and what the end result was. And I was quite sure Pepper was, at that moment, considering alternative methods of disposing of Steven Angelo.

A ragged copy of Cosmo caught my attention while we were sitting in the hospital waiting room. One article in particular claimed to share secrets on how to please a man in bed, tonight and every night. Although I found the piece quite enlightening, the research was probably suspect. My gaze caught Stryker's and my heart leapt. I couldn't help wondering what he'd think about cherry popsicles in the bedroom. Self-consciously I smoothed my riotous curls, which I hadn't bothered to comb before heading to the hospital. Letting out a sigh, I forced my mind back to business.

After Pepper called for an ambulance, she called Karen, who in turn called Stryker and our little ragtag group set off for the hospital.

Stryker looked like a man caged. I sure wouldn't want to be Steven when he's finally released from here. We all decided to wait to call Detective Adams until Karen and Stryker could, "interrogate him."

Jonathan, on duty again, approached us looking down at a chart, stopping in front of me he held out his hand. I took it and he pulled me up from the uncomfortable emergency room chair I was sitting in.

"Well, he'll live. Tazers aren't fatal," turning toward Pepper he added, "But Pepper, you probably shouldn't be using one on a regular basis."

"Well, I would have shot him if Beau hadn't taken my Colt. Then there would be no worries." She said shooting a glance at Stryker, who in turned rolled his eyes.

Pepper wasn't known for her discretion. Her openness so appealing under normal circumstances could also be something of a drawback.

"I don't think you should be doing that either." Looking back at me he said, "Do you have the tazer with you?"

"Yes. He's not going to get the chance to try anything else." Pepper said.

Holding out his hand to her, Jonathan said, "Maybe you should give it to me so you won't be tempted again. I'm trying to discourage him from pressing charges." Pepper grudgingly handed it over to Jonathan. "He wants to charge you both with assault."

"Assault? He broke into my home in the middle of the night. That can't be legal."

Jonathan placed the tazer in the pocket of his lab coat and then held up his hand as if to say, *"I don't want to hear it."*

"We're going to be releasing him in a little while. I gave him something for the headache, packed his nose to stop the bleeding, and told him to keep his genitals iced to keep the swelling down." Looking up and over his reading glasses at me he said, "Nice shot by the way. I had no idea you'd be using that crutch as a weapon when I gave it to you last night.

"I assume you will be taking him home with you, Mattie."

"Absolutely not. Why would you assume that?"

"From what he tells me he's your husband."

# CHAPTER 21

G reat," Steven said in his familiar mocking tone, eyeing Stryker, Karen, Pepper, and me as he hobbled out of the doors leading from the emergency room. "Me and the menagerie. Maybe we can pick up a stray dog, or maybe a raccoon, and make it a par-tay."

Stryker grabbed him by the arm, leading him out into the early morning sunrise. "Yuck it up, funny boy. Your ass should be in jail right now for murder." Even with his mirrored sunglasses on, Stryker's glare was undeniable.

With a petulant look on his face Steven whined, "I can't *even* believe you're accusing me of murder." His voice still had a Munchkin-quality to it because of the gauze packed in his nose to stop the flow of blood.

"Why? You draw the line at extortion?" Stryker asked, dragging Steven with him. Stryker out sized him by six inches and about twenty-five pounds.

I had to hand it to Steven though, he might be a butt, but he wasn't easily intimidated.

"I'm not extorting anything. That property is mine fair and square. She left me without a word and didn't sign any divorce papers. Anything that is hers is mine."

"Wow . . . you're a real stand-up guy, aren't you?"

"I didn't come here for a fight. I just want what's mine then she'll get her divorce. Who are you anyway?"

"I'm her bodyguard. Pretend I'm not here."

"Okay you two, stop right now." I said stepping in between them. Turning toward Stryker I said, "I appreciate everything you are doing for me but Steven is my problem. I'll take care of him. Besides, don't you have something important to do?" I asked him.

"I'm doing it. I'm protecting you."

"Really? From him?"

Stryker shrugged his massive shoulders.

Back in my kitchen, Stryker remained silent, standing at the door. His arms crossed over his broad chest, leaning back against the wall, he glowered.

I didn't really believe Steven had anything to do with Roger's death but I'm not sure if he played a role in trying to drive me crazy. Until I had some answers, he wasn't going anywhere. Unfortunately, Stryker wasn't going anywhere until he had some answers either.

"You really know how to pick 'em, O'Malley." Stryker proclaimed.

"So you've said."

"Well I think it bears repeating."

# CHAPTER 22

I limped into the *Drunken Monkey Tavern* for Karaoke with Virgil, and thanks to Pepper I was wearing a clean long-sleeve t-shirt and jeans. I was also armed with just enough cash to get myself a pleasant buzz. I sat nursing a Corona while waiting for Sami who was going to meet me here after her last class. I could use a friend right about now, especially a friend who could kick some ex-husband butt.

I felt a little guilty about leaving Pepper with Steven but she insisted she could handle him since, "Beau was good enough to give me back my gun, and Harry's not going to let him get away with anything." It was already obvious Harry wasn't a fan of Steven.

Keeping my eye on the door for Sami, my stomach clenched.

*DAMN.*

He strode in, the crowd seemed to part, men guarded, women watched him covertly from under heavily mascara'd lashes. He portrayed the classic bad boy; dark good looks, eyes dark and smoldering, tall and broad-shouldered, dressed in black leather, overall bad attitude.

Just seeing him cheered me up.

When he spotted me, he stopped dead, as though re-evaluating his choice of drinking establishment for the evening.

A platinum blond in a short, hot pink, zebra-print skirt seated at the bar, crossed her long legs, smiled, and cooed, "Well . . . hello there handsome." Raising her black eyebrows suggestively.

Stryker rolled his eyes and came to sit across from me at the small table I'd managed to snag when I first got here.

"Buy you a beer, Marine?" I asked.

"Why not?" He shrugged. I noticed he was looking a little tired and distracted. I set off for the bar to order his beer.

The blond in the zebra skirt seemed to have gotten over his rejection and moved on. She was now making an effort to acquire the attention of some other unsuspecting male. Her luck vastly improving this time, but her choice of species much lower.

Returning, I placed Stryker's beer on the table in front of him. He looked at it for a moment then knocked back half the bottle. Setting the bottle back on the table in front of him he proceeded to peel the label off while asking me, "O'Malley, what are the odds we'd end up at the same place to get drunk tonight?"

"Actually, pretty good since this is the only bar in town."

Stryker nodded, "Touché." Leaning back in his chair he settled in to listen to the music.

"Okay, do you want to tell me what you and Karen are keeping from me? And don't say, *nothing*. I know better."

Stryker shifted uneasily in his chair. Took a long drink. Then stared at me for a full minute before answering.

"What has Karen told you about the person that killed Kevin and Sam?"

"Nothing. She's never discussed them with me."

"Well, in a nutshell the unsub we were profiling was abducting his victims, taking them into a cornfield, cutting out their brain, and hanging them on a pole like a scarecrow. And the most disturbing part was he started sending the brains to Karen. The media dubbed him Headcase."

"Really? Really? *That* . . . was the most disturbing part?"

"Yeah."

"Oh my God. That is so wrong on so many levels. Tell me he didn't do that to her family." I said softly, behind the trembling fingers I had placed to my lips.

"No . . . he didn't. I'm positive it was the same perp, but he didn't take their brains. Don't ask me why 'cause I don't know. The best I can figure, he was interrupted and didn't get a chance to finish. But I know it was him."

"Roger's brain wasn't taken was it?"

"Not that I'm aware of." He answered avoiding my eyes.

We sat silently for a long time, not looking at each other. He was clearly hiding something from me.

"Stryker, do you believe true evil can be destroyed?"

Our eyes held briefly, before he dragged his gaze away. "I don't know," he muttered brusquely. He ran a hand through his thick hair and let the strands trickle through his fingers. "And, don't ask me what I do know because I'm not sure about anything."

I raised my bottle and touched it to his. "To evil being destroyed."

He made no comment, but drank in thoughtful silence.

We sat there for a long time together, yet separate, in our own thoughts.

"Steven didn't kill Roger."

Stryker shrugged, clearly not convinced, his hand closed around his bottle, taking another long drink.

"He doesn't have it in him. Look at the size of him compared to Roger. He couldn't have dragged Roger all around town. And, why drag Roger all over town?"

"Mmmhmmm." Stryker, forever noncommittal, was nodding slowly, his eyes focused on me.

"You have to trust me on this." I insisted.

"Based on . . . ?" Stryker asked, not bothering to disguise his amusement.

"Do you have real issues with him, or are you just trying to get on my nerves?" I asked.

"Issues," he said without faltering. "Nerves? Now that's just a perk." He tilted his head and shrugged. His admission didn't surprise me.

"So what's the issue?"

"My gut tells me he's guilty of something, just not sure of what . . . yet," Stryker answered. That was all he was prepared to give right now. He was a cop, not a fortune-teller. I knew this.

Leaning in toward him, I set my elbows on the small table and laid it all out for him.

"Okay, does his puny physique and weak chin give the impression of a serial killer? *Absolutely!*

"Does his arrogance and disagreeable nature give off vibes of over compensation? *You betcha.*

"Does his superiority complex come off like maybe he'd rather his sexual partner's be submissive . . . or preferably dead? *Totally.*

"Not to mention he's just the right size to crawl through a doggie-door undetected. But I still don't think he killed Roger." I sat back in my chair and took a swallow of my beer, satisfied I'd made my argument.

He let out a short, derisive laugh.

"Wow! You just presented a great argument . . . for the prosecution. Nice job, O'Malley." Stryker leaned back in his chair and did a slow soft clap.

Refusing to let myself sound defensive, I said, "Stryker, don't you see. Steven is a coward. He steps in after all the work is done. He's not going to get his hands dirty. He's a vulture; he sweeps in after the prey is down.

That's why he waited to confront me when he knew I was hurt and he thought I was alone. He just wants my money. He's more . . . I don't know . . . serial extortionist than serial killer and . . . "

"Jeez O'Malley, land your plane." Stryker said, cutting me off.

It wasn't until I was finished that I'd realized I was saying all this through clenched teeth and wondering why I was still defending Steven after all he'd done to me.

Glancing over at the door, I sighed as I watched Sami walk in. In fact, everyone watched Sami walk in. Wearing red cowboy boots, tight jeans and a white, heavy cable knit sweater, which hung off one shoulder leaving it bare, she caught the eye of every male there. Like Stryker, she draws attention everywhere she goes.

"Let's just agree to disagree, okay." Stryker said standing as Sami approached the table.

I sighed, "Okay."

As if to prove his point, he leaned over and kissed the top of my head, then stood back, pointing a finger of warning at me, "Stay out of trouble."

I got up from the chair and hugged Sami. "Can I get you a beer?"

"Sure honey, thanks." Turning to Stryker she asked, "You're not leaving on my account, are you Stryker?"

"No. I was going anyway." Winking at Sami, he turned to leave the bar.

Sami grabbed his jacket and said, "Cut her a little slack, would you? She's having a rough time right now. She's been working hard on that novel and finding Roger dead and now her ex showing up. Things are just piling up on her right now. " I could hear her pleading my case from my position at the bar.

"And you are telling me this . . . why?"

"I don't know Robotica; sometimes your movements are so lifelike I forget you're not a real boy." Sami smiled her most beguiling smile.

Stryker shook his head and laughed as he walked away.

Coming back to the table with two beers I asked, "Are you ready for a little karaoke? Looks like Virgil's getting ready to start."

"That's why I'm here. What shall we sing tonight? In The Jungle?" she asked, watching Stryker stalk out.

We sat back to peruse the list of songs we could choose from tonight.

# CHAPTER 23

Branches whipped at my face; my heart pounded so hard I thought my chest might explode. I stopped and turned around taking a stand on the path. A vague silhouette slipped behind the trunk of a large oak tree.

"Who's there?" I called out.

No answer.

I turned and ran some more, then whirled around in time to catch sight of a moving shadow.

My breath caught in my throat. I ran faster. Which wasn't easy since my knee was stiff and the stitches pulled.

The path forked up ahead. With no time to think, I veered to the right.

I got off the path and slipped into the woods, leaves and twigs sounded like small explosions under my boots. A twig snapped on the other side of the path. I steeled myself for a battle with an unknown entity and tried to quiet my harsh breathing. Wind slipped through the trees, making eerie, scratching sounds as branches and leaves commingled. The surrounding trees were imposing, as they wrapped their branches around a secluded site as if protecting it from outsiders. I jogged the remaining length of the path and down the slope.

The oddity of the scene hit me forcibly as I crept along the path following a rhythmic chanting. Stopping, I peered through the shrubs toward the flickering firelight. Several torches lit the scene, helped by the glow of a bonfire as a group of people stood in a circle, their faces obscured by dark hooded robes as if performing some sort of ritual. If it had not been for the chanting I would have found it almost frightening.

Sensing movement behind me I turned, lights exploded around me as the pain came crashing down on the base of my skull, pain radiating down my spine. Dazed, I shook my head. Large hands grabbed my jacket, smashing me against a massive oak.

"Where . . . are . . . they?" he said menacingly. I shook my head again, trying to focus.

My shoulder was rammed against the tree trunk, my collarbone felt like it popped out of the socket.

"Where did he hide them?" Beefy hands tightened around my throat and I choked as I tried to suck in air. His hands squeezed like a vice while the pressure on my collarbone increased.

From the edges of my consciousness, I heard someone call, "Mattie?"

The hands loosened their grip, as I yelped, "Sami help . . . " he dropped me face first in the dirt.

Moaning, I pulled myself up onto my hands and knees. That's when I saw the boots—steel-toed work boots covered with a permanent layer of white dust. I watched as one of the boots hauled back and took aim for a kick. The blow caught me in the stomach and sent me flying. Rolling away from him, I curled into myself turning my back to him.

With the next kick, he leaned down closer to me and threatened, "Just have faith sugar, we'll play again." With a sinister laugh, his boot struck me in the back once more, colored lights flashed and popped like and electric kaleidoscope. The night edged in and blotted out everything.

# CHAPTER 24

Jerking myself up, I clawed my way out of the nightmare and grasped for air, the harsh rasp of my rapid breathing disturbing the early morning quiet. Shuddering, I scanned my bedroom.

I was in bed. My bed. Sweat soaked my body despite the fan whirring overhead. Heart pounding, head thundering, I gasped as I tried to catch my breath.

With a grave sigh, I told myself, it's just a dream . . . it's just a dream, which seems to be my mantra these days.

My bed faced the window, giving me a perfect view of the sheer curtains rippling in the breeze, framing the same view my kitchen window held. Lifting a trembling hand, I pushed my fingers through my tangled hair, moaning as I made contact with the large goose egg forming at the back of my head.

Pulling my grandmother's quilt around my aching body, I climbed stiffly from bed, and ambled over to take in the fractured pale early morning light that snuck in through the multi-paned glass window. The skies were gloomy, gray clouds threatening to break loose at any moment. A cool, late October breeze flowed through the open window of my bedroom as I hugged the quilt close to ward off the early morning chill that threatened to settle over me.

I tried to block out pictures of Roger . . . my eyes stung and my throat grew tight remembering Roger . . . the way he had been . . . forever young . . . forever handsome . . . alive. However, there was no undoing what had been done. Blinking away promising tears, I steeled myself to accept the situation as it was and deal with it.

Turning from the window, I headed for the bathroom. First, a long hot shower. Then coffee. I absolutely needed coffee.

A half hour later, I stood in my comforting turn-of-the-century kitchen, in my sock feet, as I watched the coffee drip with unbearable sluggishness into the glass carafe, thoroughly enjoying the solitude. I tugged at the turtleneck I pulled on and felt a little warmer in the *Life is Good* sweatshirt I pulled on over it.

How long had it been since I was alone in this kitchen. Seems like forever. Everything seems like forever.

Finally pouring myself a cup of coffee, I headed for my back porch then stopped. Recent events caused me a little apprehension. So, instead I sat down at the round pine table with the claw foot pedestal, which has been in our family for generations.

I love my old house I thought, as I looked up at the low ceiling with its wall-to-wall wood beams, arched doorways, built-in glass fronted cabinets, and crown moldings. My great grandfather built this Tuscan-style farmhouse for his young bride in the early nineteen hundreds, handling all the finish carpentry himself.

Roger had been pushing me to put in a modern kitchen, but I'd refused. I loved the authenticity and charm of the old house that had been in my family for generations. There was a feeling of stability, of things never lost, of family and strength and security. I finally felt as if I'd had all those things. For a while, anyway.

It was almost six o'clock when I heard a soft tapping at the back door, jolting me out of my reverie. Stryker stood on the other side of the glass, his gaze watchful, and his mouth set in a grim line. Harry stood on hind legs beside him, both paws resting on the window. Harry grinned, his tongue hanging out the side of his mouth.

Stryker wasn't nearly so chipper.

I shivered as I unconsciously raised my fingers to the turtleneck trying to make sure it hid my black-and-blue neck. I fleetingly remembered looking into the bathroom mirror before my shower and the shock I'd felt at the bruising on my neck, but I shoved that aside.

*Later.*

I didn't have the luxury to sort through my emotions right now, as I watched Stryker watch me.

Rubbing my nervous hands down the front of my jeans, I walked over and turned the lock. Harry pushed against my leg wagging his tail. I bent down, grimacing in pain, to pet him.

I made an effort to find a voice. "Good morning, Harry Allen O'Malley. Did you move out and not tell me?"

Straightening, I looked into Stryker's tired eyes.

*God those eyes killed me.*

"Good morning to you too, Stryker. And don't you have a home of your own to go to?"

It was the first I'd used my voice since I awoke. I sounded rather husky, as if I'd been in a smoky bar drinking whiskey all night. Obviously, the abuse my throat took the night before had taken its toll on my vocal chords.

"I went home, after I dropped you off, for a change of clothes," his voice sounding almost as husky as mine.

Remembering him at the hospital last night gave me cause.

Sami called him from the park after she ran off my attacker. He was waiting at the entrance to the emergency room when the ambulance arrived; I remember thinking he must have already been in bed when he got the call that I had been attacked in the park. He was standing there in his FBI issue sweats, his face taking on a ghost-like pallor under the incandescent lights.

The look on Stryker's face was devastating. I felt worse for him than I did for me. I knew I was gonna be just fine. He looked at me as if I would never be fine again.

"Harry wanted to ride along. I hope that was okay." His faint southern accent seemed a little stronger this morning. It had slipped out before, but only when he was tired.

He hadn't dropped me off until three this morning, sending Sami home earlier with the assurance he would get me home safely. Since it was barely six now, he looked as tired as I felt. And about as beat-up.

"Absolutely. Harry's crazy about you. Besides, he needs a strong male influence in his life. Tag, you're it." He smiled as I tapped his chest with my finger.

Stryker sniffed the air appreciatively. "You gonna share some of that?"

I pointed to a chair and retrieved a second mug from the cupboard.

He sat down at the table and stretched his long, jean clad legs out in front of him. His hair was damp and disheveled; he'd obviously showered on that trip home, but hadn't taken the time to shave. A day's growth of beard darkened his strong jaw line, making his mouth seem more menacing than usual.

Eyeing my *Life is Good* sweatshirt he said, "Well, aren't you the cockeyed optimist."

I shrugged, "Just keepin' the faith."

Carrying the steaming mug to the table, I sat down, accessing him. I found it hard to believe we'd only met a few weeks ago, and yet he had already embedded himself in our lives.

Harry had collapsed at Stryker's feet, resting his chin on his paws. They both looked very male, very relaxed, and very comfortable in their surroundings. Stryker's gaze was sharp. He said nothing.

I massaged my temples with my fingertips, feeling the weariness spread. Stryker's brooding silence didn't help matters any.

There are many kinds of silence. Companionable. Hostile. Frightened. Defeated. Angry.

I ran my finger around the rim of the mug. A circle. Everything seemed to come to a circle, when what I really wanted was a nice straight line leading to the stealthy figure that keeps beating me up.

"What's on your mind?" I asked, taking a sip from my cup to hide my nervousness.

His handsome face displayed his annoyance, "You really screwed the pooch this time O'Malley." Stryker's tone was grim.

Choking on coffee I just swallowed, I coughed. Grabbing my throat, the pain unbearable. Getting myself under control I whispered, "I don't even know what that means."

"It means you fucked up big time. What were you thinking walking in the park by yourself last night? Setting yourself up as bait again? If I remember correctly, it didn't work out so well the last time you tried it."

"No," I croaked. "I just wasn't thinking. Sami left the bar before I did and I forgot I parked my car on the other side of the park. I had to get to my car, didn't I?"

Looking into his coffee cup, he said, in a voice so low it caused my heart to thump, "You could've called me."

Anguish squeezed my heart. "I know." My tone was quiet. "But I didn't."

Stryker closed his eyes and shook his head. "No shit." His words came out in a whisper.

# CHAPTER 25

A brisk knock sounded on the door. "That's probably Stryker." I murmured. He seemed to have disappeared after everyone else started showing up this morning. However, when I opened the door, it was Detective Adams on my doorstep.

He inclined his head politely. A younger, slender woman stood impassively beside him. Her police shield conspicuously clipped to her waistband, her Beretta semi-automatic barely noticeable under the flawless cut of her wool blazer. A simple silver clip tamed thick, curly blond hair into a low ponytail at the back of her head.

This morning Adams looked tired. He wore the same brown suit he'd worn last night to the hospital, but this morning he'd changed his wrinkled pale yellow shirt for a clean crisp white one.

Walking into the living room he said in his usual gruff manner, "Good morning, ladies. I'd like to speak with you for a moment . . . " turning his head toward the woman standing next to him, "Along with Detective Abigail Rhodes here." He said by way of introduction.

*Abby Rhodes? I quirked an eyebrow as I looked in her direction.*

Shaking her head, she smiled saying, "I know. My parents were hippies from the Beatles' era. What are you gonna do?" she shrugged.

"Ms. O'Malley, is there anything you can remember about your attacker? Maybe the way he smelled, facial hair, did he have an accent. Anything at all will be helpful." Detective Rhodes asked.

"Only that his voice was low and raspy. *Kinda like mine right now.* I think I've heard it before but I just can't remember where. I'm sorry.

"Maybe Sami can give you some information. But I really don't think she saw him."

"I'm on my way to see her now but in the meantime maybe something will come to you. Just give me a call if you remember anything." She said handing me her card.

Karen, Pepper, and I were standing in the middle of my living room; Steven was sitting on the chair with his legs propped up on the ottoman, examining his fingernails, looking totally bored, and Stryker was still suspiciously absent.

I explained to Detective's Adams and Rhodes again about the attack on me in the park last night. Thankfully, Sami came looking for me when she remembered she hadn't seen Ladybug outside the bar. She was looking for me in the park when she heard my screams and came to my rescue, scaring my attacker.

"Have you heard anything about how Roger died?" I asked, looking at Detective Adams.

"M.E. says overdose." Adams said, glancing over at Karen.

"But Roger didn't do drugs. Someone must have forced him to take those. He wouldn't take an aspirin if the top of his head was coming off. This makes no sense." I said, following his glance to Karen.

She shook her head, her thick blond hair swaying. A cloud passed over her pensive face.

Looking back at Adams she asked, "What kind of drugs, Detective?"

Glancing down at the folder in his hands, he read aloud, "Opiates. Precisely . . . Vicodin, OxyContin, and Darvocet. Prescription drugs that doctors are prescribing too readily, if you ask me."

"How long had Roger been dead before Mattie found him?"

"M.E. says eighteen to twenty-four hours."

"That means he *was* dead when I saw him at the library. But what happened to the bullet hole in his forehead."

"There were no bullet holes. In his head or anywhere else on his body. He died of an overdose." He reiterated, his eyes still on Karen.

Karen stepped around Adams and opened the front door.

"Thank you, Detectives, for coming and updating us. We appreciate it."

I was a little perplexed by Karen's abrupt behavior.

"Well, okay Dr. Kavanaugh. We'll be in touch."

Turning to me, he pulled a card out of his pocket and said, "The body will be released later this morning. You can call and tell them where to send it. I really am sorry for your loss, Ms. O'Malley." His voice gruff but sincere.

Karen took Adams' arm propelling him out the door. "Thank you again, Detective." She said closing the door in their stunned faces.

"Karen! What the hell?" I asked looking down at the business card Detective Adams just handed me. "You know Roger didn't kill himself."

"I know he didn't," she said, sounding very sure. Turning her attention elsewhere, she said, "Steven, it's time for you to go. Get your things together and Pepper will take you back to your hotel."

"Oh no, I'm not going anywhere. This is my house, too." Steven said, testily.

"You either get your stuff right now or I'll let Pepper take you out back and shoot you. Your choice."

"Kavanaugh, are you suggesting violence?" Stryker asked, seeming to appear out of nowhere. "So if I killed him, you'd give me a head start?"

"Well, he chose the rules to this game when he broke into Mattie's house. The way I see it, it's in our best interest to follow."

Steven looked at her in disbelief. He started to say something then thought better of it when his gaze fell upon Stryker leaning against the wall by the kitchen door, arms crossed, and his government issue Glock resting comfortably on his hip in full view. Steven's mean little mouth closed in a tight hard line.

"Go on Steven you can do your little happy dance in hell."

"Okay . . . okay I'm going. But I'm not done with you yet," he said leveling a hate filled stare directly at me.

# CHAPTER 26

**M**attie, you need to go get all the prescriptions you've gotten over the last few weeks from Jonathan."

"Why," I cleared my throat, "does it matter?"

"Because, I think I know where the drugs came from."

"Do you think Roger was taking my pain pills?"

"That's what we're going to find out. Go get them for me."

As I went to assemble all the prescription bottles I've been collecting over the last few weeks, I still wondered what's gotten into Karen. She was acting very strange.

When I got up to my bedroom, I sat down on the edge of the bed. As I ran my hand over my grandmother's quilt she so lovingly stitched by hand, I wished she was here right now. She and my father. Even with a house full of people, I feel so empty and isolated.

With a critical eye, I scrutinized my room. Something's different. Maybe it's because Pepper's here . . . or maybe it's because Roger's dead, but something's . . . just not right. Rising from the bed, I walked over to the closet. The doors were open; I looked in and saw the empty space where Roger's clothes had once hung. I turned on the light peering in.

*"I don't even have a suit here to take to the funeral home to bury you in. I'll have to go back to your house for that."*

As I was started to turn away, something caught my eye. There appeared to be a door in the wall on Rogers's side of the closet. I never noticed it before, probably because it was painted the same color as the wall. I reached in, pushed on the space inside the frame, and it swung open at me. Startled, I stepped back and gazed at it for a moment. Reaching in, my fingers brushed over something . . . an envelope. I withdrew it from its resting place. My name was written on it in a neat, familiar handwriting.

Retracing my footsteps, I sat back down on my bed and placed the large envelope in my lap. After a few seconds, I opened it. Inside there were two letter-sized envelopes. With great care, I opened the envelope addressed to me. The other had Allen's name written on it.

Gramma Rosa's voice came through, soft and clear . . .

*Mia carissima, Mattie,*

*No, I am not a witch or a psychic, nor do I have any super powers what so ever. But, I am most assuredly dead now. And, I promise you that, while I was alive, I was the most ordinary person imaginable. And before you dream up any more ridiculous notions, no, I do not plan to return from the grave!*

*Stop listening to Bizzy Blackwell. She's as crazy as that old hoot owl who lives in the ancient oak tree in the front yard of your house. I am, however, looking forward to a nice, long rest and many enjoyable conversations with your Grandpa Paddy. (Oh how I've missed that man.)*

*When I got word of your father's death I was so very sorry you and Allen never got a chance to know him. He was a wonderful son and man; I believe he just lived in the shadows far too long. I know it will be hard for both of you. But I also know you will weather this along with everything else. It may not have seemed so for a time, but it will come out right in the end if you just look beyond the tears.*

*He loved you both very much and never wanted to leave but, circumstances being what they were, had no choice. It is not in my power to tell you what those circumstances were, you will find those out when the time is right. And most of all do not blame your mother. Violet only did what was necessary to keep her children safe.*

*I have followed the events of the lives of you and Allen. Though sorely tempted at times, I have never broken my promise to your mother, to stay in the shadows.*

*Your Aunt Patty has kept me apprised. I'm so glad you have her. She and Violet are both strong female role models. Follow their lead and you will do fine, my sweet Mattie.*

*I know that being watched from afar will appeal to your magical spirit. So, rest assured you are being watched by those of us who cherished you in life and loved you till our deaths and after.*

*So that's about it for now, except to tell you William Benzer will be expecting a call from you now that you've found this letter. He's a little eccentric but harmless enough. Ti amo, Gramma Rosa*

I looked up from the letter and stared blindly across the room as the words and the images I visualized settled over me like falling snow. It was difficult to accept the fact that a woman I hardly knew had known so much about me. I no longer doubted her love and devotion for Allen and me. But what did she mean by . . . look beyond the tears? And why was my father living in the shadows?

The tears finally came. Tears for my grandmother, for the father I never got to know, and tears for Roger, who did nothing wrong except to make the mistake of falling in love with me. Tears, especially for my sweet baby. I hope all my loved ones up there are looking out for you.

I curled up on my bed, wrapped my grandmother's quilt around me, and grieved for everything I had lost.

# CHAPTER 27

The Hopewell Funeral Home was packed with Roger's friends and clients.

I watched Stryker as he watched the crowd, mentally checking off each of the mourners as they entered. He assumed that Roger's killer would be hyped up enough to attend, and explained that often the killer wanted to be close to the action to revel in what he considered his superior intellect while the lowly police attempted to track him down. Killers were known to show up at crime scenes or the funeral, eager to be connected to the investigation and grief. It fed their egos to know they were the mastermind behind the tragedy. Stryker said it was only a matter of time before this one showed his hand.

Sensing my gaze, Stryker chose that moment to look over at me. His full lips gave a slight tug upward as he nodded his head. He seemed to understand my loss, without ever expressing the overly sentimental pity that made me want to retreat further. There was no softened edge of sympathy in my dealings with him and I appreciated that. If we could discover the truth about Roger's murder, perhaps he could rest in peace.

"The dead should be mourned, but life has to be lived. We are here today not to grieve but to celebrate the life of Roger Elliot Moore. Gone at such a young age but still leaving a large imprint on our lives . . . "

After the first ten minutes of shaking hands and accepting condolences from people I'd never met in my life, I had a knot developing in my stomach. I did not want to be here sharing my grief with strangers.

The room was closing in on me.

   . . . *I'm going to crawl out of my skin if I have to sit here much longer and listen to this person talk about someone he's never even met. If one more person comes up and hugs me, I'll scream.*

Karen brushed back a tangle of hair and tugged at my arm. "Trust me he's almost finished sweetie. Just have a little faith," she whispered.

*What?*

"Karen what did you just say?" My voice soft and trembling.

Sensing something was up she grabbed my hand and dragged me to the door, leaving everyone sitting and staring at our retreating backs. Everyone except Stryker, who was hot on our tails.

"What is it Mattie? What did you remember?" The question was sharp as she took me by the shoulders.

My eyes fell. My words were ragged, uneven, could scarcely be heard. "You said, just have faith."

She nodded.

My mouth trembled. "That's what he said to me . . . right before he pushed me down the stairs. His mouth was right next to my ear and whispered, *Have a little faith sugar, you'll be dead before you hit the bottom.* Then, the other night when he was kicking the crap out of me he said, *have faith, I'll be back.* I know it was the same guy. His voice was low and gravely, I'm sure he was disguising it, but something was familiar about it. And his breath . . . he's a smoker."

Suddenly something dawned on me . . . Have a little faith.

"Karen, I've got to leave. I've got to go back to Arizona. Right now."

Karen shook her head not understanding. "We'll talk about it after the funeral."

All the while Stryker never said a word but the look in his eyes spoke volumes. If looks could kill . . . I was getting out of the line of fire.

It was no better at the cemetery.

I sat stiffly beside Karen, who had my right hand in a death grip, and my mother on the other side crying into her freshly ironed white hanky while she gripped my arm possessively. We sat in the first row beneath the green funeral canopy, next to the pewter casket as it rested above the newly dug grave. The gravesite sat at the top of a hill. A sea of headstones fell away below, lost in the grayness of the day. Pine trees stood watch, the sentinels of our sorrow.

The minister's rich voice carried his words to us: "Almighty God, with whom the spirits of those lives who have departed to be with our Lord and with whom the souls of the faithful, after they are delivered from the burden of the flesh . . .

I looked around at some of the familiar faces.

Crimson Ravensky, Roger's girl Friday, arms clasped tightly across her chest, wore a sleek black suit with a white blouse peeking from underneath the form-fitting jacket. The black turned her pale face ashen. Her haunted eyes never left the casket.

*Was it more than losing her boss that put that troubled look in her eyes?*

Steven Angelo, my ex-husband, could be the poster boy for Funeral Director magazine. His black suit, bowed head, and somber face personified proper sorrow.

*What possessed him to come to the funeral of a man he'd never even met?*

Dr. Jonathan Harmon, looking totally put together in his well-fitting black slacks and a black turtleneck beneath a gray wool sport coat, seemed to scan the crowd.

*Is he looking for someone?*

Paul . . . *God, I don't even know his last name . . .* stood alone under a tree, looking preoccupied. He has yet to approach me to offer his condolences.

*Is he that shy or is there something to his preoccupation?*

Stryker hung back and watched the crowd behind the mirrored sunglasses he wore, despite the grayness of the day.

I felt him watching me and stifled an insane desire to run to him, bury my face in his shoulder, and weep.

Death, by its very nature, modifies the connection between family and friends. Survivors tend to assemble, using food and drink as solace to counteract loss.

Karen's house sits up on a hill across from mine on Bay Lane. A stream, too small to be called a river, careens down behind her property and empties into the bay more than a mile away. Her house, an old Victorian, was built in the late eighteen hundreds; two stories of white frame with a wide porch stretching across the front.

Five lush ferns hung in a decorous row between ornamental pilasters while white wicker furniture with colorful floral cushions took center stage. The window boxes overflowed with red and white geraniums, giving an overall cheery appearance to an otherwise dreary day.

The overcast sky had lightened and a pale hint of sun seemed to filter through the clouds. With the front door ajar, the noise level was rising faster than Echo Creek after a thunderstorm. The sizeable living room was packed sardine-style with mourners. Most held wineglasses and used hushed voices. From my seat on the porch, I could hear their dinner-like conversations.

Through the window, I observed Karen, playing hostess, making sure everyone's needs were met. She seemed watchful, her gaze flitting uneasily around the room. Her smile, when it appeared, was apprehensive and never quite reached her eyes.

Still not sure I buy into crap like this, her "aura" seemed dark. Almost as if a magnetic force field was surrounding her, hopefully protecting her.

*Jeez, I'm beginning to sound like Bizzy Blackwell.*

Pepper came out to sit with me on the porch. She patted my knee as she sat next to me. "Are you all right, honey?"

"Pepper, I'm worried. Is everything alright back home?"

"Yes, honey. I just talked to Julia and she told me all was fine. You need to take care of things here and let me worry about the other."

"You're right I know, but I just can't help worrying."

Keys in hand, I walked across the street to my house; cars were parked on both sides of the road leading to Karen's house. Some of the overflow had encroached down the lane leading to the Blackwell house.

I unlocked the door. As I reached back to close it, something powerful slammed into me with a suddenness and intensity that sent me hurtling, my hands reaching out instinctively to catch myself. I hit the floor and rolled as someone grabbed me by the hair, pulled me upright, and dragged me backward. I stumbled into him as he held me up by my hair. He squeezed his fingers around my face digging into my jaw so hard it forced my mouth open. He stuck his face against mine and I could feel his breath against my mouth. "Where did he hide it? Don't make me ask again." His gravelly voice threatening, as he shook my head, using my hair for control.

I clawed at his hand, trying to pry his fingers out of my hair. The pain was unbearable.

"Let go, let go. I don't know what you're talking about," I croaked.

Just as my assailant went for my throat again, my cell phone screamed out "Blood on Your Hands," a grinding death-metal rock ringtone that spiked my brain better than a double espresso, and startled my attacker into dumping me on the floor.

"The next time I come back I'm not gonna ask. I'm just gonna kill you."

I scrambled crab-like toward my screeching phone and with shaky hands, I jerked it open. "Allen?"

"Yeah, where are you?"

"I just ran home for a sec."

"Are you okay? You sound weird. Do you need me to come over there?"

"No, that's okay. Besides, you know me; I've always been the weird twin, right?" I forced a laugh.

"Well yes, yes you have. And thanks for living up to that. When are you coming back?"

"I'll be right there," I said as I closed my phone.

I lay on the floor where my attacker dumped me my mind whirling. What have I stumbled into?

Taking a deep breath and exhaling, I imagined myself dispelling all the anxiety from my body, a self-help technique Sami taught me.

There were at least two dozen people still wandering around Karen's Victorian living room, with its dark paneled walls and florid red-cabbage-rose wallpaper.

Slowly, everyone turned to me. Conversation died.

Ignoring them, I crossed the room to the large coffee urn that stood next to a plate of Oreos. "Thank you, Karen," I murmured while helping myself to a handful of cookies.

Stryker watched with question in his eyes as I hurried past him.

"O'Malley?"

"I can't stop now I've got to find a bridge to jump off."

"So . . . things are going that well, huh?"

"He's close."

"Who's close?"

"A very scary man," I panted . . . slowly.

# CHAPTER 28

I shook my head and closed my eyes as depression settled over me like a wet blanket of mist settling over a field in the early morning hours.

Karen had poured us both a glass of wine, which seemed to be the only thing my stomach would agree to without staging an uprising. At this rate, I'll be on amphetamines with wine chasers by morning. I had decided not to tell anyone about my attack earlier, knowing it wouldn't do any good any way.

"I can't believe he left me everything. Why would Roger do that? My God, I killed him and he left me everything." I hadn't stopped crying since my talk with Mr. Benzer earlier.

Karen was sitting at the table with me, holding my hand. "Honey, Roger loved you. That's something you'll have to live with, although it's not your fault you didn't feel the same way. He knew going into the relationship how you felt. You never lied to him, and you certainly didn't kill him."

"No, I just let him move in here and believe that eventually I'd start feeling the same way. I knew I never would. Maybe if I'd met him now instead of a year ago I could have loved him the way he deserved. He never stood a chance."

"Do you want to talk about Steven? Can you tell me what happened?"

Groaning, I dropped my forehead onto my arms, remembering . . .

Steven strutted into my studio, with his hands in the pockets of his nicely fitting khakis, jiggling his change, and whistling Girl from Ipanema. He was wearing a coral golf shirt that set off his tanned face and made his perfectly even white teeth stand out like a beacon. I thought he looked just like a Malibu Ken doll I had when I was eight. He was Hollywood handsome, his blond hair, a little long on top, was lying across his forehead as if

*someone had just run her fingers through it pulling it
into a curl in front.*

*We had an appointment to do some headshots. He
was a news anchor for a local cable station and he was
terribly popular with the women in the area, but he
wanted to branch out. Maybe go national. He was my
first celebrity shoot and I'll admit, God don't hate me, I
fell in love with him the moment he walked through my
door.*

*After that first shoot, we were never apart. We were
so much in love; I didn't hesitate when he asked me to
marry him one month after we met. I couldn't believe my
luck that I was marrying Steven Angelo. He was so
wonderfully old-fashioned he wouldn't even kiss me on
the lips. He wanted to wait for our wedding night. He
said I was worth waiting for.*

Shaking my head I snorted, "You know what? I never
got paid for those damn headshots."

Karen reached over and rested her hand on my
forearm. "There is no sense in being haunted because you
trusted him."

"Well, that trust ended when I found him in bed
with . . . with . . . a man. He turned violent and threw a
clock at me. I tried to get out of the way and tripped."
Embarrassed, I turned my head away from her.

After a moment, I looked back. "Karen, I was six
months pregnant and had to drive myself to the hospital
but the damage was done. If I would have just turned

around and left, everything would be fine right now. But I stood there, clicking away with my camera until I pissed him off. I put myself and my baby in danger and my baby paid the price."

"Don't do this to yourself. It was not your fault. This is all on Steven. Think what you like, but you could no more control what he did, than I could have controlled what some psychopath did to my family. There is evil out there and no matter how much you want to protect the ones you love, you can't always do it."

I lifted my head and looked at her. I touched her hand, brushing my fingers over her cool, dry skin. "I'm sorry. I didn't mean for us to go there."

"You know I'm never really far from Kevin and Sam," she said. "Losing a child is one of those horrors from which the heart never mends. And when you have convinced yourself you're the one responsible, it sits there festering like an open wound."

Karen's not one to give in to self-pity. But, *her* truth was more painful in some ways, than the simple fact that someone else was to blame for her family's deaths.

"Maybe it is time I talked to you about it. I appreciate you giving me my space and I'm sure it's been difficult, given your penchant for being inquisitive." She said with a sad smile while looking me in the eye.

"Stryker was point on a task force. He saw an interview I did about serial killers. He called and asked me to look at the file. We discussed the case on the phone and through email for a while, but we were getting nowhere with our profile. I remembered Professor Kavanaugh from BU. Kevin was a brilliant man, a professor of behavioral studies at Boston University.

"I contacted him, we met, and went over the files, until we finally recognized what had been staring us in the face all along. We were dealing with more than one perpetrator, mentally at least. The Sybil of serial killers if you will.

"This unsub was atypical. He didn't conform to a usual type or expected pattern. Old, young, black, white, rich, poor, male, female . . . we had nothing . . . no discernible pattern. He shot, he stabbed, he strangled."

"So how did you know it was him each time?" I whispered the question.

"Geographic locations. Anyway when I had done all I could, I returned to Boston. I called Kevin to thank him for his help and he asked me out to dinner. Three months later we were married." Karen stopped talking and looked down at the wide gold band she couldn't seem to stop twisting on her left hand.

"Wow Karen . . . three months? Who knew you were so impulsive? Now it takes you three months just to choose a pillowcase." I said trying to inject some lightheartedness into the conversation.

She blew her breath out in a short laugh, the kind a person makes when something isn't funny but she wished it were, and continued, "When it's right, it's right, and Kevin and I were certainly right. One year after that first dinner, we were blessed with a beautiful baby boy, Samuel Beau Kavanaugh. Kevin and Sam were my whole life . . . and then one day . . . " Her look was pained as she sighed heavily, wiping the tears from her eyes.

"Beau? Was he named for Stryker?"

"Yeah, he was. Beau was Sam's Godfather.

"Anyway, after Sam was born, I still did some consulting for the CBU. We had been tracking this one serial killer for more than six months; he used dumping sites all over the mid-west. Farm country, always cornfields. He would open their head, cut out their brain, stuff the empty cavity with straw, and then prop them on the pole like a scarecrow hanging. We knew we were dealing with a surgeon or at the very least, someone with a medical background. He certainly knew what he was doing." She sighed heavily, remembering.

"I captured his attention. In his mind, I was his adversary. I was the personification of the task force that was hunting him. He started sending the brain he removed from his victims . . . directly to me. It suddenly became about him versus me.

"After Kevin and Sam were discovered in that cornfield, he never showed up on the radar again. He either died, went to jail for something else, or just moved on. He finally got what he wanted from me. My grief, my fear, my anger . . . maybe it was just my attention he wanted. Pick one . . . he got it all. I can only hope *he got* a bullet between the eyes." She exhaled loudly, as if hoping to expel the demons.

"He just stopped?"

She got that faraway look in her eyes again and nodded, "It seemed so. I never heard from him again. They've never stopped searching for him, but nothing. Unfortunately, in most cases they have to wait for another victim and hope he makes a mistake."

I wondered what Karen and Stryker saw. Because, it sounds as if the agents of the FBI's effective Criminal Behavioral Unit saw a lot more than most agents did. Although, what they saw and how they handled it was somewhat vague.

"There was a rumor going around the law enforcement community alluding to that end. But, I'll never know for sure. If it's true, I owe Scarecrow a debt of gratitude."

"Scarecrow?" I asked, not understanding.

"He is someone who can get what your average, law enforcement people can't always get. Justice."

"Exactly how does he get . . . *justice*?" I asked, curiosity getting the better of me.

"A headshot."

I pressed my lips together and nodded thoughtfully, "Well then, I hope Scarecrow succeeded."

"Unfortunately, I'll never know for sure." There was no answering spark in Karen's strained brown eyes.

"Oh . . . I'm sorry, Karen. I didn't mean to bring all this up for you."

"You didn't . . . it's always there," she said composing herself.

Nodding in agreement, I said, "I'd like to hear about them one day."

"One day." She nodded, lost in thought. "But, for now I'm telling you from experience, you have to let your guilt go," she said, sounding like the old Karen again.

I drew a deep breath and resisted making an obvious comment about someone carrying guilt around. Gently, I pulled my hand from Karen's grasp and rubbed the back of my neck. I felt stiff and tired, and there was fuzziness to my thoughts that made it difficult to think straight.

"Thanks for letting Mom and Pepper stay at your house tonight. Allen and I will be fine here. I'm going to take a hot bath, then spend some quality time with my twin. Goodnight."

"Goodnight, sweetie. Call me if you need anything."

A lump formed in my throat as I walked from the room.

Later that evening, my phone rang for the umpteenth time. People had been calling all day to offer their condolences. I'd already taken a long hot bath, which did nothing to ease the aches in my back and hip, and I was on my third glass of wine. Allen had gone to bed an hour ago, after we talked for a while. He was saddened by Roger's death and afraid for me. I assured him Roger's death had nothing to do with me and there was nothing to be worried about. We talked a little about Allison, then I told him I was tired and needed to get some sleep. As he headed for the guest room, I asked him something we had silently agreed not to talk about years ago.

"Allen?"

"Yeah?"

"Do you remember him? I mean . . . do you ever think about him?"

I watched his face. His gray eyes went from soft to steely, his jaw unyielding.

"Do I remember him . . . sure. Do I ever think about him?" He shook his head.

"Never," he replied wearily, turning back toward the bedroom.

I walked into the kitchen, depleted, and sat down at the round pine table. My gaze drifted to an aged photo of my father and grandmother hanging on the wall.

Memories of the day my father died hit me. Violet hadn't lied about what happened to him. She hadn't attempted to create an easy to swallow reference her children could understand; Michael O'Malley was dead and wasn't coming back . . . ever. Year by year and bit by bit, details started to fade from my memory.

Beyond exhausted, I glared at the ringing phone, refusing to pick it up again. It stopped. Then it rang again. Whoever it was wasn't giving up. I picked it up, so as not to disturb Allen, and looked at the small screen . . . *BLOCKED* . . . I punched the green button.

"Hello."

There was a hiss, then a crackle. After a long moment, a low and gravelly voice I was becoming very familiar with, came through the line, "Have a little faith, I'm coming."

Click. Dial tone.

I felt a prickle down my back.

Shaking off any morbid thoughts initiated by the phone, I went upstairs.

# CHAPTER 29

Adrenaline pumped through me. Shifting in an instant from deep sleep to full alert, the noise that jolted me awake, the metallic rattle of the front doorknob, the faint screech as the door swung in, was startling in the silence.

*Someone was in my house.*

Already moving, I eased over the side of the bed grabbing the iron poker I'd picked up as an after-thought as I made my way to bed last night. Not really expecting to have to use it when I'd placed it next to my bed no more than, glancing at the clock on my night stand, *Jeez it was only an hour ago*, when I had finally called it a night.

My hands trembled. I fought indecision and knew it was just panic. Thoughts incomplete whirled in my mind. Shoes . . . door . . . Allen . . .

First, I had to know who was there.

The wood floor was cool beneath my bare feet as I crept into the hallway. The moon spilled in through the window above the stairwell.

I stopped to listen again. The sounds were louder now, thumps and a slight *screech*, as if a piece of furniture was being moved. Someone was opening drawers and pulling books off shelves.

I gripped the poker tightly and started down the stairs. Halfway down I paused on the landing, the dark silhouette of an extremely sizeable man was rifling through my bookcase.

The light, cast by the moon, shone across him as his gaze swept the room. I took the time to watch him. His face, covered by a ski mask, gave me just a glimpse of the discontented droop of his mouth, the venal gleam in his eye, the resistant curve of his lips, and the angry lift of his chin.

He was a dangerous man. Dangerous men have an air of reckless abandon. They are not bound by any rules . . . neither man's nor God's.

It was time to see the face of my intruder.

The sudden blaze of light from the overhead fixture illuminated harshly over the room.

Startled, he looked up.

I tried to take advantage of his confusion.

"Hey!" I yelled as I jumped the rest of the way down the steps. He had about seventy-five pounds on me. I swung the poker level with his waist, but my aim was off and I clipped him in the shoulder. Stunned for just a second, he barreled toward me. I lifted the poker again and aimed for his head. He swatted it like a fly. With one hand, he pushed me into the railing face first, and then ran out the front door he had left standing wide open.

Recovering, I ran out after him. Standing in the driveway, with bare feet and poker raised over my head, I stopped and looked around. He was gone. Well, he couldn't have just disappeared; he had to be here somewhere.

Was that a shadow?

Heart in my throat, I stepped forward and peered through the darkness where I saw the shadow. It was only a shrub catching in the wind and dancing in the moonlight.

Behind me, I heard Allen. "Mattie? Mattie you out here?"

Oh God, Allen. Taking a deep breath, I lowered my makeshift weapon and ran back up the drive toward him. "Yes, Allen I'm here." Taking his arm I asked, "You okay?"

"Yeah, you?" Allen asked the concern in his voice evident.

I nodded my head, "Yeah, I'm fine. Let's get you back inside. I'm sorry I woke you."

"You didn't. Harry did. I had my headphones on and fell asleep listening to a book on tape. It wasn't until Harry jumped up on the bed and started pushing me that I figured something was wrong."

"I'm sorry I woke you anyway." I said, guiding him up the steps to the front door and back into my ransacked living room.

"Mattie, when are you going to tell me what's going on here?"

"As soon as I know, you'll know," I said. The defeat in my voice resoundingly obvious, even to my own ears.

"Well, I finally convinced Allen I was fine and that this is just a normal occurrence around here anymore." I said, as I pushed through the swinging kitchen door. Stryker was leaning back on the edge of the counter. "By the way, how did you just happen to be driving down my street at three o'clock in the morning?

Shrugging his shoulders, he said, "Checking up on you, which appears to have been a good idea."

"I had it under control."

He closed the distance between us and grasped my chin, turning my face to get a better look. Something feral flared in his eyes.

"Obviously," Stryker said dubiously.

I edged away and raised a hand to my lip. It was already beginning to swell. "I smacked my face on the railing when he pushed me."

Characteristically, Stryker's comment to me was somewhat flippant.

"You just can't stay out of trouble, can you?"

"Apparently not."

"What the hell is he after?" The question directed more to him than me as he picked up a dish towel off the counter, retrieved a handful of ice from the freezer, wrapped it in the towel, and handed it to me.

"Here, for the swelling. Might keep you from getting a fat lip." He said with a quick smile.

I held the ice to my lip, wincing at the cold. "How the hell would I know? Probably has to do with the phone call I received earlier." I said answering his question as I walked back into the living room to access the damage in there.

"And what phone call would that be? If you don't mind my asking." He said, doggedly following me.

"Last night I got a call from my gravelly voiced friend. He said, 'Have a little faith, and after a little heavy breathing he hung up." I could feel his dark eyes as they followed me, in all probability calculating if I was about to lose it.

Stryker stood by the large front window across the room and stared outside into the darkness. I studied his profile, which appeared carved out of stone. Stifling a sigh, I turned away and looked around the room. Usually the room is quite welcoming and neat. The beamed ceilings, rock fireplace, floral furniture, and a huge brightly patterned area rug added to the coziness. Now it was a mess and I felt violated. My frustration mounted as I paced the living room. I took a long slow breath, and tried to concentrate on the smell of the remains of burning wood in the fireplace. My gaze slid around the room and rested on the Navajo rug I had hung on the wall to soften the surface. I tried to remember back to a time when my life wasn't quite so volatile.

My shoulders sagged as I turned and went back to the kitchen to make coffee.

Stryker followed me, folding his arms across his chest as he leaned back on the edge of the counter with his long legs stretched in front of him crossed at the ankles. This is what I now dubbed, the Stryker Stance.

I stole a look at my companion and noted that the half smile on his handsome face was far more dangerous than it was reassuring and his regular features gave nothing else away.

"So far you've been lucky." When I started to protest, he gave me a dark look and rammed his fingers through his hair hard enough to cause me to wince. "No, Dammit! Let me finish. You were attacked in the park a few nights ago and you just buried your boyfriend . . . "

"Ex-boyfriend," I clarified quickly, though the words as I spoke them seemed unnecessary.

Stryker cleared his throat, and if anything, his gaze became more intense, more focused. "Your ex . . . who was murdered . . . and tonight you've been attacked in your own home, from what you recalled earlier, not for the first time either."

Stryker looked to be in combat mode, his black cargo pants tucked into black boots, and a black hooded sweatshirt stretched across his ample chest.

Sitting down at the table, holding the ice to my lip, I hung my head, feeling defeated.

"Sometimes it's hard for me to strike a balance."

He studied me thoughtfully.

"Don't strike a balance. Just act like an ordinary person."

"I am an ordinary person. Most of the time," I sighed, "Or at least I used to be."

He shook his head. The silence unnerving.

Looking up at him I asked, "Do you have limitations, Stryker?"

"We all have limitations. We just learn to work with what we've got." He stared into his cup as if it held all the answers, instead of just a jolt of caffeine.

"I just wish I knew what he wanted."

Sitting down next to me, he reached out and ran a thumb tenderly over my swollen lip. "Know what I want? I want you not to get hurt anymore," he said softly. "That's what I want . . . and this sick son of a bitch caught." It sounded like an afterthought.

I drew a shaky breath and pulled away from him.

"Well, everything's fine now. You can go home. Maybe we can still salvage some of this night." I got up from the table and walked to the back door.

Holding it open I said, "Goodnight, Stryker."

"Night, O'Malley." His head down as he walked to the door. Looking back he said, "Don't forget to lock up."

"Humph," I snorted. "Like that makes a difference around here."

I walked slowly back upstairs to my bedroom knowing that any more sleep tonight was just an illusion.

After an unsuccessful attempt at sleep, I decided to get up and take a shower. I brushed my teeth and tamed my damp, curly hair into a French braid at the back of my head. I applied a little make-up to hide what was left of the dark circles under my eyes, but there was no way I was going to be able to hide my cut, swollen lip.

Searching around in my closet, I pulled on a pair of worn jeans that fit me like an old friend, a black turtleneck (to hide the bruises) and a sweatshirt; I just couldn't seem to warm-up this morning.

Elsewhere in the house, a radio was playing Mega Death, *or some other kind of chicken killing music.*

Allen was up.

I forgave him his choice of music because he'd made coffee. Its aroma infused the house.

Snatching my Sketchers from the floor of the closet, I headed downstairs. The phone rang before I could hit the bottom step. After the call last night, I wasn't in any hurry to answer it, and heaved a sigh of relief when it stopped ringing.

Allen pushed through the kitchen door with the phone in his hand. Holding it out he said, "It's for you."

Reluctantly taking it from his hand, I said a guarded, "Hello?"

"So glad you thought to call me last night." Karen's voice had a calm sardonic tinge to it. "I'm coming over, put the coffee on." *Almost too calm.*

"Wait! Mom doesn't know about this, does she?"

"No, I sent her and Pepper into town."

"Good. I've got to try and get this place cleaned up before they get back."

"Okay. I'm on my way."

After getting my living room in order in record time, Karen and I had just sat down at the kitchen table to catch our breath and drink our coffee when the backdoor swung open and Stryker sauntered in.

I got up and as I poured him a cup of coffee I said, "Good, I'm glad you're here. I want to talk to both of you about this guy who's been attacking me. I have a plan to draw him out."

Stryker stood and was standing next to me before I even realized he had moved. "Are you implying you want to use yourself as bait O'Malley?" he asked with a no nonsense tone in his voice.

"Listen Stryker."

"No!"

"Listen."

"Not an option!" Stryker turned away from me.

"I'm beginning to run out of patience here."

Turning back he said, "Wow, this is you being patient? Imagine my surprise."

"I don't know if I'll ever manage to get past your sarcasm and realize you're not a total asshole," I said, throwing Stryker a razor-sharp look, my tolerance for his sarcasm at an all-time low.

"Damn, O'Malley, that hurt," he countered, feigning a blow to the chest.

"You two have had your chance," I said pointing at Stryker. "You're the big bad marine," then turning on Karen, "And you . . . you're supposed to be able to read these fucking people like a book. In the meantime, I'm getting pushed down stairs, attacked in the park, and beat up in my own home. Not to mention what could have happened to poor Allen last night." I said trying to hold back threatening tears.

"Poor Allen?"

The anger in his voice jolted me.

I turned toward the door where he stood, not hearing him enter. "Allen, I didn't mean . . . "

"Yes, you did Mattie. You've always thought of me as an invalid. When are you going to realize I'm a man and I can take care of myself and you, too, if need be?"

I walked over and put my arms around his waist.

"I know you can, it's just that I've always felt . . . I feel . . . "

"Responsible."

Taking me by the arms, he put me away from him.

"You, my dear little sister, are not responsible for what happened to me. It was an accident. Nothing more. Nothing less. No one has ever blamed you. Not me. Not Mom. Not anyone. Except maybe you. And you can stop that right now."

I ran my hands up his arms and paused at his well-developed biceps.

Noticing the hesitation Allen drew an exasperated breath.

"You don't think I work-out every day just to look good, do you? I'm not just a pretty face you know." His smile was amazing. "I work-out so I can take care of myself if I need to. So stop worrying about me and let me help."

"I'm sorry. Allen, you're right. I've had you in invalid mode far too long. You're a man." Looking up at him with a smile, "Obviously, a big strong man," I said with a lilt to my tone.

"Ha ha, very funny. Now read me in."

Responding to the silence in the room he said, "Hey I watch NCIS, too."

After reading Allen in, from the first day this all started with me tripping over a drugged Harry, to the break-in last night, he went back across the street to Karen's to keep Mom and Pepper off my back.

"Okay, back to what we were talking about before . . . if you don't want to listen to me, you can both leave my home right now. I mean it. Just get out."

Turning my back on them, I crossed my arms in a show of indignation. Gazing out the kitchen window, across the yard in the direction of the pond where I found Roger, I tried to rein in my runaway emotions.

It had been just a few short weeks since I stood in this spot looking out at the same sweeping views, thinking my life was just about perfect. A few short weeks since my world started unraveling. The steep sloping lot was now a nightmare of knee-high weeds and cattails bending in the passing breeze. With much more rain, the softening hillside would slide down into the pond.

I was having a hard time holding it together. It's probably just the side effects from the attack on me last night, but I was exhausted and felt . . . dangerously unstable.

"I know there is something the two of you aren't telling me. I'm sure you have your reasons. But, for now I want you both out of my house." It was said so softly I wasn't sure I spoke aloud.

Karen stood behind me and laid her hand on my shoulder. I shook it off and kept my gaze focused on the spot where I found Roger.

"Okay, we'll talk later."

"That won't be necessary," I returned stiffly, feeling like a traitor.

"I understand."

A vacuum of silence followed her out the door.

Sensing Stryker's steady regard, I glanced back and found his expression full of sympathy. My heart . . . never far from the surface anymore . . . had to be showing on my face.

Stryker studied me thoughtfully. I really, really hoped he couldn't see how tightly I was strung.

Turning back toward the window, I sniffed. "I'm not a punching bag."

Tears I'd been holding back poured down my cheeks.

"Yeah." He was behind me before I even realized he'd moved. His hands were on my shoulders and he drew me back into his chest, slipping his arms around my waist. It felt good to lean back into him and let him carry my weight for a moment. It would be so easy to turn into his arms and bury myself in the comfort he offered.

Resting his chin on top of my head, we stood gazing silently out the window. Something melted inside as he pulled me securely to him. "She just wants to keep you safe."

"Yeah." I said mimicking him.

"Okay, I'm listening . . . talk to me. What do you have in mind?"

Drawing in a deep breath I said, "You know, I'm not sure this isn't about me as much as it's about Karen. Everything seems to point to your serial killer."

I turned in his arms to face him.

"But you already know that, don't you?"

His nod was imperceptible.

"Karen knows this, too, doesn't she?"

He muttered a curse as he dropped his arms and stepped away. I had no desire to argue with him right now. I had to exert all my effort to shake off this sense of foreboding. It might just be my imagination working overtime, but I had a right to a case of nerves after all that had been happening.

"Get your jacket. We're going to pay Sami a visit."

"Yes!" I yelled as I clenched my fist and thrust my arm straight in the air. It didn't matter how long a shot it was. It felt good just to be getting something going.

# CHAPTER 30

Y ou can't be serious? You . . . " Sami said
pointing at Stryker, "Are going to put a loaded
weapon in . . . her hands?" Sami asked as she
turned her stare and finger to me. "Karen will freak, not to
mention how fast she'll turn that weapon on you."
Stryker nodded with a gleam in his eyes and an evil grin
on his face. "Yep, serious as a heart attack. Sami, I need
you to teach her everything you know in the next four
hours. Think you can do it?"

"Well, I don't know if you've met her, but Mattie isn't
the most coordinated person I've ever dealt with. Granted
she's not stupid. But, really Stryker, a gun?"

"Hellooo . . . standing right here . . . can hear you." I said as I waved my hands in front of their faces. *Nothing.* Jeez, you'd think I was invisible the way they're talking about me.

"Hey! Any chance I can buy a ticket into this conversation?" *Again nothing.*

Ignoring me, Stryker continued, "Sami, I know she can do this. Please. Her life depends on it."

"Alright, if you're sure. Besides, I'm a sucker for a handsome face and a covert operation. Come on, Mattie. Let's see if we can do this without losing anything vital."

"Awesome." Turning to Stryker, I lifted myself up on tiptoe to whisper in his ear, "Thank you."

He squeezed me tight, lifting me slightly off the ground. I felt both frail and strong in his arms.

"Just pay attention to Sami. My life might depend on it, too." He said taking a deep unsteady breath.

I pulled out of the hug with tears in my eyes. "I'm not crying you know."

"Understood."

# CHAPTER 31

Driving home, traces of nighttime had crept around the edges of the clouds. The intense storm, unseasonable for fall, had eased. Strong winds had stripped trees of any remaining leaves and thunder exploded like a war was going on. I used my wipers to fend off the light drizzle splattering against the windshield. The trees along the street looked drenched, their autumn glory, now diffused. Somehow, it made things worse, making my fears more vivid.

Traveling along the road that ran adjacent to Echo creek, I let my mind wander. Holding that gun in my hand and firing it felt formidable. I had never experienced such power. I was actually holding a controlled explosion in my hands.

Sami spent the first two hours teaching me about firearm safety. Then the last two hours she let me touch one, the same one she sent home with me. A Sig Sauer–22 semi-automatic.

I must have fired off hundreds of rounds.

"Aim for the head," Sami said standing behind me. Holding my outstretched arms with her hands she whispered in my ear, "Look him in the eye. If you're going to aim a gun at a person, you, at the very least, owe them that. If you can't look him in the eye, you don't need to be carrying a gun."

As I drove, the weight of the pistol settled in the small of my back in its holster, feeling comforting and disturbing at the same time.

*I remember thinking, "It's just like aiming and shooting my camera. Except my camera goes click and the gun goes bang."*

Focused on how tonight was going to play out, I didn't notice the large truck following me until its lights filled the interior of my car. Someone struck me from behind, my head jerking as he made contact with the rear bumper of my car. Then another tap, his bumper settled against mine. I felt a sudden increase in speed forcing me forward. My heart hammered as I gripped the steering wheel tightly, the sweat collecting at the base of my neck merged with the cool air blowing in from the open window.

I tried braking. Nothing. A burning smell reached my nostrils.

I stamped on the accelerator. The lights dropped back suddenly.

I was traveling very fast. Too fast.

Too late I saw the sharp left-turning arrow. I flew past it slamming on my ineffective brakes. I lost control and hit the gravel on the side of the road. Ladybug swerved, fishtailed, and jolted over gravel and weeds. I jerked the steering wheel away from the rocks. Over compensating I spun back into the path of the trees.

I screamed and hung on, as the world swung wildly around me. Trees flew toward my windshield.

My jagged scream ended in an explosion of noise and tearing metal.

Then nothing.

The crash seemed to take forever, giving me enough time to have one clear thought. *Oh, shit.*

Everything went dark and deathly silent.

I held my breath and listened, wishing I could shut my mind off. The clock on the dashboard ticked off the seconds. Outside leaves rustled. There was movement.

Was my mind playing tricks on me? I heard branches snap despite the maddening pounding of my heart.

Is he coming back for me? I closed my eyes like I did when I was a kid and thought, *"If I can't see him he can't see me."*

Gradually, I became aware of the pain. Something sticky and warm ran down my face. I ran my trembling fingers across my forehead and cried out when my fingers touched the gash blood was flowing from.

I opened my eyes and blinked. The windshield was shattered; a tree was lying across it.

I glanced around the surrounding area searching for lights or movement of any kind. Nothing seemed to be moving.

Mentally pumping myself up, I reached for the door handle just as the door flew open and the interior lights exploded, blinding me momentarily.

I began to quiver from the inside out as terror sliced through my veins.

A second later, I was jerked roughly out of the car. I squirmed, trying to wrestle away.

"Stop!" he ground out.

"Stryker?" I whispered, hoping . . .

"Not this time, sugar." It was the gravelly voice guy. He tightened his grip drawing me firmly into his chest.

I had never felt such raw fear.

*Mattie, aren't you tired of being a victim? I heard Sami say.*

I looked around again hopeful, but again it was only in my head. I tried to remember what Sami had taught me about breaking away from someone who has me trapped from behind. Drawing on my fear I went slack, dropping my chin to my chest, my body dead weight in his arms. He drew me in tighter. Taking a deep breath, I threw my head back striking him square in the nose.

"What the fuck," he yelped and shoved me toward the ground, taking hold of his bleeding nose.

Frantic, I scrambled crab-style, my legs not able to support me. I reached the road, stood, and made a mad dash for the park. I didn't get two steps before he jerked me back by my hair, and on to the ground, the impact forcing all the air from my lungs. Gravelly voice guy had me on my back and was dragging me toward the water.

*My God, he's going to drown me.*

"Nooo!" I managed to scream at the top of my lungs.

Something was jabbing me in the back as he drug me across the ground. It was my gun. I twisted the top half of my body so only my butt was scraping the ground and with a shaking hand I removed the Sig from its holster.

I raised the gun and fired up toward the sky. Almost as if I'd planned it, the bullet hit a tree branch above us. It came crashing from the heavens, hit my attacker on the head, and he fell forward releasing his grip on my foot. While he held his head, I flipped over onto my hands and knees, stood, and hauled ass across the street, slipping into the shadowy park.

I hid behind one of the large trees, panting with fear, waiting, and listening. Peeking around the tree I saw he was still standing by Ladybug with his head thrown back, his gloved hands trying to staunch the blood gushing from his nose, a black ski mask concealing his face. He lowered his head and slowly looked around.

"You broke my fucking nose. I'm gonna kill you for this," he howled, bringing my attention back to the danger at hand. I whirled around and began to run.

My heart pounded, my lungs ached as I zigzagged deeper into the park, trying not to think about the last time I ran through here. My neck muscles tight and my body alert to every feeling, I heard every sound around me.

I stumbled through the darkness, tripped, and went skidding on my stomach, face-first in the dirt. I looked back to see what had tripped me. I couldn't be sure but it looked like a person sitting on the ground, resting, back against the tree.

Wondering why someone would be sitting out here in the middle of the night, I stood and moved closer. I sucked in my breath while stepping back abruptly. A metallic taste settled in my mouth as I forced myself to take in gulps of air so I wouldn't black out.

I dropped my head, closed my eyes, and counted out a full ten seconds before staring at him once again in disbelief.

His head tilted to one side, a straw hat perched on it.

I glanced around to see if anyone was near, and with a trembling hand I pushed the hat back, away from his face. His wide-eyed stare brought to mind a wild animal . . . *a rabid one.*

Forcing myself to move closer, I crouched and reached out as I touched the side of his neck, checking for a pulse. My hand shook so hard I couldn't be sure I felt one.

"Oh Steven," I moaned, setting back on my heels. Horrified, tears streamed down my face, not because I thought he was a good person or that I was going to miss him, but because I was getting tired of all this useless violence. As the blood pooled beneath him, the insects of the night continued to buzz around his head and unmoving hands splayed on either side of his body as he leaned against the base of a massive oak.

A hand grasped my shoulder.

Stiffening, I jumped up on the balls of my feet and came around ready to do battle.

"Mattie?" he said softly.

I know that voice, I thought, feeling slightly troubled.

The moon cast intriguing shadows over his face through the overhead branches jutting from the immense trees.

He gave me a ghost of a smile.

My hand shook as I lowered the gun I hadn't even realized I held. Though the Sig was limited to a few hours of training and practice, I was somewhat surprised to realize it felt comfortable in my hand. At the very least, familiar.

Charmingly handsome, blue eyes sparkling, and a lock of blond hair falling across his forehead, he was smiling that big crocodile smile of his as though he were actually glad to see me.

I secretly cursed the fate that had brought us to this same spot at the same time. He looked different, his face somber, distant as the waning moon. In that instant, I knew. I was dizzy with the realization of how dangerous he looked in the dark robe with the hood covering his blond hair.

Pressing his lips together, he nodded while lowering the hood. All semblance of charm seeped out of his handsome face as the hood fell away revealing features that were still quite perfect; smooth cheeks, wide spaced eyes, and firm square chin. But, the skin was stretched tight, the eyes flint hard, the smile on his lips tense. Eyes sharp and hard met mine in a moment of intimate, unthinkable understanding . . .

My hand, still shaking raised the gun again.

"Mattie, are you threatening me?" His words dropped like an arctic sleet between us, his smile never faltered.

He stood stock still.

I took a step back.

"No . . . no . . . of course not." I glanced back at Steven's lifeless body splayed out on the ground.

I took another step back.

"You remember me, don't you?" He smoothed back a lock of light-colored hair that had fallen into his hate-filled eyes.

He lunged for the gun.

Wrestling for control, I gasped softly as the gun went off in my hand.

We stood motionless, staring into each other's eyes in disbelief.

I could almost imagine the bullet slicing through my body. Maybe it had. Maybe I was just too numb with terror to feel anything.

He staggered back a step and looked down as he pulled up the robe to expose his thigh. Blood was oozing through the jeans he was wearing beneath the monk's robe. His face twisted in a spasm of pain.

Slowly he looked up. His eyes glittered. "You shot me," he said, foolishly stating the obvious.

"I didn't mean to," I cried out turning back to Steven. "I . . . I was just trying to . . . "

At that moment an electric charge buzzed down my spine and hummed in my brain. My legs gave way, my vision blurred, and the last thing I remembered was . .

# CHAPTER 32

I had no memory. No idea of what happened, or how long I'd lain unconscious in this place. A place, I'm sure that is just below the earth's surface where the souls of the dead live. *Probably hell.*

My head ached, feeling as if it's split wide open. I tried to focus on other parts of my body; everything hurts and my head continues to pound. With something restraining me, I am lying on a hard surface. I shifted position painfully, and like a dreamer slowly awaking, I began to make out shapes in the murky shadows around me as my eyes adjusted to the darkness.

I was lying on a table.

No, I'm strapped to a table.

Taking in a long, shuddering breath, I swallowed back my fear. I'm going to be sick. I'm groggy and in pain and I want to sleep. Maybe I am sleeping, maybe I'm dreaming and this is just a really bad dream. I need to wake up. It's a terrible dream and I will myself to wake up . . . now.

I take another deep breath and choke back bile as my head throbs. With one more deep breath I realize, to my horror, I am awake. I really am, and this really is happening.

*Don't panic O'Malley.*

"Stryker?" I jerked my head up quickly. Too quickly. Gently laying my head back down I realized the voices are in my head. There is no one here to save me.

Fear pounded through my brain. Panic seized me as I looked around frantically, searching for a way of escape.

Never had I felt more alone.

Never had I been more determined.

The building groaned softly.

I bit back a scream.

"Are you awake?" a voice asked softly. Puzzled, I know I've heard that voice before.

I don't answer. *Make him think you're dead, O'Malley.*

"You should be awake," said the voice again, coming from the door.

A light came on suddenly; I tried to jerk my hands up to shield my burning eyes but the straps held my arms down. I knew the voice on the other side of the door. It was someone I knew who should be assisting me but was not.

"What do you want? Let me out of here." I yelled, struggling with the unmoving straps.

I looked around, my eyes finally adjusted to the illuminated space. I was laying on one of two stainless-steel tables. I turned my head to take in the rest of the room. It looked like something out of an old movie . . . *an old Frankenstein movie to be exact.*

Across the room flat-bottomed glass beakers were spread out on a make-shift counter constructed from large wooden slabs; many of the beakers contained a green liquid. Surgical instruments were spread out on top of the table next to me. And, what looked to be a human organ floated in some sort of clear fluid in a glass container. It almost appeared as if it were suspended in air.

My gaze continued on to the other side of the room and stopped as my eyes landed on an object propped against a crumbling wall. It was a white cane just like Allen's, white with reflective tape wrapped around the lower part of it.

A sob filled the room: *mine.*

The doorknob turned slowly and he limped in. He had wrapped his thigh in white bandages that were now turning red from the flow of blood that seeped through them. He still wore the same bloody jeans he'd been wearing when I shot him.

*Oh my God, I shot Jonathan.*

I shuddered at the thought.

"Jonathan?" While I didn't remember everything that happened, I was beginning to be certain about a lot of it. The last time I saw Jonathan, he wore a monk's robe. That was noticeably gone now.

*Play dumb, Mattie.*

"How are you, Mattie?" His voice, even though barely a whisper, made me wince. "Do you remember what happened?"

With great effort, I shook my head trying to focus on him. At the same time, I thought if only my head would fall off then maybe the pain would stop.

"Where is he, Jonathan?" my voice shook, my teeth chattered. I willed myself to calm down.

He didn't look capable of thought. His face was ashen, his eyes blank.

"What did you do to me? It feels like the top of my head is about to come off," I asked softly.

"Now you know how poor Steven felt."

"Poor Steven?"

"You really don't recall?" Shaking my head no.

He continued, "You shot me." My eyes opened wide with registered memory.

"Ahhh . . . you do remember."

"It was an accident."

"The hell it was."

"Where are we? This looks like some kind of operating room."

"You're partially right. This was my father's room. I used to sneak in here when I was little," he said as he limped further into the room. "This is where I first got my love of medicine. I knew I wanted to be a doctor and follow in my father's footsteps."

I watched as his trembling hand went to his thigh.

"How serious is the wound?" I asked. "Untie me so I can take a look at it."

"It was a through and through. I'll live. No thanks to you."

"You tried to take the gun from me. Why?"

"Because you finally realized who I was. Didn't you?"

"What? I don't understand." I said nervously.

"Yeah, you do. You remembered it was me with Steven the day you came home early and caught him in bed . . . with a man," he said as he pulled my gun out from behind his back.

Thunder crashed inside my head, the day rushed into me like waves in the ocean. A man with long brown hair and a scraggly beard peered out from under the blanket. Looking into Jonathan's eyes now, I knew I was looking into those same feverish eyes. Only then, he was coming down from the orgasm he'd just acquired with my husband. Now, I can only hope it's an infection from the gunshot wound.

"Jonathan, I need to sit-up. I'm going to be sick."

"No, you'll be fine." He said as he moved closer to the table. "As a matter of fact, maybe you and I will have a bit of fun before I kill you."

"You're doing all this because I took pictures of you and Steven? You can have them. Just let me see Allen."

Jonathan tightened his grip on the gun and I could see his jaw take on a more pronounced line. There was a definite light of madness in his eyes.

"This is not about that," he responded angrily. He took a deep breath and said, "Allen is safe and sound, Mattie. Not to worry about that. Now, where is he?"

Staring at the barrel of the gun, I remembered what Sami told me as she handed it to me. *"Never pull your weapon unless you are prepared to use it, because the other person will be."*

"Who? What do you want? You want me. I'll let you have me if you'll only let Allen go."

"Well, I think I'm going to have you anyway as you don't have a bargaining chip here." He said, with an arrogant grin, while lifting himself onto the table and lying down next to me. "Now, why don't you just relax and we'll have a bit of fun." The placid lover's timbre to his voice sent a wave of disgust piercing straight through my brain.

He pressed his body into mine. I shuddered as I felt the hardness of him press against my leg and he ran his right hand over my breast, all while holding the gun in his left hand above my head.

"Please, Jonathan, I need to sit-up. I'm going to be sick. Could I use the bathroom, please?" Hearing the pleading in my own voice repulsed me.

He reached up and started stroking my hair. "Take a deep breath. You'll feel much better."

Revolted by his touch I shivered and turned away. Taking a deep breath did nothing to appease my roiling stomach. Lifting my head I turned toward Jonathan, and just as I was about to plead again, I heaved my guts out.

Jonathan jerked back and rolled off the table but not before I emptied part of my dinner on him.

"God . . . disgusting."

Breathing quickly and heavily through my nose I begged, "Please, just let me sit up. I know I'll feel better if I can just put my head between my knees." I pleaded, still taking in deep breaths so I wouldn't choke to death on my own vomit.

"Alright, but you'd better not try anything." He limped over to one of the racks, got a towel to wipe himself off, picked up another, and brought it back to me. He undid the straps he used to secure me to the table and helped me sit up, handing me the towel.

I tried to wipe myself off as best as I could, taking my time while trying to figure out what to do next. "Jonathan, why are you doing this?"

With wild eyes and a sweat soaked his brow, his breath came fast as though he'd just run ten miles uphill. "Enough!" he shouted. "Where . . . is . . . Scarecrow?" his voice softer, his jaw tight, and his teeth clenched.

"Scarecrow? I don't understand." Remembering what Karen had told me about the phenom . . . Scarecrow.

*Stall for time, O'Malley. Help is coming . . . it has to come.*

"So, your father was a doctor?"

"Yes, my father, Matthew "Harm" Harmon, was a gifted surgeon as well as a respected psychiatrist."

"So, your father was a surgeon and a psychiatrist? Wow, what was he going to do with those degrees . . . brain surgery?" I asked as I giggled. Oh, God . . . I must be more scared than I thought.

"Yes. My father was going to perform the first successful brain transplant," his tone calmer now.

Boy! I was going to get whiplash trying to keep up with his mood swings.

"Brain transplant. That sounds pretty futuristic."

"My father was ahead of his time. Until he was killed."

"I'm sorry. How did he die?"

*Keep him talking, O'Malley.*

"He was shot in the head. As a matter of fact he was shot right between the eyes," he said evenly, looking me directly in the eye.

"That's awful, Jonathan. I'm so sorry. It's hard losing your father. I know. We lost our father about twenty years ago."

"No, you didn't."

"Umm . . . yes we did. He died in a car accident out west."

"No, he didn't! Now where is Scarecrow?" He was getting agitated again.

"Let me see Allen first, and then I'll tell you." Regaining some of my strength, I shook as I stood. My hands gripped the edge of the stainless steel table keeping me upright as I looked him in the eye. While the voice in my head urged me to be strong, I took a step toward Jonathan but stopped when he raised the barrel of the gun and pushed it into my chest. In Jonathan's handsome condescending face, a storm was brewing. I looked into his terrifying blue eyes and felt the temperature drop suddenly and drastically. I shivered in the claustrophobic room as though standing before an open meat locker.

"Why did you kill Roger? And Amber. What could they have possibly done to you?"

"I didn't kill Roger. That was just a bonus, if you will. And I don't know anything about any Amber."

"Were you and Steven were in this together?"

"No, it was all coincidence . . . you bringing him into the ER the morning Pepper zapped him. I hadn't seen him since the morning you found us together. What was that, like five, six years ago?" He was obviously remembering that time fondly.

"You know you shouldn't have gotten so upset that day. What we had was nothing. It was you he loved. I was just something he needed to get out of his system."

"It was nothing? Just something he had to get out of his system! Are you freaking kidding me? What the two of you did that day devastated my life . . . forever." Shaking my head and sweeping the hot tears away with the back of my hands, I continued, "Did you know I was six months pregnant the day I found you in bed with my husband? Hmmm, judging by the look on your face, you didn't. Yeah, I was. The same day my husband, the one you claim loved me, threw an alarm clock at me causing me to trip and fall on my stomach. Can you guess what happened?" My hands instinctively protecting my stomach, as my demanding eyes bored into him.

Looking right through him, I said quietly, "You're a doctor . . . do the math."

"Well you know, some things are just meant to be," he said matter-of-factly.

"Yeah, kinda like your father getting his head blown off . . . huh."

His hand flew out so fast I didn't have time to dodge the fist that hit me square in the jaw knocking me back into the table. "My father was not meant to get his head blown off, as you so aptly put it." His voice was devoid of emotion, all traces of compassion now gone. "He was a great man destined to do great things. Some people had to die so he could do his work."

Rubbing the side of my face I said, "You say you didn't kill Roger or Amber. But, if you didn't do it, who did? And, what about Steven? You're not going to tell me you didn't do that either, are you?"

"Don't you see, Mattie? Neither Roger nor Steven had anything to do with this. They just happened to be in the wrong place at the wrong time. Besides, it's okay to admit I did you a favor. You really wanted to be rid of both of them, didn't you?"

"No! How can you say that?"

"Come on, Mattie, you have to see the favor I did for you. You needed someone to save you from them."

"What I see, Jonathan, is a man who thinks he can get away with murder." I hurled back at him. "But you won't; not this time."

He smiled coldly and gave a short dry laugh. "Oh, Mattie, don't you see? I already have. Now, because I'm tired of arguing with you, I'm going to go bring Allen in." Waving the gun at me he said, "Now step back and sit down. If you try anything, you won't be the one I shoot. It'll be Allen; and we both know how much your blind brother means to you." His laugh was short and derisive. "Do you understand?"

I nodded. "Yes, I understand. I won't do anything. I promise."

"Like I'm interested in your promises. You had better be prepared to tell me where Scarecrow is." Giving me one last glance, he backed out the door and locked it behind him.

Why does Jonathan think I know anything about Scarecrow? Maybe he thinks Karen or Stryker told me. It doesn't sound like anyone really knows much about him. It sounds like he's more rumor than real.

Think, Mattie, think. Why does this deranged lunatic think you know this guy? What could possibly make him think that? Crap! My head is pounding again. *That punch to the face didn't help much.*

The door opened, drawing me out of my reverie. I stood as Allen walked through the door, with Jonathan close behind, the gun pressed into Allen's back. I awkwardly walked toward him, my legs not quite belonging to me. Jonathan shoved Allen forward. Catching his arm, I turned him toward me. "Allen, are you alright? Did he hurt you?"

Lifting his hands to my face, Allen asked, "Mattie, are you okay? Jonathan came to the house, told me you were in an accident, and offered to bring me to the hospital. What's going on? Where are we? Jeez what is that smell? Did somebody puke in here?" *Leave it to Allen.*

"Yes, I got a little sick but I'm fine now. Anyway, Jonathan assumes that I know the man who killed his father."

"I'm not assuming anything. I know Scarecrow and I know that he killed my father. Now, what I want from you two is to know where that coward has been hiding for the last twenty years."

"Jonathan, you're crazy. Whatever you *think* we know . . . we don't."

Moving closer to me and pointing the gun between my eyes he said coldly, "Don't . . . call . . . me . . . crazy. I know what I know. Raven told me. Scarecrow should have cleaned up his own mess. There were three of them in the area the night. The assassin, Scarecrow, pulled the trigger, firing that bullet right between my father's eyes. Raven was the cleaner and unfortunately he died before he could tell me who the third person was."

*The assassin? The cleaner? WTF!*

"Why would Scarecrow kill your father? I don't understand."

"I'm sure Karen has told you all about the alleged serial killer, Headcase?"

"Ummm . . . yeah," I said, not sure what I was agreeing to.

He raised his eyebrows and nodded, "So, she has spoken of him. Reverently . . . I hope."

"Jonathan, I don't understand. What do you know about any of this?"

"Let's just say they got in Harm's way," he giggled like a schoolgirl.

"Got in harm's way? I don't understand," shaking my head. Suddenly, it became terrifyingly clear . . . Jonathan's father was Headcase and he killed all those people.

"Headcase, the media mockingly named him, was my father. A gifted surgeon, indeed. Those damn people just couldn't see it. They took away his license to practice medicine. So, he had to show them. He had to show the know-it-alls that deemed him unworthy, just how brilliant, skillful, and truly worthy he was."

It hit me then, knocking the wind out of me. I struggled to draw a breath . . . "No," I whispered, "Your father killed Karen's family and all those others and you knew about it?"

"Of course, why do you think I became a doctor? I'm going to pick up where my father left off. Roger's brain was just a preview of what was to come. The next brains I'm going to extract and send to Karen are going to be yours and Allen's. That's poetic justice.

I jerked my arms up involuntarily as if to ward off a blow.

"You see, my father never got a chance to take the brains of Kevin and Sam. Scarecrow put a bullet between his eyes before he finished his job."

"I don't understand why you think we know anything about any of this."

"Why would you know anything about this? You know this because . . . Scarecrow is your father."

My heart caught as if on something sharp. I began to shiver violently. The coldness I felt went all the way to my core. Looking up at Allen, I stared at his sweet innocent face with its too-old eyes, and knew without any doubt, he thought he knew the truth.

He thought our father was alive.

He thought our father was an assassin.

That went a long way in explaining why he was so pissed at him.

On impulse, I reached for him. Feeling the strength of his grip as his long fingers entwined with mine, I felt my trembling ease.

"Roger's brain. You . . . took Roger's brain and . . .
sent it to . . . Karen?" I stammered, trying to make some
sense of this. "Oh. My. God."

"Ahh I see they didn't share that little tidbit with
you. I wish I could have been there to see her face. Her
and that damn smug Stryker. So superior, both of them."
Jonathan shook his head as if trying to clear it. "I had you
all fooled, didn't I," he cackled.

"Steven's brain, which is right there by the way," he
said pointing to the container sitting next to the surgical
instruments, "was slated for you. I thought the scarecrow
hat was ingenious. What do you think?

Now, will daddy come out of hiding once he finds out
his children are dead?"

"Why do you keep saying that? He's not our father.
Our father is gone. Please, Jonathan can't we stop all this.
Besides, you need a doctor in case your leg is infected. At
least let me take a look at it." I said.

"You stay right where you are." He swayed, waving
the gun at me. "Tell me what I want to know or I'll kill
your poor blind brother right now," he said in a mocking
tone.

Before I knew what was happening, Allen took a mad
swing at Jonathan, clipped him in the jaw, and knocked
him back toward me. But, Jonathan having the advantage

of sight, punched Allen in the gut. Allen doubled over and dropped to the floor, his arms clutched his middle. Jonathan reared his good leg back and kicked Allen in the chin.

I lunged forward and pushed Jonathan. *"Leave him alone!"* I dropped to my knees beside my twin.

Jonathan grabbed me by my hair and yanked me back up to my feet.

Pointing the Sig at the furrow between my eyes, he said, "Don't move again, or I'll shoot you just like your anomalous father shot mine." His eyes took on a maniacal look.

Holding the gun on me, Jonathan was barely able to stand. His hand shook and he was sweating profusely as he leaned back against one of the stainless steel tables trying to keep himself steady. His eyes darted from me to Allen, who was still lying on the floor, not moving.

Glancing around the room for some kind of weapon, I just barely caught a glimpse of a shadow in the doorway. Before I could move, Jonathan looked over at the door. I heard the muffled sneeze of a silenced automatic just as Jonathan felt the bullet slam between his eyes and into his skull.

I stood mute, watching in horror as Jonathan's head jerked backward, blood and tissue sprayed out the back of his head. The puke green wall behind us was splattered with blood and I felt his blood dripping down my own face. For the second time tonight, the metallic smell of blood made me nauseous. As if in slow motion, Jonathan stumbled, his lifeless body yielded to the floor, pushed by some unseen force.

*This can't be real.*

My knees buckled and I collapsed into a kneeling position on the floor next to Allen. My clenched fists pressed hard against my mouth. I couldn't move. I couldn't breathe. It was almost as if I were viewing this from somewhere else. As if I were someone else.

"Mattie, what happened?" Allen groaned, waking me from my stupor.

I was obviously in shock otherwise I wouldn't have been able to look at Jonathan lying on the floor, blood seeping out of the back of his head.

"Mattie, what happened?" Allen asked again. "Where's Jonathan?"

"He's . . . " I stopped, a guttural sound coming from my throat. "He's dead." I answered in a whisper that echoed in the silent room. My gaze took in the now empty doorway. If it wasn't for Jonathan's brains splattered all across the room, I'd have to wonder if I only imagined someone was there.

My lips trembled uncontrollably, "Are you all right, Allen?" I asked, thanking God he couldn't see that he was covered in blood and brains.

"Yeah, I'm fine," he said, sitting up and rubbing his jaw. "You should see the other guy though," he said with a chuckle, but his eyes were full of fear. "Mattie? What happened to him?"

"Poetic justice Allen, poetic justice," I said with a self-deprecating laugh. "Come on Allen. Let's get the hell outta here." After helping Allen stand, I staggered across the room and retrieved the cane Jonathan had placed in the corner to taunt me. On our way out the door I grabbed a scalpel to use as a weapon, just in case Jonathan hadn't been working alone.

# CHAPTER 33

G od help us," I whispered into the still night as I stared up at the old hospital. I felt a chill as cold as the arctic sea settle into my bones as we hurried along a broken sidewalk to the front of the building. The threat of rain hung heavy in the air as dark shadows fingered out from the surrounding woods. Crickets softly chirped as we stood near the crumbling fountain with its crying angels, cracked basin, and weed choked concrete. I felt a presence, an evil cruelty, as if the building itself were glaring down at us, daring us.

I drank in the oddity of the old building. The leaded glass windows, so thick that a brick would probably bounce right off them, hid layers of dust and dirt. The stone blocks looked to have been lifted into place by hand and ivy climbed eerily upward toward the most striking aspect of the entire place. Carved angels, with arms raised toward the heavens, lined the rooftop. At one point in time, I'm sure the angels were meant to be guardians, offering hope to all the desperate people who passed through those vast doors.

The angels that happened to still be standing, some one hundred years later, were left with broken wings, raised arms that looked as if they had been amputated, and in some cases beheaded. The angels, once a sign of hope, now seemed to mock all those held captive here.

Heart thudding and nerves stretched to the breaking point, I told myself this decaying aged structure, which appeared so daunting, was just brick and mortar.

Even so . . . I shuddered as I thought of all the tortured souls who had resided here, cared for by doctors, *doctors like Jonathan's father . . . ?*

Souls left in limbo.

"What? Where are we Mattie?" Allen asked as I squeezed his hand in a death grip.

Before I could answer, someone ran up behind us. I turned, stepping in front of Allen, wielding the scalpel in my out stretched hand.

"Mattie, Allen, come on we've got to get you out of here," Coop's worried voice tunneled through the dark night.

I jumped when I heard his voice. "Nicky, is that you? What are you doing here? How did you find us?" my questions all running together.

Reaching out he extracted the scalpel from my tightly clenched fist. "I'll explain later. Come on we gotta go."

I closed my eyes, trying to block the images of bloody water and the chunks of Jonathan's brain that circled the drain. I was aware of the stinging as the water hit me like sharp needles pricking my skin, but I didn't care. My mind, deadened to all feelings, was numb from the inside out. Letting my body fold into itself, I slipped down into the tub drawing my knees into my chest. I closed my eyes and let the water beat down on my face. Dropping my chin, the cooling water pounded the back of my head.

When the water turned cold, I attacked my wet body with a towel and tried to erase any leftover matter, imagined or otherwise. There was a strange taste in my mouth. I wasn't sure if it was my imagination or if something had flown into my open mouth when

Jonathan's head exploded. Gagging at the thought, I tilted over the toilet again but nothing came out. My insides were empty.

"Mattie?" Karen called from outside the bathroom door.

Straightening, I reached for the toothpaste again.

"I'll be down in a minute," I answered, putting paste on my toothbrush. I tried again to scrub the offensive taste out of my mouth.

I threw the toothbrush into the trashcan.

A kitchen cabinet hinge creaked. Glass clinked against glass. I stopped, feet glued to the pine floorboards as I stood in the middle of my living room staring at the kitchen door, paralyzed, feeling light-headed and still sick to my stomach.

Karen entered, "There you are." Her husky voice trailed off as our eyes met.

She blinked twice, then said, "Here," and held out a cup, "You obviously need this more than I do." She smiled while her eyes continued to study me skeptically.

I hesitated, and then accepted the cup.

"Sip it. You don't want to get sick."

*Too late for that.*

Although the hot liquid went down easily enough, I waited to see if it was going to revolt against me.

She stood silently waiting for me to say something.

Hesitantly she asked, "Do you want to talk about it?"

"No!" I glanced at her sharply, surprising myself as much as her by the outburst.

I'd left home yesterday strong and sure of myself; I'd returned bruised and vulnerable. Emotion came at me in waves. First apprehension. Then anger. I could handle this. I had to.

Karen took a deep breath, creating a barrier between herself and the weight of that one small word. "Whenever you're ready, Mattie."

Realizing what was at stake for her I said softly, "Karen, please. I know there are things you need to hear but I can't talk about it just yet. Please give me some time." My voice broke.

Her poignant brown eyes clung to my face.

"You take all the time you need. In the mean time I'll see if I can find something for you to eat and . . . maybe, just maybe, a little wine," she said. "Oh, Detective Adams stopped by. I told him, as your doctor, I couldn't allow you to be interviewed just yet. He said to tell you he'll be back in the morning."

I nodded.

Karen sighed, resigned as she softly closed the door on the awkward silence that had fallen between us. The events of the last few weeks left Karen shaken and hollowed out. I wanted to tell her what she needs to hear but I can't. Not now. Maybe not ever.

I sat and let myself sink into my comfortable and familiar sofa. Harry laid on the bearskin rug that I brought from Arizona and had thrown on the floor in front of the fireplace. Raising his head, he looked at me for a moment, sauntered across the room, and laid his head in my lap. I stroked him behind his ears as he purred like a cat; the sound like a lullaby. I wrapped my arms around his neck and laid my cheek on his head. "Thanks, Harry," I whispered as I kissed the top of his head.

With my trusty sidekick in my arms, I tried to put my concerns in perspective.

If Jonathan was to be believed, which I highly doubt, he didn't kill Roger or Amber. Why would Jonathan admit to killing Steven and sending Karen Roger's brain, but deny everything else?

Great! I'm trying to make sense out of something said by a lunatic.

An unexpected shiver of unease scuttled down my spine.

*If he didn't do it . . . who did?*

# CHAPTER 34

I shuffled down the stairs. Stopping halfway, I took in what should have been a very comforting scene.

"I see the Hopewell swat team has arrived for duty," I said, eyeing Coop, Sami, and Karen sitting in my living room.

"Mattie!" Karen said her face lighting when she saw me. "Did you get any sleep?"

"I'm fine." That was true enough, although it would take more than a few hours rest to recuperate from what happened earlier tonight.

"Where is everyone else?" I asked noticing a large void in the group.

"Well . . . Pepper and Violet flew out to Arizona earlier. Pepper had some things that needed taken care of; she said you would understand. We talked Violet into going with her. Allen wouldn't leave; he's over at my house and Stryker is with him."

Holding up her hands, "And before you go all ballistic, he's just talking to him. Believe it or not Beau can talk to people."

I knew Stryker would handle Allen with as much care as needed. At least I don't have to worry about his safety for the time being. I was more concerned about why Pepper agreed to take Mom to Arizona with her.

"I know you all have questions but could I have some coffee before we start." Turning toward Coop, "You did bring coffee didn't you, Nicky?" I asked inhaling deeply.

"You know I did, Mattie. It's in the kitchen. Let me get you a cup."

"I'll come with you."

As soon as the kitchen door swung closed I walked into Coop's receptive arms, and he let me cry unguarded.

Just the two of us standing in the middle of my cozy kitchen, me hanging onto him for dear life and him rubbing my back with his large comforting hands and murmuring into my hair everything would be fine.

Sometimes it felt as if my father were holding and comforting me.

*I just want my father back.*

I stood there in his arms finally beginning to feel safe. From where we stood, I could see the picture of my grandmother and father. I found it very comforting. As I studied it something clicked, something that had been bugging me.

Son of a bitch, now I know what it is.

I pulled away so I could look up into his handsome face.

"I need to talk to you about something."

"Fire at will."

That phrase might be more apt than he'd intended.

"Did you know my father? Or anything about him?"

His gaze shifted to the kitchen door then back to me but he said nothing.

"Or, maybe I should ask, *do* you know my father?"

Stepping away from him, I walked over to the window and looked out onto my yard, careful not to let my gaze wander as far as the pond. When I turned back around Coop sat at the table, his arms crossed over his chest.

"Come here, sit down, and tell me what you think you know."

I sat down next to him and picked up my favorite coffee cup with a picture of Wonder Woman declaring, *"Saving the World makes me Thirsty."*

The coffee did nothing to warm the hollow coldness in my stomach, but I sipped it as I glanced over at Coop.

I sat back and inhaled the aroma putting my jumbled thoughts in order.

"You were an Army Ranger, right?"

"Right."

"Special Forces?"

"I was."

"You were away from home for a long time, weren't you?"

"Twenty years."

"Can you tell me what your job was?"

"No."

"Can you tell me where you were?"

"Everywhere."

"Did you ever work with my father?"

"Ask me anything but that."

"Don't you think I have a right to know?" I pleaded.

"You have every right to know, but I have no right to tell you." His voice held genuine regret.

"Well then," I said as I pushed back from the table and stood. Dazed, disoriented, and exhausted I started for the door then stopped. "Nicky, how did you know where to find Allen and me tonight?"

"I got a call."

"From Scarecrow?" I whispered, my trembling hands hovering over the door leading from the kitchen.

Silence.

Looking back at Coop, I watched as his head dropped to his chest.

My stomach churned and my cheeks were feverishly hot as tears trickled down my face. Gaining control of my emotions, I shrugged and said philosophically, "I guess there's no sense standing here dwelling on what you can or can't tell me. I'll see you tomorrow."

Pushing through the door back into the living room, I made my way upstairs feigning a headache. I know they are all disappointed in me right now but it can't be helped given everything I've learned in the last twenty-four hours.

"Damn!" I glanced at the clock as I tossed off the covers.

I padded barefoot down the stairs toward the kitchen, tripping over Harry who has been following close on my heels. My protector.

My house was eerily quiet as I pushed through the swinging door, into the kitchen. I wonder where my posse is.

I eyed the half-empty bottle of wine on the counter. Giving myself a mental shake, I reached into the cabinet and grabbed a water glass. Turning on the faucet, I let the water run while looking at my reflection in the window over the sink. I realized beyond the darkness any number of things could be lurking and watching me.

"Crap! I'm scaring myself."

I knew Jonathan was dead and he could not hurt me anymore. But, I couldn't get past some nagging thoughts.

After downing a full glass of water, I set the empty glass in the sink, turned back to the kitchen table, and sat down. My gaze went straight to the picture hanging on the wall of my father and grandmother.

Gramma was looking up and smiling at my father, full of pride for her son and unshed tears in her eyes. Looking closely at the picture, I think I finally have one of the answers I had been looking for. My father was wearing a uniform just like the one I saw Coop wearing in one of the pictures in his shop.

Celebrating the fact that something else was falling into place I reached into the cupboard picked up a wine

glass, grabbed the opened bottle of merlot off the counter,
and headed back up to my bedroom.

# CHAPTER 35

I stretched and arched my back coming out of my wine-induced coma. I woke to a muffled, dull thumping and blamed it on the wine.

Sunlight snuck through the gauzy curtains of my bedroom windows. In defense, I buried my face in the pillow managing to block out the light but not the thumping in my head. I was awake.

The house was quiet, but the sounds of the day drifted in from outside. A fall breeze set the chimes on the back porch tinkling and rustled the curtains lightly. It was a beautiful day, cool and smelling faintly of fall and burning leaves.

Thinking aspirin and coffee, I pushed myself up in bed. It was then I realized the thumping wasn't in my head, but downstairs. Someone was knocking on my front door.

*Ding, dong. Ding, dong.*

Jeez . . . now the doorbell.

Still groggy, I stumbled out of bed, rummaged through the clothes on my floor. Finding a pair of red plaid pajama bottoms I pulled them on under the oversized Red Wing hockey jersey I'd slipped on last night before going to bed.

*Ding, dong.*

"All right, all right, I'm coming. Jeez, wait a second will ya?" I started out of the room then stopped and went back to the bed for Gramma's quilt to wrap around me.

Looking around, I called out, "Harry. Come here boy." No response. Great; he bolted again.

Making my way down the steps, I hesitated just a second before I opened the front door.

"Good morning, Ms. O'Malley. I hope we didn't catch you at a bad time." Detective Adams said, eyeing my outfit.

"Umm . . . no, no," I said pulling the quilt tighter across my shoulders.

"Is it okay if I come in?"

My legs weren't working right, but somehow I stepped aside. "Please come in, I was just about to make some coffee. Would you like a cup?" I asked while pushing the screen door open for him to enter.

"Sure, that would be great," he said as he crossed through the door in front of me and didn't pause until he reached the other side of the living room stopping in front of the fireplace. I let my eyes follow him. Both my mind and stomach churned. He turned back to face me.

"Okay. Let's just go into the kitchen and sit down."

Following me through to the kitchen, he took a seat at the table pulling out his small notebook and placing it on the table in front of him.

I set about making the coffee then asked, "Did you say, I hope 'we' didn't catch you at a bad time?"

"Yeah. Detective Rhodes went across the street to get your brother. They'll be along in a minute or two."

"Allen? She's talking to Allen?"

"Yes. I understand he was with you last night. Is that correct?"

"Well, yeah. But I don't know what he can tell you."

"You'd be surprised at the things a blind person can garner from a situation that a sighted person would probably skim right over."

"You're right. I'm just being overly protective again." I fell silent and went back to making my coffee.

Karen, Allen, and Detective Rhodes came through the back door just then.

After Allen and I recounted what we could remember from last night, Detective Adams turned to Karen and asked, "What do you think Dr. Kavanaugh? Was he a whack job?"

"Whack job is not a technical term Detective. If you are asking me if he was mentally ill, that's hard to say. However, I never picked up on it. He was probably self-medicating. You might want to ask the medical examiner to look for that. Many mental illnesses can be controlled with the correct medication."

"So, you're saying a medicated whack job could blend into the crowd and wouldn't stand out like a sore thumb."

"Yes basically that is what I'm saying. However, something changed and the medication wasn't enough anymore. There had to be a stressor that pushed him over the edge. He was finally at the point where no pill could allow him to pass for normal and I believe that stressor was Mattie. For some reason he is associating you with Scarecrow, whom he blamed for his father's death."

"Me? I didn't do anything. How could I possibly know anything about his father's death? Why do you think I know anything about Scarecrow?"

"Calm down Mattie, I'm profiling him, not agreeing with him."

"I know I'm sorry. And just for the record I totally agree with Detective Adams, Jonathan was a nut bar."

I sat at the kitchen table for a long while after the others left thinking back to the night before. After attempting to piece together Jonathan's rants, and trying to decipher the probable from the improbable, I have to admit it was all just too difficult to accept as plausible.

From under the table, I heard Harry's low growl, followed by the peal of the doorbell.

I walked through the living room to the front door with Harry's toenails clicking at my heels. I opened the door and stood there staring for just a second longer than necessary.

"Hey, Paul," I said trying to hide my surprise at finding him on my doorstep. "I've been meaning to call you. Come on in." I pushed open the screen door, letting him into the living room.

"Sorry to be disturbing you so early but I was going by and I wanted to stop and offer my condolences. Mr. Moore was a real nice man. He's gonna be missed." His baseball cap, pulled low across his brow, was making it hard to see his face.

"Come on in." I took his arm and pulled him inside. "I was just about to make myself some breakfast. Would you like some coffee?"

Following me in to the kitchen, he said, "Uh . . . no, thank you. I don't drink coffee. I just stopped by to look at those pipes up in the master bath. Mr. Moore called a few weeks ago, but I never got around to it."

"Don't drink coffee? How do you stay alive?" I smiled gesturing to the table. "Sit down. There's probably something you can drink in here," I said opening the refrigerator door.

"No, thank you. Nothing." Looking down at the floor he explained, "I've been working over at that new subdivision across town. You know, over by the old asylum. They're puttin' up some real nice houses. Eventually that whole area will be homes and shops."

Wow, that is probably the most I've ever heard him say at one time. It always seemed to me Paul wasn't playing with a full deck but Roger said he was just shy and an excellent plumber. Glancing up at him I noticed some bruising around his eyes.

"Paul, are you alright? You look tired." He was a large man, so burly his navy blue t-shirt rode up his arm exposing white skin above his tanned arms.

"Oh, I'm fine. Just puttin' in a lot of hours, that's all. Now if I could just run upstairs and take a look at those pipes I'll get out of your hair and let you get on with your day."

"Sure. Go ahead. You know the way." I watched as Paul pushed back out the kitchen door. Something seemed familiar about the way he walked. I wondered what? Shaking my head, that's just ridiculous.

I checked out the contents of the refrigerator. Coop had left some muffins for me, but for some reason I didn't think I wanted anything from him just now. I reached for the loaf of bread, made toast with peanut butter, and poured myself another cup of coffee.

I gulped down half the steaming coffee before I headed to the back porch to look for Harry. I hesitated for a full minute before I finally turned the knob.

"Mattie, you've got to stop this. Jonathan is dead. There is nothing to be afraid of."

*And you've really got to stop talking to yourself.*

Stepping onto the porch felt good, it felt familiar. The morning air had a chill, but I leaned into it, pleased that it cleared my head. I looked out over my back yard and breathed deeply. Someone was burning leaves. Fall was definitely in the air and everything was getting back to normal.

"Harry. Harry, come on boy." I really don't know what I expected.

*I guess things really are back to normal.*

As I called to Harry, I went around the house to the front yard and walked past Paul's large panel truck to get to the front porch.

Wrapping the quilt around my shoulders I sat down on the swing to finish my coffee. Before I called out a search party, I would wait to see if Harry showed up on his own.

It was a brilliantly sunlit morning in early November, but its beauty was deceptive. I shivered, thinking after all the long days of the unknown, I exalted in the sensation of familiarity, wrapping the feel of it around me like Gramma's warm quilt. The worst was past. I would survive, and the whole world seemed brighter, sweeter, and happier.

After going over our experiences from last night the consensus was that there were probably two forces at work here.

One . . . Jonathan trying to avenge his father. And two . . . maybe Roger hid something in my house that the gravelly voice guy is trying to find.

The turmoil staggered in my mind, so I shut down as my gaze scanned the neighborhood.

Across the street, Mr. Hadley, my elderly, widowed neighbor, was outside sweeping off his front porch. He lifted one hand in greeting and I waved back. His beds of yellow chrysanthemums, not quite ready to concede to the falling temperatures, were sprinkled with the beauty of white impatiens and bronze zinnias. On a bench, in the center of Mr. Hadley's park like yard, sat a small sculpture of a young woman reading a book, ringed by the incredible flowerbeds.

Mrs. Hadley passed away just before I moved in. Karen told me Mr. Hadley set the sculpture out as a memorial for his wife. I took a moment to wonder if anyone would ever care enough to do something like that for me.

*Doubtful.*

Paul's voice startled me and pulled my attention away from the view.

"I just need to get some tools from my truck. I won't be much longer and then I'll be on my way."

"Okay. Do what you need to do. I'll be out here soaking up the sunshine."

Paul sauntered over to the back of his truck. It was then I noticed the lettering on the side of the big box truck . . . Paul Ravensky Plumbing . . . no job too big or too small.

Another unexpected shiver ran down my spine.

"Paul?" I called to him guardedly as I walked over to his truck.

"Yeah?" he called back to me. His face buried in the bed of his truck.

"Paul, are you related to Crimson?"

# CHAPTER 36

I touched a shaky hand to the side of my head and discovered a large lump and something sticky in my hair. *Damn I think my skull is cracked wide open.* Closing my eyes I fought a wave of nausea.

I opened my eyes slowly. When I was finally able to turn my head, I recognized I was in the gazebo down by the pond where I found Roger.

"It's your own fault, you know," Paul said loudly. "If you would a only told me where he hid the papers, this would be done and over now."

"Jesus. You're making my head hurt worse. What are you talking about?"

"Mr. Moore. Him and his partner smooth-talked my sister into investing in some property they was selling. She found out he was selling that same property over and over. I told him Crimson changed her mind but he wouldn't listen to me. We can't afford to lose that kind a money."

Painful as it was, my mind flashed back to the files in Roger's office. The ones with the same address on all the contracts under different property company names.

"How do you know that was what he was doing?" I asked trying not to move my head in the process.

"Crimson heard the two of them talking one night after she came back to the office to get something she forgot. He had that other guy, Joel, doing his dirty work for him."

"God, Paul it's you who's been attacking me isn't it?" I asked. I knew I had to keep him talking so I could make a run for it.

"I didn't want to hurt you but Mr. Moore wouldn't tell us nothing. We had no choice but to see what you knew. Crimson said you'd tell quick enough if you thought you was going crazy."

*Oh my God!*

"So you drugged Roger and had him pop up all over town for only me to see, trying to make me think I was going crazy," I said slowly trying to make sense of what he was telling me.

At least he had the decency to look guilty as he nodded his head.

"But why did you kill him?"

"That was an accident. Crimson forced him to take too many of those pills. She didn't know it would kill him. Honest. They was prescription drugs. Not something we bought off the street."

"And Joel? Did you hang him in Roger's shower?"

"I didn't mean to hurt him. I just wanted to scare him. But when I heard you come into the house, I had to quiet him."

"What happened to his body?"

"I don't know why they never found it. I never went back there."

"What about the lady in Roger's pool?"

"I didn't do that . . . honest." His eyes were as big as saucers.

"What about Amber? Are you the one who stole my aunt's car and ran her down?"

He nodded, looking down at the floor of the gazebo. "We didn't mean for that to happen, either. We just wanted to scare you but she stepped off the curb right in front of the car. I tried to swerve around her but I couldn't turn fast enough."

"So, let me get this straight. You accidently gave Roger an overdose and killed him. Right?"

Paul nodded . . . yes.

"Then, you accidently hanged Joel. Correct?"

He nodded again.

"And then you ran over Amber with a stolen car while you were trying to scare me."

"Yep."

"You two really aren't very good at this are you?"

"We never meant nobody no harm . . . really."

Actually, I believed he wasn't capable of killing anyone. Accidentally or otherwise.

"Paul, why did you keep saying "Have a little faith? What did you mean by that?"

"Crimson did some background work for Mr. Moore and found out about your baby. She told me you'd crack once we threatened your baby. She said you'd get the inn-u-endo." *This was said very slowly.* "I didn't know what that meant but Crimson said to say it."

My heart cringed thinking of what they could have done to her, but I knew in my head they would never have gotten close enough to do anything.

"Oh my God Roger had me checked out? Did he know? Did Crimson tell him what she found out about me?"

He looked down at his feet and shook his head. "Nope. She thought it was best to keep that information to herself. Just in case we needed it for leverage someday."

His speech became very slow and deliberate. Obviously, Crimson was the brains behind all this and I knew she could be much more dangerous than Paul ever thought of being.

Softening my voice I said, "Paul, don't you understand Crimson is using you?" I was sitting up now leaning back against the bench across from Paul who wasn't really paying much attention to me.

"No!" he said shaking his head. "She's my sister. She wouldn't do that to me. She's taken care of me all these years since our father was killed. They called him Raven, you know, like the bird. I like to think of my dad as a bird."

Raven? Suddenly I remembered Jonathan's remarks about Raven. He'd told him Scarecrow killed his father. "When was your father killed?" I think things are coming full circle here.

"That's none of your business." Startled, I looked over and saw Crimson standing on the ground just outside the gazebo with a gun pointed at me.

*Dear God, please don't let me die here.*
*Focus, O'Malley.*

I looked around. I could have sworn that was Stryker's voice.

*Like I don't have enough problems. Now, I have Stryker in my head . . . again.*

Whether he's in my head or not, he's right. I needed to focus. I willed my muscles to relax and managed, despite the pain, to focus on my task.

With my hands held up in front of me, I said, "Okay, let's just calm down and talk about this. Crimson, I can help you."

"Shut up! You're not going to help us. How stupid do you think we are?"

"I don't think you're stupid. I think someone took advantage of you and you did what you felt you had to do. No one can blame you for that."

"She makes sense, Crimson. Maybe she can help us." Paul pleaded with his sister.

"Paul, don't you see? She's just like her father." Slowly walking up the steps, she crossed the gazebo and went to her brother. "Paul, do you know what our father was?"

Paul shook his head no as his eyes remained on his feet.

"Our father was considered a cleaner. Do you know what a cleaner did?" Not waiting for an answer she continued. "Our father cleaned up the mess her father made after he assassinated someone. Our father had to dispose of the subject after Scarecrow "connected" with them. Connecting being a pretty word for killing. Her father was a professional killer."

"How do you know *anything* about my father?"

"After my father died, I found some papers he had hidden in his desk. You'd be surprised what I know about your father and the others."

*Others?*

"Crimson, let's stop all this right now. We don't need to pay for our father's sins."

"Our father had no sins. It was your father who sinned," Crimson said unemotionally. She was beginning to sound a little like Jonathan.

I didn't like how calm she had become. I could only hope she would just pass over to La-La land with her brother.

Bracing my hands on the floor of the gazebo, I tried to push myself up onto one of the benches.

Crimson pointed the gun at me, but her eyes were vacant as she said, "Stay where you are. Don't try anything."

"Crimson, more deaths aren't going to help matters," I said softly while pulling myself up onto the bench.

"Maybe for you. But it'll give Paul and me time to go through your house and find those papers. Once we destroy them no one will ever know we had any connection."

"I thought that was what you were doing while I kept her down here," Paul mumbled.

"I was, but then her nosy brother walked in. Luckily for him, he's blind. Otherwise, I would have had to kill him instead of just hitting him over the head."

*"I have had about as much of these nut-jobs hurting me and my family as I'm going to take," I thought as a new anger pushed me.*

Realizing Crimson didn't care about killing one more person, I figured I was going to have to find a way to get myself out of here quickly.

The sky darkened with the threat of an afternoon storm. I heard thunder off in the distance. Paul had taken to muttering to himself as Crimson paced the gazebo in front of me.

"Shut up, Paul! I can't think."

Lowering his chin to his chest he mumbled, "Sorry," sounding like a little boy who had just been scolded.

Crimson sprang to attention, her voice shrill, "What was that?"

I definitely liked it better when she was ignoring me. "What?"

"That!"

I picked up the distant sound of thunder cracking.

"It was just thunder, maybe," I said, though I hoped for something a little more powerful . . . like an AK-47.

Paul sat on one of the benches, as far away from the steps in the gazebo as he could get. Head down, he looked as if he might be praying.

*I'll drink to that.*

Crimson, on the other hand was definitely losing it. She moved to the opening by the steps. She gripped the gun with shaking hands and waved it back and forth looking out across the vineyard. Just then lightning struck an apple tree right behind us in the orchard. The crack was deafening.

Crimson jerked causing the gun to fire.

*"Ruff . . . ruff!"*

Harry burst through the cattails that surrounded the pond and jumped into the gazebo as he knocked Crimson back onto the bench across from me.

I wrapped my arms around his neck, "I'm so glad you're here, buddy."

Harry nudged me with his nose, *"Ruff!"*

"Shut that mutt up," Crimson warned waving the gun violently around the small space.

I stood up and urged Harry out of the gazebo. "Go on, Harry. Go home to Allen. Okay buddy?" Pushing on his backside I aimed him for the steps. Crimson still waived the gun, so Harry thought it meant, "Let's play." He jumped up on Crimson with his front paws on her chest and his mouth around the hand that held the gun, wanting to play tug-of-war.

The gun went off again, and this time the bullet grazed my upper right arm. I screamed as the gun went flying through the air. Harry pounced on Crimson with both front paws as he pushed her backwards. She hit the railing full force, flipped over it, and landed into the muddy pond below. Still believing it was a game, Harry jumped over the railing, followed her, and landed on top of her.

Forgetting the pain shooting down my arm, I scrambled for the gun, hoping to get to it before Paul. I turned and aimed the weapon at Paul. But, I didn't have to worry about him because he still sat in the same place, mumbling to himself, as he rocked back and forth.

*I guess he's gone to his happy place.*

Crimson screamed. I hurried over to the rail in time to see Harry pull on Crimson's jacket. She splashed all around as she tried to get up, but Harry had a different thought. He just knew she wanted to play.

"Get this dog off me! Now!" she screamed.

Harry howled.

Stryker burst through a cluster of apple trees and stopped short as he took in the scene in front of him. He saw Harry as he thrashed around in the water with Crimson and me as I stood in the gazebo, looking down on them with her gun still in my hand.

He walked over to me with a big grin on his face and asked, "You okay?"

"Yeah, I think so," I touched the gash on the side of my head and winced as I looked over my shoulder at Paul, "He gave me quite a whack with a flashlight. But he seems to be ready for a rubber room now. Crimson is the brains behind all this. He only did what his sister told him to. I think he's really harmless enough."

Stryker holstered his weapon. "What happened to your arm?" he asked. Blood dripped down my arm and just as I looked at it, I became dizzy. I swayed and reached for Stryker, who caught me just before I fell face first on the floor of the gazebo.

Setting me down, he looked at my blood-soaked hair, pulled a scarf out of his jacket pocket, wrapped it around my arm to stop the bleeding, and glared at Paul. He let his glare shoot over to Crimson, who was still trying to get away from Harry. I'm pretty sure Stryker was thinking about whacking someone upside the head.

I placed my hand on his arm and gently shook my head no. Glancing down at my arm I asked, "Where'd you get this scarf?"

Stryker shrugged his shoulders, "I don't know. I think one of the cops gave it to me the night you were attacked in the park. I must have forgotten it. Why isn't it yours?"

"Yeah it is. I was just wondering how you came to have it is all," I said perplexed because I wasn't wearing it that night. It has been shoved to the back of my underwear drawer ever since I moved here. Who could have taken it out and left it in the park?

Just then, red and blue flashing lights pulled up and Detective Adams jumped out of his car. Holding his hands up in front of him, palms out, he said, "I know, you've got to take her to the hospital." Shaking his head, he reluctantly said, "Go ahead. I'll catch-up with you there."

"Thanks, Detective. Come on, O'Malley. We need to go get your head examined," he said with a smirk, as he wrapped his arm around my waist. He stopped and gazed up the hill to where his truck was parked, then looked back at me. He shook his head and said, "No way O'Malley. You're hoofing it this time."

Leaning into him I said, "That's fine. I think I can make it.

# CHAPTER 37

Lying in the bed in my small hospital room, I summed up my present condition as being in a world of hurt, but relieved it was all over. I had one hell of a headache, *another concussion,* but I could handle it. My upper arm was bandaged and in a sling. I was going to have to spend one night in the hospital for observation.

A soft knock pulled me out of my daydream and Stryker stuck his head in the door. "You up for a little company?" he asked.

Sighing I said, "Sure, I might as well get it over with. Adams must be chomping at the bit to talk to me."

The door swung open wide and a little red headed person burst into the room, arms outstretched, and yelling, "Mommy Mommy . . . Faf here, Faf here."

"Oh my . . . " I sobbed, reaching out for her with my one good arm. "I see honey. Faith's here . . . Faith's here."

She stopped at the edge of the bed, turned, looked at Stryker, and demanded, "Boo up. Boo up," she said reaching up to Stryker. He easily picked her up and sat her on the bed next to me.

I cried as I hugged my beautiful little girl. I looked over her head at Stryker standing there rocking back and forth on his heels, grinning like the Cheshire cat and asked, "Boo?"

He grinned and tilted his head to one side, "Yeah, that's kinda what she calls me," he said bashfully. "She had a hard time saying Stryker." He smiled at Faith.

"Cute."

Before I could thank him, the door was pushed open again. This time the people who came through didn't seem quite as happy to see me.

Mom, Pepper, Karen, Allen, Sami, and Coop filed through the door making the small room even smaller.

Faith held out her arms to my mom and called, "Up Gran-Gran, up.

The big smile on Mom's face told me all I needed to know as she reached for her granddaughter. Faith jumped over into her Gran-Gran's arms and kissed her loudly on the cheek.

With tears in her eyes and her face pressed into that curly mop of red hair, my mother looked over at me and whispered, "You have a lot of explaining to do.

As everyone was leaving my room I called to Karen, "Can you stay for a second? I need to talk to you."

Turning back to me she said, "Sure. What's up?"

"I just want to apologize for lying to you about Faith. I know I should have told you but I'd been protecting her for so long it just seemed the natural thing to do."

Sitting on the edge of the bed Karen took my hand in hers. "Mattie you don't owe me an apology. You did what you had to do to protect your daughter."

"I know but I feel bad about all the secrets and the lies."

"Oh honey, we all have past secrets that have led to present lies."

# CHAPTER 38

S winging on my front porch, I shivered as I pulled my grandmother's quilt tightly around me trying to ward off the cold that had finally set in alerting us that winter was surely on the way.

I watched as the big black truck pulled up to the curb in front of my house. Stryker easily jumped out and strolled up my walkway. His gaze never left me. I shivered again, but it wasn't from the cold this time. I hadn't seen him since my release from the hospital.

He stopped at the bottom of the steps and softly said, "Hey, you."

"Hey, yourself," I said, trying to catch my breath.

"Where is everybody?"

"They're all inside playing with the littlest member of the O'Malley clan."

Stryker nodded as he climbed the steps onto the porch. I scooted over and gave him room to sit on the swing next to me.

He was silent for a few minutes before asking me, "How'd you keep her hidden for so long?" Shrugging he continued, "Hell, why'd you keep her hidden for so long?"

I sighed deeply. I'd been waiting for someone to ask me that question. I really thought Mom or Allen would be the ones with the questions, but Pepper had probably answered the majority of them by now. They were just waiting for me to heal before they tag-teamed me.

"The why is easy. When Faith was born, they handed me this tiny person all bundled up and she just stared up at me. When I looked down at her this feeling hit me, as if I'd been struck by lightning. It was love . . . that instant inexplicable love you can only feel for your child. In that moment, I knew there was no way in hell Steven would ever get his hands on MY daughter. I couldn't trust his judgment anymore. I couldn't trust him anymore.

"The how was a little harder, but not by much. I don't think Steven cared enough about me or the baby to give us any real thought after I left that day. So, I let him believe I miscarried. Pepper called him, he pushed her a little about where I was, but she handled it."

Stryker nodded, as if he could see that.

"I was on bed rest for two months until I could safely deliver her. I lived with one of Pepper's friends, Julia, a midwife. When my baby girl came into this world, she was a mass of red curls and healthy lungs."

He smiled as if were imagining it. "Why'd you name her Faith?"

After a deep breath, I said, "Because that was all I had. The doctors couldn't tell me how much, if any, damage was done from the fall. The only thing they were positive about was that she had a strong heartbeat. As for the rest, I knew I just had to have faith."

*Hmmm . . . ?*

"Well, she's gorgeous and willful. Just like her mommy."

"Thanks." I glanced over at him. "Stryker—I'd just like to thank you for not making this any harder for me."

"Hey I'm a smart ass—not a jackass."

"Debatable, but thanks anyway."

"So, what now, O'Malley? What are you going to do?"

"Well, I've thought about that. As you know, Roger left everything to me in his will. I guess I'll wait to see what's left after the whole lot's been sold and all his debts are paid. Anyway, remember the building I showed you downtown . . . The Humphrey House?"

He nodded with a smile on his face, obviously remembering the other things that happened that day, too.

"I'm going to buy it. I'm going to open the bookstore I've always wanted. Owning my own business will make it easier for me to come and go . . . with Faith . . . you know."

"Sure, that makes sense." He paused in deep thought for a moment. "Have you given any more thought to your photography? I mean . . . you're very talented."

Looking at him skeptically I asked, "How do you know? You've only seen a few pieces of my work."

"Weeeelll . . . " he drawled. "Actually, I've seen more than you know. Remember when I went to Arizona to check out Steven?"

I nodded, remembering.

"I went to that gallery in Scottsdale where you have some of your pieces hanging. By the way, Reggie and Cameron said to tell you hello and they want you to send more stuff." Stopping to take a deep breath, Stryker continued. "I also went to ASU and talked to your photography instructor. Do you remember Professor Landor?"

"You were busy, weren't you? And, yes, I do remember her. She was wonderful. But how do you know Professor Landor?"

"She's kinda my mother."

"What! What do you mean she's *kinda* your mother?"

"Okay. She is my mother. While I was out there I dropped by to see her and asked if she remembered you. She told me you were one of the most talented students she'd ever had. And, she'd often wondered if you pursued your art. In fact, she has one of your prints hanging in her home. And trust me, I know my mom. She wouldn't hang just any old thing in her home."

"Wow . . . I don't know what to think here. First, I'm impressed she even remembered me. That makes me feel good knowing someone appreciated my work. Second, why didn't you tell me?"

"I didn't really have the time. If you remember we've been kinda busy."

I nodded, remembering. "So, where are you going with all this Stryker?"

"I don't know. It just seems to me that someone with all that talent should be doing more than just selling *old* books."

"Well, thank you for that but I just don't know. After Steven and Jonathan . . . you know that was the last time I'd picked up my camera. I don't know if I ever want to look through a lens again."

"I'm just asking that you give it some thought. That's all."

I nodded agreeing to think about it.

"Not trying to change the subject, but . . . what have you found out?"

"Well, O'Malley . . . I don't think Roger was who you thought he was."

"I've already come to that conclusion on my own."

"Okay, here's what I know. The redheaded woman in the pool was Elaine Patterson. She lived in Roger's house but we've found nothing in his finances to indicate she was renting from him. It looks like she was . . . living with him." He paused, waiting for me to get angry, I suppose. "We're pretty sure Paul and Crimson killed Elaine, either just to get her out of the way or because they mistook her for you. I'm sure they'll tell us eventually."

"I don't know Stryker. Paul said she was already dead when he got there."

"Well, that's something Detective Adams is going to have to work on then."

"Okay, so Roger's dead and Elaine's dead. What happened to Joel or Joey . . . whatever his name was?"

"There has been no sign of Joey Coulter, aka Joel Simmons, dead or alive."

"Hmmmm," I grunted giving that some thought. "I still don't understand what Roger had to gain by staying here with me when he had her."

"O'Malley . . . Roger was selling off your property. The vineyards. He had people investing in your vineyards and winery. I think he hoped you'd be willing to sell by the time he had all the investors lined up. He was plain and simple . . . a con-artist."

"Okay . . . have you been able to locate the money?"

"No. That's the one piece of the puzzle we're missing. There is no money trail. But, according to the investors that have come forward there is quite a chunk of change that has gone astray. Any ideas?"

After a little deliberation on my part, I think I had the answer.

"Come on. I think I know where we might find some answers."

Taking him by the hand, I led him into the house and up the stairs.

"Ummm . . . O'Malley, do you think this is a good idea?" he asked, glancing around to see if anyone was watching us.

"Get your head out of the gutter, Stryker. I'm going to show you Roger's secret hiding spot."

Crossing my bedroom, I opened the closet doors, and turned on the light. Tapping the wall where the frame was hanging, the door popped open.

Stepping back, I motioned Stryker forward to look inside. Reaching deep inside he pulled out a large envelope and after handing it to me, he reached back inside. This time he pulled out a long narrow duffel bag and set it on the floor.

Kneeling down beside the bag, he unzipped it exposing a boatload of money. All hundred-dollar bills. Thousands of dollars.

Looking up Stryker asked, "How'd you know?"

"I found it one day after he moved out. Not the money, though. When I looked in, I only found a letter from Gramma Rose. Once I pulled that out, I didn't look any farther. Things being as crazy as they have been around here I'd forgotten all about it until you just told me the money and files were missing. It just made perfect sense for him to hide it here. He stayed here to be close to the money . . . not me," I said with some regret.

Setting back on his heels and shaking his head he said, "You sure know how to pick 'em O'Malley."

"So you've said."

# EPILOGUE

W elcome to the grand opening of The Past and Present Bookstore," I said as I greeted my guests. "Come in and help yourself to appetizers and drinks."

I looked across the room to where my mother sat on the soft leather sofa, in the living room area of the store, reading to her granddaughter. They have become inseparable over the past few months. Violet is even thinking about selling her house in Florida and moving back here to Hopewell.

*I think she's secretly hoping Mr. Wonderful will follow.*

My eyes wandered to the front window where my newly published book *Keeping Faith* was prominently displayed. After speaking with an agent Karen knew, it didn't take long to find a publisher.

Back in the far corner of my store was a mini-version of Coop's Coffee Café. This full service coffee shop was run by, no other than, Skky with two k's.

My eyes moved further around the room toward the wide stairway with the oak banister. The sign above the stairs read . . . *Captured Moments.*

I was displaying some of the black and white desert prints I had taken in Arizona. Once things are settled down a little, I'm going to get out and take some photographs of all the wondrous beauty northern Michigan has to offer.

Open for a month now, tonight is the actual grand opening for my bookstore and my book launching. Everyone in town will be here. People tend to show up for events that offer free food and wine. I sighed as I remembered the last time all those same people were gathered together . . . Roger's funeral.

Everyone I love is here tonight. Sami's upstairs giving tours of the photo gallery. Coop is back in the coffee shop serving our guests.

Allen brought Allison back for the grand opening. She's lovely and it's obvious she adores him. I'm sure there are wedding bells in their future.

Pepper is mingling with the masses. She was so instrumental in getting this whole thing off the ground, that I'm going to hate to see her go back to Arizona.

Even Clarisse Duggan came up from Florida for the opening, surprising Violet. It seems she has her sights set on Detective Adams.

Karen is in the back helping Coop. Maybe there is hope for those two yet.

*Who knows?*

Stryker is noticeably absent . . . again. He left town shortly after all the cash was returned to the investors Roger and Joel scammed. I haven't heard from him since, but a few months ago Faith got a ghost-shaped stuffed doll in the mail. It had the word "Boo" printed across the front and I can only assume it was from him.

I sold Roger's mini-mansion and his real estate business. After selling off all his assets, I had enough money to pay cash for the old Humphrey House building with enough left over for the remodeling. I even had two apartments finished off on the third floor. I could rent one for extra income. The other one is for Faith and me just in case we need to spend the night here sometime. Allen and Allison are using it this week while they're in town.

I looked down at the envelope I'd been holding in my hand. A familiar shiver scuttled down my spine.

The envelope was addressed just—**MATTIE O'MALLEY**—in bold, block lettering. There was no address, no stamp . . . nothing.

*Obviously hand delivered.*

I opened the envelope and pulled out a single sheet of white paper. Printed in the same block lettering in the middle of the page was a solitary message . . .

**ONE DOWN—TWO TO GO**

I dropped the paper as if it had suddenly burst into flames and watched as it drifted to the floor, settling at my feet.

"Hello, Matilda." I heard Mrs. Blackwell's greeting from the recesses of my mind.

Giving myself a mental shake, I returned her greeting, "Welcome to The Past and Present, Mrs. Blackwell. I'm glad you could make it."

Reaching across the counter for my hand, Mrs. Blackwell looked me in the eye and said in a voice that she obviously thought would give credence to her words, "My dear, your aura is positively purple." Shaking her head, a shrewd glint in her eyes, she added, "Not a good thing my dear, not a good thing at all."

# The End

# ABOUT THE AUTHOR

**DEBORAH STEMPIEN** spent 28 years running her own business before deciding it was finally time to do what she had dreamed of doing for years – *write*.

photo courtesy of
Rebecca Nickert

Writing a novel had always been her dream, though she told very few people until she was a "grown up." After numerous starts and stops, she realized it was time to sit down and actively pursue that dream.

Her first novel *Past Secrets, Present Lies* is the result of that pursuit.

A passionate writer, you will find Ms. Stempien currently working on the second novel in the Mattie O'Malley Mystery series *Fatal Secrets* (working title).

Debbie lives in Michigan with her husband. She is devoted to her family and enjoys spending as much time as possible with them.